THE CROWN AGENT

THE CROWN AGENT

STEPHEN O'ROURKE

SANDSTONE PRESS

First published in Great Britain by
Sandstone Press Ltd
Willow House
Stoneyfield Business Park
Inverness
IV2 7PA
Scotland

www.sandstonepress.com

The publisher acknowledges subsidy from Creative
Scotland towards publication of this volume.

ISBN: 978-1-912240-76-0
ISBNe: 978-1-912240-77-7

Jacket design by Ryder Design, Sheffield
Maps by Camilla Seddon Illustration
Typeset by Biblichor Ltd, Edinburgh
Printed and bound by CPI Group (UK) Ltd, Croydon, CR0 4YY

For my mother Patricia and my father James

Midway upon the journey of our life I found myself within a forest dark, for the straightforward pathway had been lost.

Inferno, Canto 1, Dante Alighieri

The mind is everything: what we think, we become.

Buddha

PROLOGUE

Cumbrae Island. Midnight, 2 January 1829.

A storm was gathering over the Firth of Clyde. Flecks of sleet slid across the glass. Above Sandy's head the lamp launched yet another beam over the seething water.

The kettle whistled and he slid it from the hotplate. Then with a well-practised flick he opened the stove and shovelled in some coal. He wiped his hands, stretched, and frowned at the storm glass. The liquid inside, clear all day, was frosting quickly now, and as if in answer the wind rose with a wolf's howl, licking round the tower. It was going to be a long shift, but he'd see it through till noon then hand over to Tom, presently sound in his bunk.

Sandy lifted the *Greenock Advertiser* and tried to concentrate on the shipping notices. An inky little three-masted schooner accompanied every entry on the yellowing paper. *Hunter,* sailing for Madeira on the third. *Cormorant,* bound for Bermuda the same day. *Minerva,* voyaging to Cape Town the day after. He patted a few pockets in search of his pipe and tobacco.

A bell clanged in the distance.

He stopped. Yes. There it was again. And again. But not regular, he thought, his stomach tightening. Haphazard. Like something unhinged.

He leapt to the window. Beam after beam swept the water. The clanging continued. Round came the beam again, and suddenly there it was. A stricken ship, her sails in rags.

Sandy's whole life was the lighthouse, and he knew the King's Regulations like the words of a song. Grabbing a hurricane lamp he clattered down the spiral stairs to light the beacon.

'Tam, wake up man! There's a ship foonderin' oot in the firth! A schooner, must be a trader!'

The wind whipped the grass at his ankles as he trudged uphill, the lighthouse beam raking the sky. For a moment he stopped, turned and raised a rain-lashed hand to his brow. The clanging drifted in the wind. 'It can only be a mile out at most,' he thought.

Breathing hard, Sandy reached the beacon. A wall of rain drenched him as he set the lamp down and fumbled for a rag. But just as he turned to light it, he heard footsteps.

'Tam here, quick man. Gie me a hand wi' this lamp, will ye?'

If Sandy had managed to light the beacon on Cumbrae that night, Dan Porter at the Cloch Lighthouse ten miles to the north would have relayed the signal along the coast to the Custom House at Greenock. There, the officer on watch would have noted the incident in the log and dispatched a team of marines to investigate. At first light a rescue mission would have been mounted.

But as it was, the stricken ship was not reported until late the following morning and Sandy never did light the beacon, because those words proved to be the last he ever spoke before he was struck dead with a single blow of the lighthouse axe.

1

Some stories can never be told. Some mysteries are so rooted in darkness they can never be set down, even now, here in my study, where a cheerful fire crackles in the hearth. But truth is as truth does and in these, my winter days, it's time to reveal the secrets of my life.

I begin more than fifty years ago, with the mission that led me far beyond the compass of my youth. Those memories, despite the warmth of this fire, plunge a cold blade of fear through to my very bones.

I was sick at heart with Edinburgh. My father, a senior officer in the East India Company, had shipped me home aged seven. Since then I'd measured out my life first at the Morningside School under the strict eye of the Dominie, then as a student at the College, and finally as a surgeon in the city's Infirmary. My path had been steady, my future assured. But each evening as I turned for home I'd think of the empire beyond Britain's shores. 'Mungo Lyon,' I'd sigh, 'there surely must be more to life than this.'

Then, on a bitter morning in January 1829, everything changed because of a pair of Irish navvies named William Burke and William Hare.

I was twenty-seven and alone amid the hanging mob on the High Street. I remember snowflakes and silence, the minister closing his eyes, the Bible under his chin. Someone pulled a handle and Burke dropped like a sack. His neck snapped like a dry twig leaving the rope quivering. His last breath fogged the air, then disappeared with the mob's cheer. That was the end of Burke, but not of an affair which had shaken the city's medical Establishment to its core.

Just a few weeks earlier Burke and Hare had stood trial for mass murder, but Hare turned King's Evidence against his accomplice and walked from the court a free man. They'd sold their victims' bodies to my friend and mentor Doctor Robert Knox, a Fellow of the Royal Society of Edinburgh and the city's most celebrated anatomist.

Knox was ruined, and shortly after the trial was expelled from the city. I admit it, of course. He, together with other surgeons (whom I won't name, even all these years later), paid handsomely for bodies from the Resurrectionists. Nobody approved of grave robbing, but the medical students needed to practise dissection. How else could they learn?

The arrest of Burke and Hare for mass murder, however, and the Lord Advocate's investigation which followed, made villains of us all. Folk spat at my feet as I entered the Infirmary, and my noble art became a thing of shame. Then came the Procurator Fiscal's questions, but time and again I denied everything. I was of no use, he eventually reported, and I thus avoided any part in the trial.

My connection with Knox marked me, however, and the Infirmary's Trustees lost no time in restricting my right to practice surgery. Then I lost a patient in difficult circumstances and was banned altogether. After that I hardly knew what to do with myself so, after lingering round the patients each evening making notes, I'd trudge home to bed. My sister Margaret, always writing at her desk in the drawing room, sensed much but said little.

One morning in Spring, as I sat reading a journal and smoking my pipe, a runner came with a note.

Be at my club at noon.

It was signed by the Lord Advocate.

What could Scotland's most senior government minister possibly want with me? Naturally I prepared myself for yet more unpleasant questions.

'His Lordship is expecting you,' said the doorman when I arrived. 'You'll find him upstairs in the Day Room.'

A long clock chimed twelve. A fire crackled and pipe smoke drifted over the back of a chair. Hearing my footsteps he turned and I immediately recognised his mutton-chopped face.

'Doctor Lyon! Do take a seat. Delighted you could make it. Henderson, some sherry if you please.'

He offered his tobacco pouch and I caught the aroma of Turkish Blend. I lit my briar. The sherry arrived.

He asked about my work and even sympathised with the cares of my profession.

'It's been a trying time, Lyon. But I've spoken to the Prime Minister and have his assurance there will soon be legislation to, shall we say, regularise things.'

Thereafter we chatted like old friends, but all the while he was sizing me up like a Bengal tiger. He nudged things round to family, and so I told him how my parents met at a Company ball in Calcutta, then settled in Bombay where I was raised by my ayah, Ranjita. I told of how my mother had died giving birth to Margaret, and how we were sent home to live with my maternal grandfather, the General. I was a little surprised to discover he knew my father, but then Scotland is a small place. When my father finally returned we had lived together until his disappearance, and presumed death, three years ago. With that, other than mentioning Margaret's debility which kept her home, there was little else to say.

The clock chimed the half hour, followed by more footsteps. Just as I thought my interview had ended, the Lord Advocate give a satisfied nod.

'Take lunch with me, Doctor Lyon. There's someone I want you to meet.'

At the top of the stairs was a ruddy faced gentleman, catching his breath.

'Doctor Lyon, allow me to introduce Sir John Foster. Sir John is the Collector of His Majesty's Customs at Leith.'

Sir John proved excellent company, and I observed that the reputation of His Majesty's Customs men for enjoying fine wine and good food was well-founded. He spoke of Leith (which is the port of Edinburgh) and Scotland's blossoming trade routes, all swelling the funds of the Exchequer. Wine from France, tea and jute from India, sugar from the Indies and tobacco from the Americas.

'The consumption of our nation is unrelenting,' he said, 'and Britain the shopkeeper of the world. But we must jealously guard our trade routes, because they're at the heart of all our success.'

As he said this, he shared a wry smile with the Lord Advocate. 'Your father understood that, Doctor Lyon, being of our number.'

'My father was an East Indiaman, Sir John, not a Customs Officer.'

They exchanged a glance.

'Doctor Lyon,' said the Lord Advocate, 'Sir John isn't referring to the Customs.'

'Then to what?'

Sir John drained his wineglass and lit a cigar. As the smoke filled the room, I had the sense I was on the verge of something extraordinary.

2

'Britain has enemies, Doctor Lyon,' began Sir John, 'and maintaining our advantage depends on some remarkable men . . .'

'. . . and women,' murmured the Lord Advocate.

'Apologies, my Lord – and women – who serve this country in secret.'

My father? A secret agent?

'But what has this to do with me, gentlemen? I'm a surgeon, not a spy!'

I looked to the Lord Advocate, but he met my eyes serenely.

'Doctor Lyon,' continued Sir John, 'you're educated. You understand the world. And you've few ties to bind you. Now if we consider that recent business with Knox . . .'

'Oh not this again!' I rose to my feet. 'My Lord, I told the Fiscal everything. If you've brought me here to charm out secrets I'm afraid you're wasting your time.'

'Sit down Doctor Lyon,' retorted the Lord Advocate, and he spoke with such authority that I complied at once.

'Now listen to me. We know the account you gave of yourself in that matter. It's what first brought you to my attention. Do you think my aim in the resurrection business was to discredit Edinburgh's surgeons? Hardly. I'd no interest in bringing a prosecution against Knox. But not through lack of evidence. For it may interest you to know, Doctor Lyon, that of all the surgeons whom we questioned, you were the only one who didn't point the finger of blame at Knox.'

I swallowed hard. I was green as grass, stubborn and full of anger. What's more, I was afraid. But could he see something in me that I couldn't?

The clock chimed two and the Lord Advocate rose to leave.

'Well, Doctor Lyon, it's been a pleasure but I'm afraid I have some rather pressing business. So I shall leave you in the capable hands of Sir John.'

'But, my Lord,' I protested. 'My work at the Infirmary?'

'Will be taken care of.'

And he left.

3

'Well Lyon,' began Sir John, pouring two brandies. 'Tell me this. Are you familiar with the town of Greenock, on the west coast?'

I'd seen mention of it in the shipping pages, but it might have been China for all I knew of the place. The railways were still a decade away, and even Glasgow was a city I'd visited only once. I had taken a carriage that time, but thanks to navvies like Burke and Hare the city could also now be reached in a couple of days by canal.

'Greenock's on the River Clyde, twenty miles west of Glasgow,' he continued, 'and it's Scotland's largest port. Every day its Custom House regulates more shipping than anywhere outside London. Last year its receipts exceeded half a million pounds.'

I turned that figure over. If half a million pounds was the duty paid, say at five percent, then the annual value of goods going through the port ran to more than ten million. A huge sum.

'Now think of this. Customs receipts rely on trade routes, and that means safe passage in and out of Britain's ports. That means lighthouses, Lyon, and His Majesty's government has committed a fortune to building them. The keepers of these lighthouses are the guardians of our trade routes, so any irregularity is a serious matter.

'Now then, Lyon,' he said, edging closer, 'let me tell you about a ship. At the beginning of the year the *Julietta* was spotted in the Firth of Clyde, her sails torn and listing to her starboard side. She was a triple-masted schooner, sailing from Jamaica with a cargo of sugar. But viewed through the telescope there was no sign of life.

'Now drifting like that she posed a danger to navigation, so the steamboat *Comet*, under the command of an officer of Customs and twelve marines, was dispatched from Greenock to invest-igate. When they boarded the *Julietta* they found the entire crew dead. It was fever had killed them, Doctor Lyon. Yellow fever.'

'What did they do?' I asked, wide-eyed.

'They hurried her dead ashore and buried them in lime. Then she was towed to quarantine and her hatches left open. And so she remained, for forty days.'

'But surely none of that is unusual?'

He swirled his brandy and frowned.

'Of itself, Lyon, no. Yellow fever is rife in the Indies. But there were certain other . . . irregularities. Three things.'

He gave me a sharp look, but I held his eye.

'What three things?'

'First, the *Julietta* has sailed between Greenock and Jamaica for many years, and its voyages are well recorded. After the incident Gabriel Birkmyre, my brother Controller at Greenock, inspected the records and discovered that the *Julietta* returned to Greenock every three months, averaging just over six weeks to cross the ocean.

'Now that's slower than you'd expect for a sleek keel like hers, even allowing for a sluggish turnaround at Jamaica. What's more though, whenever she arrived at Greenock her cargo of sugar was always below capacity. It was the same with her return trips to Jamaica, carrying manufactured goods. Always below capacity.'

I agreed that for a cargo ship this seemed unusual.

'Second,' he continued, 'three days after the *Julietta* was quarantined, Birkmyre learned that one of his Customs officers had disappeared.'

'From Greenock?'

He shook his head. 'From Campbeltown. Further west on the Kintyre peninsula.'

Again, I agreed that while this was unusual it could also be just a coincidence.

'But then there's the third point,' he said, and leaning in I caught the brandy on his breath. 'After the *Julietta* was rescued the keeper of a nearby lighthouse was found dead. He'd been murdered. Almost certainly by his assistant, who's also missing.'

I stared at him for what felt like an age.

'Smuggling?' I suggested. I glanced out over the ordered little world that was Edinburgh. Such a word, smuggling, seemed out of place in this dawning industrial age. It seemed to come up from a darker world.

Sir John tapped his ash. 'It's possible. Perhaps that's why Birkmyre notified the Chancellor of the Exchequer's office in London.'

'A significant step.'

'But the right one. Commander Birkmyre knows his business.' He sighed. 'The wheels of state grind slow, however, and it was weeks before I received my orders. I'm to open an investigation and report back by the end of the month.'

'By the end of the month?' It was already the tenth of April.

Sir John gave an impatient wave of his hand and leaned closer.

'There's not a moment to lose. I need someone resourceful, someone able to go west immediately. More importantly, however, it has to be someone unconnected with the Customs or any branch of government. Whatever the devilry behind all this may be, Lyon, I'm convinced an outsider is best.

'When I raised the matter yesterday with the Lord Advocate he suggested you. Naturally, I was sceptical. But now that we've spoken, I think you'll suit very well.'

There was a pause while he leaned back, gazing at me. It was time to decide, but in truth I already knew what my answer would be.

'I'll need more information,' I said.

Sir John handed me some papers. 'Read these before you leave. Then cast them on the fire. But not the money, of course.'

There were half a dozen pages followed by three more pages of some foreign code. There were also five hundred guineas in five guinea notes.

Sir John was speaking again, but I was only half listening.

'I suggest you write to the Trustees at the Infirmary and tell them you're heading west for a short while to pursue an interest. Let's say . . .'

'Marine science?' I suggested.

From boyhood swims against purple sunsets on the Malabar Coast and the return voyage from India, breathtaking and terrifying, the sea fascinated me.

'Perfect,' replied Sir John rubbing his hands. 'That'll give you the cover you'll need. Well time marches on, but two more things before I go. The first is this. You'll have two points of contact when you arrive in Greenock. Agents whose expertise is local information. Their knowledge of your mission is on a need to know basis, but they'll contact you when the time comes.'

I frowned. 'How will I know I can trust them?'

He smiled like a schoolmaster. 'All my agents have been issued with this codeword.' He scribbled it on a scrap of paper and showed it to me. Then he rolled it up and flicked it into the fire.

'Remember it.'

I nodded. 'And the second thing?'

'Is this. Greenock is dangerous, Lyon, so I hope you know how to look after yourself. Be on your guard. Trust no-one.'

He drained his brandy and ground out his cigar.

'Good luck,' he said, then shook my hand and left.

I sat in a daze staring from the fireplace to the table strewn with cups, glasses and ashtrays, to the papers in my left hand and the banknotes in my right.

I'd never seen so much money.

4

I strode onto Princes Street in the fading afternoon light, waved down a cabby and directed him to Morningside. All I could think about was Sir John's parting words, and I asked myself how I'd react if I had to fight or turn tail, kill or be killed. I could ride well enough, was a reasonable hand at fencing and could shoot straight and true. But I'd never had to fight for my life at close quarters.

The motion of the carriage jolted my mind back to the pages I'd memorised then burned. The Member of Parliament for Greenock was Sir Guy Stewart, and I was to lodge with him on the recommendation of the Lord Advocate. I was also to present myself to Commander Birkmyre.

The information turned to the murdered lighthouse keeper Sandy McLeod, his runaway assistant Tom Hamilton, and the missing Campbeltown Customs Officer, whose name was Crawford McCunn. Sandy's whole life had been the lighthouse on Cumbrae. He was from the nearby island of Bute, where his father had been gamekeeper to the Marquess. He left a sister and an aunt, both in Rothesay.

Tom Hamilton was a native of Greenock. He'd been a fisherman, and part owner of a ketch plying the route between Scotland

and Ireland. When Tom was bought out by his partner, an Ulsterman by the name of Hugh O'Neill, he decided to enter the lighthouse service and took up his first posting at Oban. From Oban he was transferred to Cumbrae, and he'd been there less than a year when Sandy was killed. Tom was *'five feet eight inches, broad and swarthy with black hair and green eyes.'*

Crawford McCunn had followed in his father's steps and joined the Customs in Campbeltown, where he'd risen to the rank of Officer. He was *'tall, of slender build with sandy hair and light blue eyes.'*

There was more on the *Julietta*. An examination of the crew had been conducted before their burial. They were only eight in number and were described as either black or Hispanic. Every one of them bore a curious symbol tattooed on their upper left arm in the form of a Double Eagle.

Around the base of the symbol ran the legend *sine unitate nihil sumus* which my College Latin allowed me to translate as *'without unity we are nothing'*. It wasn't a device I'd come across. I decided when I reached Glasgow I'd visit its university and find out more.

One of the dead was described as *'a gentleman, dressed elegantly and found in his own furnished room aft, below deck'*. He was *'about six feet, forty or forty-five years, short black hair and beard,'* while his clothes, which had been burned, were *'colourful, of good cloth.'* A solid gold signet ring the size of a walnut was on the little finger of his left hand. The ring bore the hallmark of Achille Pontellier, a renowned Parisian jeweller, and carried a seal in the same curious form of the Double Eagle, together with the initial *'M'*.

Why was he on board a schooner carrying a simple cargo of sugar?

The pages of foreign code were copied from a journal found in his possession. The original was with Commander Birkmyre. I'd squinted at the pages, turning them this way and that, and had a notion that the words were French or Italian – but it might as well have been Persian for all the sense I could glean. I didn't burn them, however, because I'd had an idea of my own about what to do with them.

Margaret had been an invalid since she was five years old. That had been a hot summer, filled with days exploring rockpools by the sea and lazing on the banks of streams. There was a deep pool in the Braid Burn close by our grandfather's house where we swam at every opportunity, daring one another in dives and launching ourselves out over its smooth surface from a rope swing. One evening, however, returning late from our pool, Margaret complained of a head cold and a dull pain in her neck. By morning she had a fever and was unable to raise herself from the bed. For weeks she suffered excruciating spasms in her legs. At times her mind wandered.

Slowly Margaret improved but she lost the use of her legs, and the doctor engaged by my grandfather diagnosed a 'debility of the lower extremities'. Throughout her childhood Margaret was carried from room to room, invariably accompanied by a pile of books until, on her twelfth birthday, I presented her with her first rolling chair which I'd constructed at College. Margaret was now twenty and on to her third chair, each one built by me. She had never surrendered to her infirmity, however, and after years of effort she sometimes managed a few paces with a stick.

Among her many accomplishments, Margaret was highly adept at languages.

My thoughts were interrupted as the carriage jolted to a halt at the corner of Morningside Place and, calling on the cabbie to wait, I hurried into my father's square villa, as solid and dependable as he'd been in life.

I found Margaret as ever in the drawing room, but first rushed upstairs to retrieve my doctor's bag stocked with the elementary medicines and equipment of the day. How much the practice of surgery has changed in my lifetime through antiseptic, sterilisation and steel! In the days of my youth, however, that battered case contained all the tools of my antique trade.

There was a leather pouch which unrolled to reveal a platoon of scalpels. There was a saw and tourniquet, bandages packed into wads, rolls of catgut for stitching, a dozen iron needles drawn out in the shape of the crescent moon, coloured bottles of laudanum, rum, iodine, mercury and talcum powder. Added to that was a tin of liniment, followed by the ranks of lances, pincers, scissors and forceps to complete my regiment of arms.

I could smell gangrene at twenty paces and amputate a limb in forty-eight seconds with the patient unconscious – slightly longer if not – so long as two or three orderlies were on hand with a set of straps. Though many of my colleagues considered it beneath their dignity, by the time I was twenty-five I'd delivered more babies than I care to remember, some in the bedrooms of the rich, but most on wooden slabs in the poor house.

I could stitch wounds quicker than a Leith seamstress and sew a man up neat as a bird for the oven, for all the good it often did. We were trained to know our instruments as a redcoat knows his rifle, to sharpen and repair blades, mix and weigh medicines to form pastilles or potions, and look a terrified child in the eye with the calm at the centre of the storm. I'd known many a jittering surgeon, drunk on his own rum, grow still when it counted, and work away with the precision of a watchmaker before tumbling out of the Infirmary at dusk and back into the comfort of a bottle.

Margaret laid down her pen and turned the wheels of her chair as I bustled downstairs.

'Whatever's your hurry Mungo? And what are you doing back at this time?'

She beckoned me over, tutting at my appearance and smoothing my jacket. Lyon by name, lion by nature she used to say, with a ruffle of my fair hair. Her own hair was light too, blonde like our mother's, arranged in pretty ringlets round her face, pale as ivory.

'There's no time to explain,' I replied breathlessly, 'I'm headed for Greenock. I'll write as soon as I can.'

She stared into my eyes with real concern. 'Mungo,' she began, but I had to cut her off.

'It's all right Margaret, really, I'm fine. It's just that something important has come up and I've been given orders to leave. I'm sorry to startle you – truly sorry – but I'll explain later.' I took her hand. 'Really, I'm all right.'

There was a pause, then her face set firm and I saw iron in her eyes. 'Take your overcoat,' she said. 'It's damp in the west.'

As she turned back to her writing I bent and kissed her cheek but she waved me away.

'Just come back safe, Mungo.'

The cabbie was waiting and I'd less than twenty minutes to make the barge. But just before leaving I turned and ran back up the stairs, past our startled housemaid Lizzy to my father's bedroom where, concealed in his closet, was his flintlock service pistol, powder and shot. I buried it in my bag and had just dashed back down again when I suddenly remembered what it was that I'd meant to ask Margaret. Swiftly I returned to her side.

'Margaret, there's something I need you to do for me.'

I drew out the pages of code which had been copied from the journal onboard the *Julietta* and handed them to her. She turned them gently in her hands.

'I can't say why, Margaret, but could you—'

'It's Spanish,' she murmured, scanning the text. 'Written in code. Rather challenging I'd say.'

I hesitated. 'Do you think you could—'

She cut me off with a smile. 'I'll do what I can, Mungo. Now go.'

I scribbled the address in Greenock and left. It was typical of Margaret, God bless her, that she didn't so much as blink at my request and I often wonder how much she guessed that day. She had an unfailing sense for things even then, and later I discovered she'd known something of my father's work.

The ding of the blacksmith's hammer faded behind me as the carriage bumped onto Morningside Road. Children played hopscotch in the gloaming. Across the road a man admired the church steeple. His face was pitted like a smallpox victim. Had I seen him earlier on Princes Street?

As night fell my carriage arrived at the canal terminus, where I quickly bought a ticket and boarded a barge. Soon I was laid out in a cramped cabin with a lantern swaying above. Over my shoulder was an open porthole, and I drifted asleep to the clop of the Clydesdales hauling me west toward Glasgow.

5

I woke in the dead of night and drew my watch to my eye. Its pale face showed just after two. Why did I have the uneasy sense someone was listening?

I crept to the porthole and peered out. The barge was tethered, rising and falling gently in the water. I'd just laid my head back on the pillow when a floorboard creaked outside my cabin.

Now there are different creaks. There's the creak of timber as a ship idles at anchor, for example, or the first twist of decking under a relentless sun. But this creak was the careful tread of a man.

The door handle began to turn.

'Who's there?' I cried. I scrabbled for my pistol.

A clatter of footsteps answered, followed by silence.

With a trembling hand I opened the door. The cabin opposite was closed, the stairs to the upper deck empty. I heard shouting above and then a face appeared. It was the captain.

'Is everything all right?' he called. 'I've just chased some fella off the side.'

I told him what had happened.

'Ach, just some chancer nae doot,' he grumbled. 'Just be sure and lock your door, sir. We'll be moving off again shortly.' He eyed my pistol disapprovingly. 'Goodnight, sir.'

Somehow I managed a few hours' sleep before waking to the dawn chorus at six. We'd reached a stage post, and fresh horses were being harnessed for the next leg.

The ceiling was so low I had to stoop while washing with a pitcher and bowl. Then I ventured out in search of breakfast. I emerged on deck to birdsong from the branches crowding the banks as the barge glided through the Lothians. The sky was moving from pink to blue, and my breath curled before me like tea from the pot, swirling and condensing on the tip of my nose.

Spying the captain at the far end of the deck I strolled down and greeted him.

'Morning sir,' he replied, 'fine day.'

He called his wife to fetch me up some tea. She emerged moments later wiping her hands on a greasy apron and handed me a pair of fried eggs and bread on a china plate; furnished with the tea I enjoyed a meal in the open air fit for the King himself. Then lighting my pipe and just to pass the time, I inquired of the captain whether there were other passengers.

'There's six berths and they're aw' full,' he replied, carefully negotiating the contours of the waterway, 'and with this weather and nae wind I reckon we'll make Falkirk in guid time the night.' He lit his pipe. 'Well, there'll be a bit dinner for ye aboot twelve if you fancy it,' he added, then reverted to his contemplation of the water, with the occasional languid call to his mate leading the horses. The old barge went along through field and heath with such serenity that morning that my heart soared, and the vision sits like a picture in my mind to this day – the last of old Scotland before the coming of the railways.

Making way for my fellow passengers as they emerged I returned to my cabin and began a letter to Margaret.

We were always close, and I dare say the loss of our mother was the reason. As an infant she would ask me over and over to describe mama just once more, how she would talk, dress, laugh and walk. Her favourite was my candlelit memory of our mother in a ball gown, kissing me goodnight then descending the stairs toward father in his uniform. Margaret would ask about her dress, her hair, the dances, who else was there and what the carriages looked like. Rather than disappoint her I'd enlarge the story to include every detail down to the marble floors of the Maharajah's palace, until even I was no longer sure what was true and what I'd imagined.

We played together constantly as children, and I remember one summer spent writing secret messages. Our code word was 'Falconer', our mother's maiden name. For the first eight words of the message, an A would be replaced by an F (being the first letter of the code word), a B by a G and so forth. We would then do the same for each subsequent set of eight words, replacing A with the next letter in the code word each time (except for A itself in the code word, which became B). Thus the sentence:

'The quick brown fox jumped over the lazy dog.'

became:

'YMJ VZNHP GWTBS KTC OZRUJI TAJW YMJ QFED EPH'

Then the whole message would be turned backwards and run together thus:

HPEDEFQJMYWJATIJURZOCTKSBTWGPHN-
ZVJMY'

It was a rudimentary but effective system – suggested in a letter from my father now that I think back – and so for the rest of the morning I wrote to Margaret explaining everything I knew. By noon I'd the entire thing encrypted and written on the back of a rather dull letter describing my journey and plans for marine observations. If the pages were intercepted the series of letters would attract suspicion, but it was the best I could do. Sealing it up I returned on deck and when the next barge passed heading toward Edinburgh I passed it over together with the postage money.

Afterwards I ate pickled ham and barley bread in the sunshine and talked with my fellow passengers. There was a young woman and her bawling infant travelling to Glasgow, then onward to Ireland.

'It's nae right,' she muttered, dandling the baby, 'me left wi the wean and nae money, while he's ower in Belfast, drinking nae doot.'

I noticed the child had a rash at his neck, and it occurred to me some liniment might ease the pain.

An old man travelling alone nodded at her words, cooing at the child all the while. I imagined him travelling for family or professional reasons. Two sailors with canvas bags ate heartily and swigged from their bottles of porter, but there was no sign of the sixth of our party. The captain's wife returned on deck with tea, and as the cups were passed round I remarked to the captain what a shame it was their remaining guest was missing out.

'Och him, he's one of our regulars. He sells gear all over the country, or so he says, but he's no feeling too grand the now. Probably the drink if ye ask me,' he added with a wink.

'I wonder if I know him,' I said, feigning interest. 'What does he look like?'

'Who? Himsel?' replied the captain. 'Och, you'll see him soon enough. He's in the for'ard cabin opposite your own. He's full of stories and has a limp in his leg he says he got at Waterloo, but mair likely he got it falling over a chair.'

Smiling at the captain's description and feeling the benefit of the meal, I stayed on deck to smoke a pipe.

'How do you find your cabin?' I asked the old man.

'Oh, fine,' he replied. 'I slept like a bairn in a cot.' He frowned. 'I couldnae see myself whit the problem was.'

'Problem?'

'Him. The feller ye were just askin' aboot. I wis settled in the front berth opposite your own when he came chapping at the door.'

He shook his head.

'Och, he's an awful lookin soul, puir man, what wi his face aw pock marked. Well, he asked me if it wisnae too much trouble but could we swap berths. The barge rocks a bit at the back, so he reckoned. Anyway, that was that.' He looked at me. 'And you, son? Did ye sleep?'

'Sorry?'

'In your wee room, did ye sleep well enough?'

My mind had slipped out of focus.

'What? Oh, yes, yes, I did thank you.' The others stopped talking and turned.

'Excuse me,' I blurted, stumbling to my feet, 'I've forgotten something.' And followed by their wide eyes I hurried below.

The door opposite was still closed as I entered my cabin. Everything seemed just as before. My bag was still on my bed – or had

I left it on the chair? The air was still. Once again, however, I'd the uneasy sense someone was listening. I went through my pockets quickly. All the money was still there.

After a while I sat down on the bed. The silence seemed to grow deeper until I heard the horses' clop and the barge drifted onward. Now that we were underway again I began to think more lightly of things. Perhaps it had simply been a thief who'd tried my door in the night. Perhaps the man in the cabin opposite was simply a commercial traveller, as the captain had said. Many people bore the marks of smallpox.

For some time I didn't move until, thinking of the child's rash, I dug the liniment from my bag. I was about to return on deck when I hesitated, returned and reopened it. Hands trembling I rummaged through it again and again until finally I emptied it onto the floor. My father's pistol was gone.

6

'You're a fool, Mungo,' I muttered, chewing my lip. 'Think, man.'

I was being watched. Watched and hunted by someone who now had my pistol. And I'd a sense that whoever this man was, he wasn't alone. I thought of Sandy's murder, and my cabin felt like a coffin.

My heart was dunt-dunting like a drum. A large part of me wanted to turn tail back to Edinburgh, find Sir John and return the money. Where was the shame in that? But whether from youthful pride or plain stubbornness, I was determined to go on. I sat down and I thought, and I kept right on thinking until I decided that, just as soon as darkness fell, I'd take my chances and escape.

This was my plan. We were due at Falkirk around eight o'clock. The captain had explained the barge would have to go through a series of locks to join the Forth and Clyde Canal. I would wait until the barge came to a halt at the first lock, then make my move.

That afternoon passed as slowly as any I've ever lived, and all the while my mind ran over every eventuality, fearful as a rabbit.

To pass the time I kept myself occupied at the porthole gazing out on forests, fields and cottages and counting off the milestones as they glided by. It was a mild day, but around four the listless air grew heavier with the scent of daisies, docks and nettles, and sure enough it wasn't long before dusty rain began to patter on the water. The rain became a downpour as the sky grew blacker and blacker, but with the change in the weather a calm descended, my spirits lightened and I felt a fresh resolve.

With a keener eye now, I surveyed the cabin and returned the scattered equipment to my bag. Then I looked in the small mirror above the water bowl. I hadn't shaved in a while, but as yet the overall effect was merely scruffy. My tweeds were hardy enough, but I cursed my leather town shoes which were ill suited to the country.

Eventually as twilight fell the rain eased off. The captain called 'whoa-there,' then made his way to his mate on the towpath. A lantern glowed from the side of the barge, but otherwise all was gloom. This was it.

I tiptoed up the stairs and emerged on deck. The captain and his mate had moved towards the first lock and were busying themselves with the mechanism. They were soon joined from a hut by an employee of the canal company.

A gangplank stretched to shore and it was the work of a moment to cross it. I reached the towpath, crossed it and disappeared into the bushes. As far as I could tell no one had noticed and, while it would soon be discovered I was gone, I hoped that where and when might remain a mystery long enough to give me a start.

I emerged through the foliage into a barley field and following its edge downhill came to a path which led south a few miles.

Then, spying another path, I struck out along that, my feet slipping in the mud from time to time but otherwise no different from the country lanes of my youth. It ran west along a stream for a couple of miles, then up through a wood. The light was all but gone now, the birds grew still and bats swooped. After a while I found myself following the perimeter of a substantial farmhouse and coming round through the gate made my way into a courtyard. A pack of dogs barked and growled as I crossed to the door and knocked. There were footsteps, a bolt was drawn back and the man of the house appeared with a lantern in his hand.

'Quiet lads!' The dogs grew still. 'What's this?' he said. 'Where have ye come frae?'

Apologising for the hour, I explained I'd got lost on the road from Falkirk. But he was already beckoning me in, tut-tutting at the condition of my shoes and leading me through to the kitchen where I found his wife and child by the fire. It was a good solid house, warm too, and my host was about my age and build, only broader. He welcomed me to Auchengean Farm, introduced himself as Davie Wellburn and in a trice there was broth and fresh bread before me at the table. In turn I made a play along the absent-minded professor lines, that I'd just been making some notes when I lost my way. But there was a twinkle in Davie's eye.

'Whit have ye got in the bag?'

'Oh, just medical supplies,' I replied. 'I'm a doctor, I always carry it.' I paused for a moment and furrowed my brow. 'The thing is, Mister Wellburn, I really need a horse for the road and wondered if I could,' I didn't know how to say it, 'well, if I could buy one from you.'

He was surprised, for sure, and explained that though there were two horses on the farm they were like family.

'But I've a neighbour, John Armitage over at the Glen. He's a horse would do ye fine fur the road I'm thinking. How aboot I take ye over there the morn?'

'Oh no,' I said, rising. 'I couldn't put you to the trouble.'

'Och it's nae trouble at all, Doctor. We've aye got a bed ready. And sure, where else would ye go at this hour?'

I hesitated. The last thing I wanted was to bring trouble to their door. But in my complacency I convinced myself I was safe, that I'd evaded whoever hunted me. After all, as Davie said, where else could I go?

So I agreed, and we sat comfortably together in front of the fire. I was asked my opinion on the health of the bairn and dandled him on my knee. Then, as my eyelids grew heavy, I was pointed in the direction of a bed and was soon sound asleep.

I woke sharp in the middle of the night. The dogs were barking again. I crept to the window and through the gloom made out horses, murmurs and a figure crossing the courtyard. There was silence for a moment, then the front door was battered loud enough to wake the dead.

Davie appeared on the landing carrying an ancient hunting rifle.

'It's you they're after, isn't it?' he whispered.

I nodded. 'I'm sorry to bring trouble to your door, Davie.'

He stared over the banister. The battering continued.

'Open up!' The voice was menacing.

Davie grimaced. 'Well, they dinnae sound like they're the law, that's for sure. I'll gie it a wee bit and then I'll have to open the door, but if you're wise you'll get oot o here. Good luck to ye, man.'

He gave me his hand.

'I'll never forget this,' I said, his decency overwhelming me.

I returned to the room, grabbed my bag and stole to the window. I counted four horses in the courtyard. I raised the sash, tied my bag securely over my shoulder and crept out onto the ledge. At the same time Davie open the front door and in they barged.

By now I was out on the ledge with the roof on either side. The slates gleamed in the drizzle. I took a deep breath and heaved myself up and onto them, but my shoes slid down again and caught in the gutter.

'There he is!'

The shout came from the courtyard below followed by a gunshot, and a ball whistled by. One of them leaned out the window beside me and aimed a pistol directly at my head. I kicked out and connected with his hand enough to deflect his aim. There was a deafening report as the gun discharged into the air.

As I beetled up toward the crest of the roof he clambered out of the window and followed me. It was a desperate scramble, and just as I had put my hand to the top ridge he seized my ankle.

'Caught ye now, doctor,' he grinned, and just at that a rare surge of rage came over me. He gave a start of surprise as, instead of continuing to struggle away, I pulled my ankle up, hauling him higher until, with every ounce of my strength, I kicked down. His grip slackened, and before he could recover I kicked down again.

He gave a sharp cry as he slid away then tumbled from the roof, followed a moment later by a thud as his body struck the ground.

As their shouts of confusion turned to anger I slid to the far side, clambered partway down a drainpipe and jumped the rest of the way down. A searing pain shot through my leg as I landed and flailed forward. Then came more shouts and barking as, with no idea where I was going or what I was doing, I clawed my way through a great tangle of brambles and disappeared into the dark.

7

I crashed through the undergrowth, all the while following the run of the ground downhill. I slipped more than once, skidding sideways in the mud, and before long was bedraggled as any scarecrow. At one point I stopped and listened, but there wasn't a sound, and digging out my watch found it was past one. My chest heaved with every breath and my leg throbbed. Resting against a tree I began to despair at the thought of the hours till dawn, certain in the knowledge that my pursuers would be close on my heels, their determination to capture me only increased by the death I'd almost certainly inflicted on one of their own. That thought spurred me on as I forced my way through heather, bracken and scrub.

It flashed through my mind that I should hide up a tree, scrape out a burrow, or double back. But all I could think was to run.

I soon faced a dilemma. A muffled roar had grown and grown in my ears until all at once I stumbled onto a riverbank. The forest gave way to a streak of sky, the treeline just visible opposite, and the sheen of the water told me this was no mere stream. It must have been thirty feet wide and as deep as I was tall. In desperation I snapped a branch from a tree, immediately regretting the mark this left, and jabbed it into the freezing water. It didn't strike solid ground, and all the while the current pulled like a dog new to a leash. It was no use, I couldn't cross. So which way should I go?

I figured that by turning right and following the bank downstream the going might be easier, and perhaps I would reach farmland and the chance of cover in a barn. To my left, however, the cause of the din was all too apparent. A hundred yards upstream the whole river fell in a great curtain of water, tumbling down until it formed the smooth stretch in front of me. Though the ground rose sharply that way I'd be above my pursuers, and I told myself that the river would surely narrow to a point where I could risk a crossing. Since I daren't double back there was nothing else for it and shutting out the pain in my leg I began the ascent round the waterfall.

The going was tough, and with every step I fought my way through fern, bushes and saplings. Sweat streamed into my eyes, thorns scored my face and soon my hands were sticky with blood. The cascade pounded in my ears now, until with a final lunge I reached the head of the falls.

Sprawling on the mossy ground by a boulder I drew a sleeve across my brow and fought to regain my breath. Then, inch by inch, I peered round the boulder.

Three figures were searching the bank. During the climb my mind had raced with the idea they'd divide on reaching the river, but that hope vanished with the glow of a lantern. Their heads were bowed searching the ground, and a moment later my stomach lurched as one beckoned to the others. Their heads rose in unison toward the waterfall and I ducked out of sight, but it would make little difference. They'd found my trail. I heaved myself to my feet, hitching my bag more tightly over my shoulder as I did so, and staggered on.

Above the falls the river bulged to form a small loch. The forest retreated round its shores allowing grass to skirt its banks. I sprinted pell-mell in a wide sweep, from time to time leaping streams as here and there they dribbled down to feed the river. The waterfall faded only to be replaced by the pounding of my own heart, and with my lungs bursting I reached the head of the loch into which the river dropped in a plashing cascade. It was still too wide to cross, however, so on I pressed through rowan and pine. A pair of grouse clattered into the air in front of me and I stole a nervous glance over my shoulder.

On and on I climbed. From time to time a rock or ridge barred my path, each time I turned inland, but on one occasion I slipped and plunged waist high into the icy torrent. My breath whistled through my clenched teeth as I inched along the sheer stone bank, my shoes slithering on the rocks below.

The banks grew closer, the water running in ever narrower courses shallower and shallower, until finally the forest thinned out and I emerged onto moorland beneath a starlit sky. I'd climbed about two hundred feet up a narrow ravine, and by this point the river was young and playing over falls. A pair of sheep turned and trotted away, and over a rise I made out a hill shepherd's cottage. Smoke curled up showing a fire still smouldered within, but otherwise nothing stirred. All was so calm it was hard to believe three men hunted me, and I realised the next decision I took could be life or death.

There was a sheep track running away to my left, while a set of stepping stones forded the river to my right. That gave me an idea.

I darted toward the river, being sure to leave heavy footprints, and even managed to stage a fall leaving a handprint in the mud. Then I started across the stepping stones leaving muddy prints all the way, with more heading downhill on the other side. As mud gave way to heather, however, I tiptoed to the side and doubled back in a wide arc, all the while treading softly as a deer. My false trail now set, I pressed on a good half mile further up the slope until I found a narrow point and waded back across the river. I was now a good distance above the cottage and, finding a dip, lay down in the heather. Its white walls were barely visible in the gloom and all was silent save the river.

I didn't have to wait long. By the time I'd caught my breath the lantern emerged from the treeline and moved toward the cottage. Their voices carried in the still air. They were arguing over which way to go. Moments later a fist pounded on the cottage door while the lantern crept round in a wide circle below. They must have roused the shepherd because a bolt was drawn followed by harsh voices and I felt sorry for leading them to him. His bewilderment must have satisfied them, however, for having searched the cottage they were quickly back outside. A voice cried out and the lantern moved to the river, across it, then down.

'There's more of them heading down,' said one. Just as I'd hoped, they were picking up my false trail.

I gripped the heather, for I sensed their doubt. Everything was still, I hardly dared breathe, and then the lantern swung away down the hill, growing fainter and fainter.

I rolled onto my back and let out a sigh of relief. I was soaked to the waist, exhausted and cold. I was about to get to my feet when I saw two figures climbing toward me. They'd divided, one downhill two up, and they were advancing one on each side of the river.

I buried myself in the heather. They moved closer, their laboured breath louder and louder until finally they seemed on top of me. If they saw me now I was dead, simple as that, and I committed myself to my maker. The moment stretched out in my mind as I lay there, helpless as a new born lamb until the tension broke.

'Anything?' came the call from the far bank.

'Naw, nothing, I cannae see a thing.'

Their voices came from higher up the hill. They'd somehow passed over me in the dark. The thrill of escape coursed through me, followed by the realisation they could turn back at any moment. I listened, stock still, but for the time being they were intent on searching ever higher. To the thump of my own heart I counted fifty, another twenty for good measure, then crept forward an inch at a time until I was halfway back to the cottage. Then I half lifted myself and began to run.

On and on I ran, gradually lifting myself higher, quicker now, until I was past the cottage and down the sheep track. I'd come within an inch of being found. But for the moment at least, I'd given my hunters the slip.

8

A rosy dawn spread west as I stirred from under a hedgerow, my breath curling in the iron chill. The air resounded with bird calls. Stretching and knuckling my eyes I reflected on the few hours since my escape from the farmhouse. I hadn't stopped running until reaching level ground, and even then I'd followed one lane after another until, unable to take another step, I'd collapsed on the verge.

I swiped away the worst of the mud caking my clothes and turned to what remained of my shoes. Wincing with pain I peeled them off followed by my socks, their thick wool sticky with blood. I fished the liniment from my bag, coated my feet and bound them with bandages. Returning the liniment, I spied the flask of rum, hesitated, then lifted it and took a generous swig. The spirit burned giving fleeting comfort and hauling the socks and shoes back on, I stood and took in the unbroken country on all sides.

It was time to move but not on foot, for my hunters would be back on horseback. I needed a horse too – and quickly.

The first opportunity proved a disappointment. After several miles a farm hove into view, smoke curling from its chimneys, and I marched up and rapped the door. It cracked open an inch and the wary owner barked at me to state my purpose, but no sooner had I begun than the door slammed shut.

I soldiered on and after a while the river from the previous night reappeared, only this was its lower reaches. Two men approached carrying shovels. I froze at the sight of them until I realised they were workmen. Wide-eyed, they stopped speaking and looked me up and down. They barely answered my passing greeting and though I could have asked directions I hesitated, by which time they were past. It was a harmless encounter, but it left me realising how fearful I'd become in less than a day.

After three more fruitless farm calls I reached a signpost which really did cheer me. *Glen Farm* it read, in tall white letters, then *J Armitage, Esquire.* It was the neighbour Davie Wellburn had mentioned. A boy answered my call and when I asked for Armitage he pointed to the yard, and there I found him working on a cart wheel, a heavy-set old countryman in a leather waist-coat. He stroked a white beard and looked me in the eye as I explained my purpose. If he was surprised by the sight of me, he didn't let it show.

'Just wait here a wee minute,' he wheezed, and limped out of the yard. I did as I was bid, pacing all the while. When a full half hour had passed I grew concerned. After an hour I was just about to leave, when Armitage and the boy rounded the corner leading a handsome chestnut stallion.

'He'd new shoes a week ago, and I've slipped on an old saddle fur ye,' said Armitage with a grin. 'He's a beauty, no?'

We closed the deal at twenty-five guineas including an old pair of boots, a price which was at least seven too many, and I handed over the five guinea banknotes which he scrutinised, giving me many looks as he did so. Satisfied, however, he sent the boy into the house for some cold chicken pie. All the while Armitage watched in silence and I feared lest he ask me any questions. But apart from peering at my doctor's bag he seemed uninterested.

Finishing the pie, I thanked him and mounted the horse.

'Wherever your headed,' he replied, 'I've nae doot ye'll be lookin' fur the high road. Ye'll strike it ower there, aboot four mile south. Good luck now.'

It was a relief to be on horseback and in no time I spied the dusty high road. I didn't trust it, however, and a mile short turned west over moorland.

Clouds scudded across the sky but cresting a bluff the sun burst through and I saw for miles in every direction, the grass rippling in the breeze. Falkirk's chimneys and steeples bristled in the distance and from there the canal headed straight west while the road twisted like a bootlace. My horse picked its way down from the bluff, then along the banks of a burn. Slowly the clouds returned and the sky grew grey. I pressed on.

Toward the end of the day and with the light fading, a fork in the road appeared. One way led west, the other north by a bridge over the canal. I kept back and moved into cover.

A lone rider waited, watching the road.

The darkness grew. A second rider approached. Together they dismounted and conferred, pointing first in one direction, then another. They were my hunters from the moor. Through the gloom I made out a twisted lip on the face of one. The other – a short fidgety man with his back to me – turned only once, darting his eyes from side to side. As for the third with the smallpox marks, there was no sign of him. I felt sure he was their leader. He was somewhere nearby, planning my capture with a spider's resolve.

Twisted Lip swore and spat on the ground. Through their mutterings I caught the word *Denholm*. They lingered at the junction, seeming in no hurry to leave, until a carriage and four horses came thundering toward them. It was the mail coach, and a guard stood at the rear with a blunderbuss in his hands. The sight of it unnerved them as well it might. Mail guards often shot anyone loitering on the highway, such was their fear of robbers. They quickly remounted and trotted west.

With the mail coach gone I crossed the canal. The day was hurrying to a close now. It was time to find shelter. As my horse picked its way, head bowed, great earthworks appeared in the landscape. I reached the ruins of a guard tower and suddenly realised this was the Antonine Wall, the last outpost of the Romans I'd learned of as a boy.

My horse settled inside the ruins. Green and pink lichen patterned the ancient brickwork, and the moss at my feet was dry and yielding. The clouds, which had scudded across the heavens all day, now halted in the windless sky. Here and there a star peeped through and a sliver of moon glimmered in the firmament. I thought of those ancient Roman guards staring north into the unknown.

I committed myself to my Maker, remembering just two days earlier I'd been cursing life's predictable path. An owl hooted. My horse whinnied, and in silence I gave way to sleep.

9

I woke to swirling mist, my face numb and fingers blue. Fear of the unknown clutched my heart.

Forcing myself up I rode on. A light breeze gradually dispelled the mist and the day grew bright until, from a rise, I spied the smoke of Glasgow, thundercloud black. Villages appeared, then towns, their labourers and domestics crowding the roads, heads bowed.

As I crossed the city limits it began to rain. The dirt track gave way to cobbles. Smoke hung in the air, coal dust was quick in my mouth and then, as millworks sprung up all around, the din of their steam looms pounded like an anthem to progress. Despite the noise and grime it was good to be back among people. The streets grew busier toward the river.

Glasgow was booming. Its cotton industry blossomed on the back of immigrants from Ulster, and while the days of the Tobacco Lords had gone with the loss of the American colonies, their fabulous wealth still echoed all around. James Watt's steam engine was king, and already powered everything from ships to printing presses. The city had a swagger quite unlike fusty Edinburgh. Steel and ship building hadn't come to Glasgow yet, and there still lingered signs of the city's mediaeval roots in stone crosses, twisting lanes and mossy chapels.

I sold my stallion in a farrier's yard for twelve guineas, a price the merchant could easily expect to double. At the Gallowgate I entered a corner washhouse, where a penny secured me a hot bath and a shave. Then I inspected my clothes and shoes and made good use of a brush and some dubbin. Much improved, I headed for the river to find passage to Greenock. Turning a corner under the sign of *The Silver Dollar* I reached the Broomielaw, its quay stretching along the north bank of the Clyde.

If the streets before were busy, the Broomielaw was seething. Two carts laden with milk cans rumbled close by, their drivers bawling at me to look where I was going. There were boys running errands, the drowsy cry of a newspaper vendor, barrels being rolled through warehouse doors past old men chewing plugs of tobacco, fishermen mending nets and cranes lifting crates in net slings. Meanwhile a host of puffer boats thronged the inky water, their funnels smoking, furnaces roaring and engines clattering. Their crew called one to another while here and there stood a noble puffer captain, arms folded and a pipe clenched in his teeth, the master of all he surveyed.

Back from the water's edge dim passages led to a warren of backstreets. Two pigtailed Chinamen in matching red suits disappeared through an arch and down a staircase, a blue lantern glowing above. From somewhere on an upper floor came a woman's bawdy laughter. To me it was mayhem and confusion, but there was also an order to it all, and I began to see that from this quay Glasgow connected with every port the world over.

Picking my way, I reached a shipping agent's office and presented myself to a frock- coated clerk. He was making ready to close but stopped on my approach.

'Can I help, sir?'

'I'd like to purchase a passage to Greenock, if I may. Perhaps there's a boat later?'

He scanned a list.

'Well ye just missed one a half hour ago, and I'm afraid there's nothing for the rest of the day sir, ye see it's a limited service. But there's a passenger ship leaving tomorrow morning if that might suit ye?'

'I was really hoping for something this evening.'

He scratched his chin.

'Well,' he replied, with a glance over his shoulder, 'ye could try Archie McGregor. He doesn't normally take passengers. It's just small cargo he carries – but ye never know, he might make an exception fur ye, sir. Ye'll catch him a couple o hunner yerds along there. It's a bonny wee puffer. The *Strathspey*.'

I thanked him and wandered along the quay, searching for the name of each boat I passed. Finally I found her. Her captain was busy on deck.

'Hi there below,' I called. He looked up and cocked his head.

'I hear you're heading downriver to Greenock. Can I join you?'

He slowly rubbed his forehead.

'Greenock, is it? Well, I'm just waiting for a delivery of engine parts that's to go tae Dumbarton, so I am, then I wis thinking of making a start. But it'll no be Greenock until aboot seven the morn. So if that suited ye, how aboot I get ye back here at nine?'

I quickly thanked him and disappeared back into the twilight.

It was time to visit the University.

10

Back then the University was a medieval college on the High Street. I slipped through the gate and into the quadrangle, its solemn clock tower rising above me. A side staircase led up to a studded oak door. It swung open as a student shuffled out, a sheaf of papers in his ink-stained hands. I dodged round him and entered the library.

Glasgow University is ancient, and it showed in its vast collection of tomes. Candles burned in wall sconces below a dark panelled ceiling, while ranks of shelves and twisting stairways led off the reading room.

I set about researching the Double Eagle. A cabinet with rows of drawers from A to Z stood before me. Each drawer contained a stack of handwritten cards bearing the name of a book and its location. Recent additions were in fine copperplate. Other cards were as old as the library itself, written in a monk's spidery scrawl. I finally located two crumbling volumes and laid them on a desk.

The first was an obscure sixteenth century work entitled *Heroicall Devices* by Marcus Claudius Paradin, Canon of the Abbey of Beaujeu at Lyons. This book catalogued a great number of symbols, and the good Canon had annotated every one. Leafing through, I came upon the following device and historical note.

'The Eagle hath always been the chief ensign among the Romans when, from the time of the Consul Marius, it was dedicated to the legions and preferred above all others. It is the King of birds, chosen for a symbol to signify a nation which hath subdued all others. But in the days of Constantine the Great, when the empire of Rome came to be divided East and West (as Wolfganus Lazius, historiographer to the king of the Romans saith) and command shifted to the Emperor's new city of Constantinople, it was the Double Eagle that came to be preferred.'

I then turned to the second book, a mediaeval work entitled *Buckland's Heraldry*. From its pages I discovered the following commentary:

'The signal of the Double Eagle is a most ancient device of Europe. It has its moderne origins in the courtes of the Byzantine Emperors, but its rootes are deepe, mysterious and extend far back in tyme unto the East and the Sumerians in Mesopotamia. In every age of mankind it denotes devyne power and authoritie and is an emblem of Scorpio: the transformation from the beetling scorpion to a soaring master of the skies.

It is the device of Byzantium and the Roman Emperors at Constantinople, of Charlemagne, the Knights Templar, the Order of the Solar Temple, the Russian Imperial Court and the Orthodox

Church; and as the Double Eagle of Lagash (a city of the Sumerians) it is the greatest of all markes in the Scottish Rite of Freemasonry, the most noble of all Masonic Rites.

It symbolises many things in many places, and its particular significance is not always clear from first encounter. But like unto the God Janus of the Romans it faces two ways, toward war and peace, East and West, good and evyll, order and chaos.'

While I'd heard of the Emperor Charlemagne and the Knights Templar, I knew nothing of the Sumerians. I'd never heard of the Order of the Solar Temple and as for the reference to Freemasonry, while I knew some of my colleagues in Edinburgh formed part of that brotherhood, I was not among them. What could possibly account for the symbol's presence on board the *Julietta*? Who were these people, united under its wings, and what was their purpose?

A faint sound to my left startled me, but it was only a rat scuttling along the wall. I hurriedly copied down the entries, trying to ignore the stares and whispers I was beginning to attract. I knew more but still understood little.

Outside the night air was perishing beneath a clear sky and sickle moon. I hurried along deserted streets. A church bell tolled eight followed by three quarter chimes.

For the second time that day I turned the corner of *The Silver Dollar* but this time I froze. My hunters stood not a stone's throw away, blocking my path to the *Strathspey*. Twisted Lip glanced round. I instinctively dived into the tavern and the door swung shut at my back. The place was crammed, the air thick with sweat, tobacco and ale. Two fiddlers played at a corner table. A moon-faced fishwife cradled a glass of gin. Lolling against the fiddlers she crooned an old Scots rhyme in time to the music. Everywhere was jostling and merriment. I edged to the counter between a pair of drunk Danes and shouted to the landlady for ale. She sized me up as she poured the beer. Trying to keep my head down and my hand over my face, I slipped a penny across the counter and headed for a quiet corner. To my astonishment I found myself sitting beside the shipping agent from earlier, his eyes closed, insensible with drink.

A fellow stumbled forward, two glasses in his hands, narrowly avoiding crashing onto our table.

'Here Jimmy, here's a wee whisky fur ye. Wake up man!'

Jimmy barely stirred but, eyes closed, stretched out his arm and, by virtue of some perfect drunken harmony, made seamless contact with the glass. He sipped the whisky then laid it down before resuming his slumber. I marvelled at the perfection of it, but that thought disappeared when, a moment later, Twisted Lip prowled in.

I ducked down beside Jimmy and pretended to sleep, and in doing so discovered his rolled-up frock coat. I slipped it on. But it might avail me little, for Twisted Lip was at the counter now and beckoning to the landlady.

Just then something happened that saved my life. As the land-lady cupped her ear across the counter, there arose from outside voices raised in song, and into the bar marched a half dozen arm-banded citizens of the Glasgow Temperance Society, with a minister of the church at their head. They were singing Psalm 100:

> *All people that on earth do dwell,*
> *Sing to the Lord with cheerful voice,*

Him serve with mirth his praise forth tell,
Come ye before him and rejoice.'

The effect of this extraordinary entrance was mixed. Many turned their backs and continued drinking. Others jeered and waved their arms as if to shoo them off. Some however were embarrassed, particularly by the sight of the stern reverend, and here and there patrons drained their glasses and began to leave. In an instant I saw my chance. Scooping up my slumbering neighbour I made as bold an attempt at a drunken stagger as I could, calling to him that it was time we were for the off.

Too drunk to care Jimmy followed like a lamb and, heads down and crooning, we were soon past the preacher and outside where the rest of the Temperance brigade thronged.

I daren't look up and continued along the Broomielaw in a drunken clinch with Jimmy until the voices died away. After a while I darted a look back. My pursuers were livid, grabbing one patron after another in their bid to find me.

I settled Jimmy into a cab, returned his coat and pushed five guineas into his pocket. Then I stole to the harbour wall and down a ladder. Archie was there, waiting.

'Permission to come aboard?' I called.

'Permission granted, sir,' he grinned. 'I was beginning to wonder if you were coming at all!'

He gave me a mock serious look.

'Now, there wouldn't happen to be some rough looking characters after you by any chance? Only I had a couple of them here a bittie earlier looking fur someone. That wouldn't be you now, would it?'

Seeing me hesitate he laughed and clapped me on the shoulder.

'Dinnae fear, man, auld Archie telt them nothing – and though I neither ken nor want to ken what they're after you for, you seem a braw enough lad to me. Now, let's get ye to Greenock. Eh, what's your name again?'

I gave him my hand. 'It's Lyon. Doctor Mungo Lyon.'

'Well doctor, it's a pleasure to have you on board. Now, let's get under way, shall we?'

Moments later, a lantern at its prow, the *Strathspey* puffed away from the harbour while the dark mass of Glasgow grew distant behind.

11

I drifted in the half-world between sleeping and waking. The Lord Advocate, Sir John, Margaret, my parents: their faces rose like ghosts and stirred the dark pools of my memory until I was back in the India of my childhood, gripping Ranjita's hand. A fire eater danced in the street. Flames bloomed from his lips, dazzling my eyes, then all became Burke writhing in the hangman's noose. Finally Twisted Lip was towering over me, fingers reaching, and all the while a repetitive drumming grew louder and louder.

I struggled and woke to the regular put-putting of the *Strathspey*'s engine. I was below deck, my head jarred against a coil of rope. Daylight streamed through a rust-pocked porthole. Sweet engine oil, a salt sea tang and something like rotten eggs lingered in the dank air. I got up, stepped over a puddle of bilge and clambered on deck.

'Well, well, good morning to ye, Doctor Lyon,' called Archie from the wheelhouse. 'Ye needed that sleep I'd say, I'm I right?'

I returned the greeting with a yawn and rubbed my neck. He passed me some strong tea.

'We're after leavin' Dumbarton aboot ten minutes ago, and I reckon' wi a clear calm morn like this we'll be tying up at

Greenock the back o seven right enough. Aye, it's a fine day, for the moment anyway. And how's that for a view for ye then?'

Most memories have faded over the years, but my first sight of the River Clyde that morning will never fade. The risen sun was strong on our backs. The air lay still as in a deep forest. The water sparkled beyond our bow ripples while a solitary seagull followed, wheeling against broken cloud. Left and right stood the green hills of Renfrew and Dumbarton, but it was the craggy peaks of Argyll looming in the distance that dominated the glorious scene.

Then it changed. A cold wind rose from the west. Dark clouds rolled in and the rain came hammering down. I hurried, shoulders hunched, to join Archie in the wheelhouse.

'Just a passing shower, doctor,' he said. 'It'll clear again in a wee minute.'

Sure enough, the battering rain ceased and the sun broke through the cloud, casting shafts of light on the simmering waters. I'd never seen anything like it. It was my first taste of the west coast's ever-changing weather.

As the morning wore on the river teemed with puffers heading upriver and down, and Archie had a greeting for every one. News of tides, harbour traffic and profitable errands were called out one to another. The *Strathspey* was just one in a great flotilla of little steamers. As the river widened, and we drew towards the harbour of Port Glasgow on the south bank, I caught my breath at a triple-masted barque in full sail. She was more beautiful than anything I'd seen since India.

Graceful as a swan she glided from the town's harbour, where I was surprised to see the occasional gentleman going to and fro in a powdered wig or tri-cornered hat, just as if dear old George the

Third were still on the throne. The crew busied themselves on deck while one fellow scrambled to the crow's nest. She was embarking on a voyage across the Ocean and I wondered what sights her crew would see between here and the sultry West Indies. Meantime three more ships waited at the quay, their masts bare, their cargos being discharged by swarms of dock hands.

Beyond Port Glasgow the river widened again. By now I could see dozens of ships at anchor. The river became a deep bowl here, a natural amphitheatre surrounded on all sides by rising hills. To the north and west, sea lochs led off into narrow passes and mountain glens, while the main body of the river swept round to the south, turning the Tail O' The Bank at Gourock to the open sea beyond. But before that turn, here, on this sheltered elbow of the river, lay Greenock.

The water was choppier now and Archie had to work the tiller hard. The waterside thronged with ships, the sky a forest of masts. I searched in vain for the *Julietta* among names like *Mercury*, *Antigone*, *Basilisk* and *Hunter*.

We were no more than a hundred yards from the river bank when all the chaos of the docks ceased, giving way to the serene frontage of the Custom House Quay. There, set back from the river, stood the Custom House, the headquarters of Commander Gabriel Birkmyre, His Majesty's Collector of Customs and Excise at Greenock.

Archie slowed the engine and nudged the *Strathspey* tight to the harbour wall.

'Now if ye dinnae mind, Doctor Lyon, I'll no hang about for any sign o the Excisemen. They aye ken where tae find me, without me troubling their door!'

We shook hands like old friends and, slipping him a guinea before he could argue, I leapt onto dry land. I watched for a moment as she steamed on downriver, the smoke from her funnel puffing in the breeze. Then, to the cry of the gulls, I climbed the steps to the Custom House and my first encounter with Gabriel Birkmyre.

12

I'd been waiting in the hall over an hour, finding geometric patterns in the chess board floor and attracting glances from the clerks as they shimmered in and out through panelled doorways. Were there enemies here, within the Customs? Had my arrival been noted, perhaps by this very clerk who now approached?

'Commander Birkmyre will see you now, Doctor Lyon.'

I was led up a double staircase, the landing dominated by the lion and unicorn glaring down from the Crown insignia. I gazed back, my neck hair bristling. I've always distrusted power, and there's rebel blood in my veins. After all, it wasn't so many years since many of my clan rose with the Young Pretender only to face the horror of Culloden Moor. The Crown wasn't always right, or just. The Lord Advocate saw loyalty in me, he said. But could I, or any man, be always loyal to the Crown and do its bidding, no matter what the cost?

Gabriel Birkmyre seemed every inch the Crown's loyal servant. A native of Greenock, the Royal Navy had been his life. He had served with distinction in the Napoleonic Wars. Like Nelson himself he'd even lost an eye, in Birkmyre's case at Aboukir Bay whilst serving aboard *HMS Culloden* under Admiral Troubridge. I suppose he believed he'd always be at sea. But it wasn't to be.

In the aftermath of war Birkmyre suffered what was politely referred to as 'a nervous episode'. Following an honourable discharge befitting his rank he returned home and into the Customs. Within just eighteen months he was promoted to the high office of Collector. While surprising to many, the decision was no doubt influenced by his distinguished war record. That, and some powerful friends. He was generally cold and distant, with precious few glimpses of warmth, except on the subject of fine wine and good whisky, for which he had a definite weakness.

None of this was known to me on that first occasion when I was shown into his office. Three windows opposite gave onto the Clyde, and Gabriel Birkmyre stood before them like a captain at the bridge, hands clasped behind his back.

I was announced.

'Thank you, Mister Ferguson,' he replied without turning. 'That will be all.'

The clerk retreated and closed the doors. A clock ticked on the mantel to my right amid stern government portraits. On my left stood a table strewn with charts, tables and open logbooks. A wine-stained goblet rested beside a burning candle, sickly in the daylight.

Birkmyre still had his back to me, one hand faintly trembling now that I noticed, the other clutching it hard. Everything about him was black, from his shoes and stockings to his britches and tailcoat. Even his scrub of hair was black flecked with grey.

'So let me get this right,' he said, turning to face me. 'You're an Edinburgh surgeon?'

I thought perhaps a few pleasantries would have been in order, but clearly he wasn't of that mind.

'I am,' I replied calmly. 'I've been barred from practice.'

I thought he'd ask more, but he didn't. I thought he'd ask about my journey but he didn't seem interested in that either.

'Doctor Lyon,' he said at last. 'I've been asked to assist your investigation here, and I'll meet that request. But I want you to know I'm far from pleased about it. In my view, civilians shouldn't meddle in Crown affairs.'

He certainly didn't waste time.

'Well, Commander,' I replied, stiffly. 'You did seek assistance, did you not?'

He seemed to hover on the verge of responding, then thought better of it and gave me a vinegar look instead. 'I want your word, Doctor, that you'll keep me informed at every stage.'

'You have it, Commander.'

'Very well,' he replied. 'Let me make this brief.'

I followed him to the table where he uncovered a marine chart of the Firth of Clyde.

'I've been annotating this from the start. Here is Cumbrae.' He pointed to a tiny island in the middle of the Firth. 'The morning after the lighthouse keeper was murdered,' he said, his finger gliding down the chart, 'the *Julietta* was spotted here, ten miles to the south. I dispatched the marines under the command of Mister Anderson, and they towed the *Julietta* to quarantine here at Greenock.' He tapped the place on the map.

I recalled Birkmyre discovering the *Julietta*'s sailing between Greenock and Jamaica below capacity.

'Perhaps illicit trade of some description?' I asked.

'Perhaps.'

He wasn't giving much away.

I peered at the chart. 'If so, that would mean a landing point. Preferably a remote one.'

'I'll grant you that, Doctor, but there are miles of shoreline round the Firth which fit that description. Assuming landings even took place here,' he added, 'and not somewhere on the south coast of Ireland, for example.'

Sure enough, the meandering coastline spoke for itself.

'Who are the main landowners round the Firth?'

'There aren't many. Four to speak of. First,' he said, pointing to the right-hand side of the chart, 'the Clyde's mainland coast south of Greenock is owned by your host, Sir Guy Stewart.' His finger moved to the far left-hand side and a long peninsula. 'Second, there's the Mull of Kintyre, which forms part of the estates of His Grace the Duke of Argyll.'

He moved his hand to the middle of the chart and an island in the Firth between the mainland and Kintyre. 'Third,' he said tapping the chart, 'there's Arran, owned by the Earl of Alba. And, finally,' he added, his finger drifting above and to the right, 'there's the Isle of Bute and the Cowal Peninsula which together form the estate of the Marchioness of Bute.'

I studied the chart. The lighthouse on Cumbrae lay between Bute and the mainland.

'These owners, what do you know of them, Commander?'

'Tread carefully, Doctor,' he warned. 'Don't toy with the likes of them.'

'I understand. But a description, Commander, that's all I ask. Just to give me an idea.'

He hesitated for a moment, balancing whether to humour me.

'Very well. The dowager Marchioness of Bute is quite frail now, and since travelling to her native France is beyond her she keeps abed in her castle in Dumfriesshire to the south. She no longer has any day to day involvement with the island.'

I pictured the fading aristocrat in her bedclothes, shivering in a draughty keep.

'You'll no doubt form your own impression of Sir Guy,' Birkmyre continued, 'but I'd say he's a sound man and a good estate manager. The Earl of Alba is a moderniser. He inherited his estates from his uncle five years ago. In that time he's improved the land considerably and even commissioned a new lighthouse. He lives here, at Dunearn Castle on Arran.'

'And what of the Duke?'

Birkmyre took some time to reply.

'Argyll is the most powerful man in Scotland, Doctor Lyon, any fool knows that. He's a man of about my own age. He inherited his father's title almost twenty-five years ago. He's a difficult man perhaps, I'll grant you, with a rather fiery temper,' and I saw that he winced a little, 'but a man of high principle.'

'Where does he live?'

'His seat is here.' He pointed. 'At Inverary Castle. It lies to the north on the shore of Loch Fyne, but he has houses at his disposal all across Argyll. He has many investments in Campbeltown.'

Birkmyre indicated the town on the map. It lay close to the southern tip of Kintyre where the Firth of Clyde turned west to the open sea.

'Speaking of Campbeltown, Commander, I understand that's

where your missing Customs Officer Crawford McCunn is from. What steps have you taken to find him?'

He shook his head. 'We searched for days and found nothing. I knew his father Hamish very well, right up to his death last year. A sound Customs man.'

I thought for a moment. 'What kind of place is Campbeltown?'

He stepped back from the chart. 'Busy, very busy. It was always a fishing port but now there's something else, something far more lucrative than mere herring.'

'And what's that?'

He raised an eyebrow.

'Whisky, Doctor Lyon. The finest whisky, of course, distilled from malted barley and produced right there in the town itself. I'm surprised you don't know that, but I suppose in Edinburgh it's all fine claret arriving at Leith. Although, I must confess, I'm partial to that too, on occasion,' and he turned the glass on the table.

'But whisky's been made in Scotland for hundreds of years, has it not?'

'It has,' he nodded, 'but for the most part illegally and on a small scale. A few years ago, Parliament passed an Excise Act. That changed everything. An annual licence to distil whisky now costs just ten pounds, and there's a new fixed duty on every gallon of spirit.

'As a result, Doctor Lyon, smuggling has died back and distilleries are springing up like wildflowers. Campbeltown already has over a dozen and the Duke is making a fortune from supplying the water. The whisky is shipped the world over and the excise revenue is growing every year. It's no small thing.'

'You must have officers to regulate it.'

He nodded agreement. 'It's hard work. I have teams of officers inspecting the distilleries, overseeing production and taking inventories at the warehouses. They have their own accommodation on site and maintaining good relations with the distillery owners is vital.'

'Quite a balancing act.'

'Indeed,' he replied. 'The challenges are constant.'

An idea came to my mind. 'What tricks might a distiller get up to, Commander?'

He thought for a moment. 'Oh there are a few. But the most obvious is distilling at night and not declaring it.'

'Do you think that happens?'

'There's always an element of illegal activity, but the owners like the new system. They make good money. Why run the risk just to make more?'

He had a point.

'And below the owners? Workers? Managers?'

He shook his head. 'There's always an element, but it's low level and sooner or later we catch them, or the owners do.'

I turned back to the chart.

'I'd like to pay a visit to Campbeltown, Commander. Can you arrange that?'

He shrugged. 'If that's what you wish. But it'll take a day or two to organise, given my resources.'

Birkmyre lifted the chart to one side and delved among his papers. 'The next thing to mention,' he said, peering at a list retrieved from under his wineglass, 'is an inventory of items recovered from the *Julietta*. Aside from her cargo of sugar there were other items in the hold, including barrels of provisions and tools. Then there were personal effects which belonged to the crew. Nothing of any note, just the usual sailors' keepsakes. Many were connected to the Roman Catholic faith.'

He handed me the list and I scanned it carefully. There were rosary beads, holy water and other such items, just as he described. There was also something else.

'It says here, Commander, that copper was found in the hold. Almost one hundred pounds weight. That seems a lot?'

There had been no mention of copper in Sir John's dossier.

'Ah, yes.' He hesitated. 'I think that was overlooked. Does it seem significant to you, Doctor Lyon?'

I thought for a moment, recalling classes with Professor Griffin on the art of distilling medicinal tinctures like rosewater, cough cordials, sleep elixirs and turpentine. Many of my colleagues thought his techniques little more than alchemy, but I found them interesting. What had jogged my memory, however, was the copper apparatus we used for distilling.

'Does copper play any part in making whisky, Commander?'

He nodded. 'They use it to make the pot stills which are at the heart of the distilling process. A whole industry of coppersmiths has grown up in Campbeltown, alongside the distilleries.'

'Very well, Commander.' I handed back the list. 'I'm told a journal was also found. Do you have it?'

He unlocked the desk drawer and lifted out the journal. It was a curious volume, bound in green calfskin with a leather strap round the middle. Birkmyre turned it in his hands before offering it to me.

'It came from the deathbed of the gentleman found aft. His pen was clutched in his left hand and this journal was in his right. Looks to be filled with some kind of foreign code.'

I hesitated.

'Go on, take it Doctor,' he said, narrowing his one good eye. 'There's no need to fear the fever. It was left in plain air for a month.'

I must admit to the strangest sensation upon first holding that journal. Its covers were soft as velvet, yet I couldn't help reflecting on the desperate closing moments of its owner's life. Despite its ocean voyage something dry and foreign lingered. Rising from its coffee coloured pages I caught the aroma of some sweet spice. The Spanish writing throughout was confident, but towards the end the script grew shaky and smudged by drops of ink. The crisp copy I'd left with Margaret conveyed none of this feeling. The first page began as follows:

servidor nombre padre vuestro de nuestro amen la que de lugar estás el en en no humilde los cuyo yo cielos mancha dios santificado de nombre sea un en tu este un nombre hacen que venga vez mucho tu española no reyno la quiero hagase hidalgo de tu vivía más voluntad tiempo una así ha cuidad en acordarme en la los rocín tierra guardián adarga como y en en más de el para de cielo

'I could hazard a guess at some words from my Latin, Commander,' I said, returning it to him, 'but its meaning is beyond me.'

Birkmyre returned it to the drawer, unaware, of course, that I had already left a copy with Margaret to decipher. 'So Doctor,' he asked, 'do you have any other questions for me?'

My thoughts returned to the lighthouse and Sandy McLeod's murder.

'Have you had any success tracing Tom Hamilton?'

'Not so far,' he replied, 'but I'm following lines of inquiry. He was seen in the *Anchor Inn* not a stone's throw along the water from here, but by the time the marines searched the place he'd gone. We'll find him though.'

'What about his old partner, Hugh O'Neill?' I ventured. But I'd hardly mentioned that name when the Commander's face twisted in scorn.

'Doctor Lyon, I've followed O'Neill for nigh on ten years. He's a rogue and a liar for sure, and a smuggler of poteen to boot, but I cannot believe he's capable of anything more significant than that. If you want me to make inquiries though, I'm sure that can be done.' He moved towards the door. 'Well, time is pressing Doctor, so unless there's anything further, I imagine you'll want to get settled.'

Our interview was over, but there was one more question I burned to ask.

'The lighthouse keeper's murder, Commander, your missing officer and the *Julietta*. Do you think these things are connected?'

I thought it was fear that darkened his face. 'I hope not, Doctor. I sincerely hope not.'

Mister Ferguson was summoned and he led me to a waiting carriage. My mind was in turmoil, but the thing which troubled me most, and set my hands trembling in the carriage as it rumbled from the Custom House, was a crest above the doors as I'd left Birkmyre's office.

It was a Double Eagle.

13

Next I called on a tailor, who fitted me out with suitable clothes for polite society. So it was close to noon when, burdened with a number of parcels, I returned to the waiting carriage.

The cabby regarded me through half open eyes. 'Where to now sir?' he asked.

'I'm to call on Sir Guy Stewart.'

He sighed. 'Yes, I know that, sir – but is it the Mansion House above that you're headed for, or his estate along the coast at Ardfern?'

There was sarcasm in his reply, but I played along. 'Do you know where he's likely to be?'

He smirked into the distance. 'Well I'd say the Mansion House rather than the estate this time o year, but he's away in London fur stretches at a time what wi his duties and that, so don't say I didn't warn ye if he's no in.'

He wheeled the horse round, hooves clattering on the cobbles, and trotted toward the heart of the town.

That morning the streets teemed with people and I saw a greater diversity of races and heard more unusual accents than anywhere else in Scotland. We passed three bearded Hindus in white dress and orange turbans, mulatto boys running barefoot on errands from the shore, freed slaves with the dark skin of Africa, Chinamen, Dutch traders puffing cigars and countless sailors from the Caribbean. Crossing the main square I even picked out what I guessed was Russian being spoken by a crew as they planned their shore leave.

Teams twisted rope for ships' rigging, the hot stench of tar drifting as the hemp glistened. Through the gates of a yard, two candle-makers gripped a copper pan and poured yellow wax into moulds. There were ironmongers and ship's chandlers too numerous to mention.

There were shops selling lemons and oranges, and shops selling tea leaves loose from great chests. There were shops selling nuts and dark raisins from barrels, and shops selling pepper and brown sugar by the pound. Between the shops narrow stairs connected to offices above, and tradesmen went scurrying up and down carrying tools, papers or charts, each according to his profession. Here I saw a carpenter, there a lawyer, up one staircase went a shipping agent, down another came a wheelwright. Everything traced itself to the ships and the Custom House, His Majesty's Red Ensign fluttering above. The whole town was a song to commerce, and from shops to public buildings the refrain was the same – sailor and cargo, home safe from the sea.

From the riverbank at Greenock the land behind is flat as a biscuit, but not for very far because it rises in a steep slope which, when climbed, gives the most breath-taking view over the town, the Clyde and the Highlands beyond.

After an arduous ascent the horse turned through eagle-mounted gateposts to the Mansion House. A colony of cawing rooks rose into the grey sky, hung there for a moment, then drifted down to brood among the branches either side of the drive.

What on earth was I involved in? I asked myself. Would Gabriel Birkmyre assist me, or was he hiding something? What was the symbol of the Double Headed Eagle doing in his office? If Margaret managed to decipher it, what would the nobleman's codebook reveal? Who could I trust and whom should I fear?

It was such thoughts that consumed me when, between stout oaks, I caught glimpses of the hills beyond the river. Then the ancestral home of Sir Guy Stewart emerged, solid as the ground itself.

A footman crunched across the gravel.

'Ah yes, Doctor Lyon,' he replied to my introduction. 'Sir Guy is expecting you.'

I was led into a red hallway. A long clock ticked at the foot of the stair. The room was cold without a fire and rather musty, but while waiting I noticed something which warmed me. It was a map of India. With a smile of recognition I picked out Bangalore, Delhi, Madras, Lucknow and Pondicherry. Heat, flies and spices crowded my memory.

'I know that look,' came a voice breaking the spell. 'It's the look of a man who's been East of the Indus and South of Kashmir, or I'm a Dutchman.'

I turned to find Sir Guy crossing the hall toward me.

'Welcome to Greenock, Doctor Lyon,' he said, shaking my

hand. 'We'd word to expect you of course, no idea when though. No matter, no matter. Always ready. Pleasure to have you here.'

I thanked him. He'd an English accent, probably from schooling there, and a clipped tone.

'You're right, sir, I was born in India. But what's your own interest in the place, may I ask?'

He laughed, eyes sparkling. 'Born there too, Doctor. On my father's tea plantation.' He pointed to the mountains of Assam in the north east. 'Brother's still there. Not been back for many years myself, but memories burn bright, very bright.' He led me to the parlour where there was a side table with drinks.

'Speaking of India,' he said. 'Offer you tea, or something stronger? Too early for whisky perhaps, but I've a fondness for tonic water and gin if you'd care to join me for one before luncheon.'

Dressed in knee breeches and a riding jacket he had a bulbous nose, large hands and flecks of fresh mud across his boots. Country scenes lined the walls and a stag's head projected above the fireplace. From the top of a bookcase a stuffed badger snarled, its fangs bared and claws flashing.

'Yes, Christopher's been back in India these past twenty years. Doubt he'll return now. Taken an Indian wife you see. Fourteen children.'

He dug silver tongs into a bucket. Ice chimed on glass.

'He tells me all the East Indiamen drink these days is tonic water and gin with crushed limes. Found I've rather taken to it myself – full of quinine you see, though can't pretend there's much threat from malaria here!'

He pressed the glass into my hand and toasted my health. The foaming drink was bitter and I winced.

'That was my first reaction too, Doctor Lyon, but you'll soon come round. Well, well. What brings you west, young man?'

I delivered the answer I'd rehearsed, though I was surprised by my own conviction.

'For many years, sir, I've had a passion for the sea. The workings of the tides, movements of the oceans and marine life all fascinate me. But they're not yet well documented.'

He pinched his nose and stared out the window.

'You've certainly picked a good place. Salt water's in the blood here in Greenock.'

I nodded.

'But the river's just the beginning. It's the Trade Winds you see, out there on the Ocean. That's what makes everything possible. Sail south till the butter melts, that's the trick, then west for the Caribbean. And coming back the current runs 'em from Florida all the way to the Irish Sea.'

'The famous Gulf Stream,' I said. I recalled a copy of the American Benjamin Franklin's chart in Old College, a souvenir of the great man's visit to the city. 'But I'd prefer to begin here, sir, with the Clyde. There's a wonderful coming together of the river, the lochs and the open sea. Yet we glimpse only the surface, while the depths remain a mystery.'

He sipped and nodded. 'Sound thinking, very sound. But what you're talking about would take lifetimes, Doctor. How d'you intend to start?'

I took another sip of the gin and tonic. He was right, the taste was growing on me.

'The Lord Advocate arranged for some Customs resources to

be at my disposal. Matter of fact I called on Commander Birkmyre just this morning.'

'Good man, Birkmyre,' he murmured. 'Very sound. See him all too rarely these days.'

I ran off a list of observations that I intended to make, including wind speeds, water depths and tides. All completely untrue of course. 'Any family, Doctor? Dependants?'

'None sir. I'm a bachelor.'

'Wish you the best of luck then.' His tone changed, and something of the politician crept in. 'But if I may be so bold, Doctor, why not some initial studies at Leith? Why all the way to Greenock?'

I put my glass down. 'To be candid, sir, and I see I must be with you, the trial of Burke and Hare gave my profession a sore knock.' I cleared my throat. 'I was barred from surgery.'

He nodded his understanding.

'Just when I needed a new challenge an opportunity arose. I'd come to the Lord Advocate's attention. He was kind, and when I sought him out he recommended coming here, to Greenock.' I let out a sigh. 'To be plain, sir, I'm indebted to you both.'

'Ah.' He cleared his throat and patted my shoulder. 'Well, a spell in the west will do you good, young man.'

There was an awkward pause.

'Yes, it's coming back to me now,' he said eventually. '*Times* had a field day with the Burke and Hare business. But what was it they printed?' He thought for a moment, snapped his fingers and began to recite the rhyme I'd heard on every child's lips for weeks on end.

Up the close and doon the stair,
but n' ben wi' Burke and Hare,
Burke's the butcher, Hare's the thief,
Knox the boy that buys the beef!

I gave a terse smile.

'Don't s'pose anyone knows what became of Hare?'

'No,' I replied. 'It's a mystery. There was a report in the *Edinburgh Courant* he'd been seen at Carlisle walking the road to London. But after that, nothing.'

I was trying to shut out my last memory of William Hare, but those weasel eyes, sharp nose and cruel, thin mouth wouldn't leave me. He'd just brought a body to the side door of the dissection theatre. Knox was pressing ten pounds into his hand. He'd caught me watching and flashed a wicked smile.

'Outrageous, when you think of it,' said Sir Guy, dissolving my thoughts. 'Simply outrageous that a man like that, a mass murderer, should confess his involvement in their joint crimes then walk from Court free to move among us.' He took a generous draw from his gin and tonic. 'Outrageous, I say.'

I'd heard Sir Guy's point before, countless times in Edinburgh. But without Hare the Crown couldn't corroborate the crimes, which was a requirement of Scots law. So the choice was a stark one. Either fail to convict both of them or do a deal with the devil and get one. After much press speculation the Lord Advocate closed his eyes, held his nose and committed the Crown to a course of action that saw Burke hang while Hare escaped justice. So all in all yes, I agreed with Sir Guy. But such was the law.

I decided to change the subject.

'Quite a house,' I said, glancing round.

He gave a grunt. 'Been in the family since the sixteenth century. Join me outside,' he added. 'Think you'll be pleasantly surprised.'

I followed him out onto the terrace. A balustrade ran in front, with steps in the middle leading to the lawn. We drew pipes and lit them, a stiff breeze catching the smoke.

Stepping over to the balustrade and resting my glass, I stood for a moment in awe. We were three hundred feet above the river and half a mile back from the shoreline, with a view over the entire valley of the lower Clyde.

High cloud painted the sky grey while low clouds scudded by, scattering rain. A sudden gap opened in the heavens, bathing the river in golden light, only to shut again like a toy box. Seagulls wheeled. The river teemed with ships.

Sir Guy watched me take in the view, then spoke in a softer tone.

'My family has been here, Doctor Lyon, from the days of the Bruce. He was our kinsman. They were Norman nobles together in France, before ever setting foot in Scotland. We came with the King and settled here. And we've been here ever since, generation after generation.'

Green lichen covered the stonework in front of me. Dampness lingered in the air, heavy with the scent of moss and the cawing of crows among the trees. Faintly at first, but growing louder, came the blows of a blacksmith's hammer, echoing up the hillside like a knock upon a door.

The wind dropped and Sir Guy took a draw on his pipe, the smoke billowing over his shoulders.

'In my lifetime, Greenock has gone from a fishing village to the port we see today. It's sometimes hard to believe, and I often wonder what my ancestors would make of it. But through all the change I serve this place as best I can.'

'In Parliament you mean?'

'Certainly,' he replied, his face growing suddenly dark, 'and anywhere else I can condemn these new tax burdens that ports like Greenock have to bear. Is it any wonder we lost the Americas?'

The politician had returned.

'I tell you, Doctor,' he growled, his hand tightening into a ball, 'this government stifles trade with its growing lists of duties and petty French bureaucracy. It encourages protectionism in an age when we should be free traders the world over. If I'd my way I'd abolish them, every one.'

He scowled over the water until, with a start, he turned back to me, draining his glass as he did so.

'Dear me, forgetting my manners. Let's get you settled, Doctor. Then you shall meet Octavia.'

Sir Guy had a footman show me to my room. It was very grand, with a bay of three windows facing the river. An oak four-poster stood against the wall, dark like all the rest of the furniture. Steam rose from a copper bath in front of the fireplace. I began to feel civilised again, and ready to do justice to a meal.

14

The three of us lunched in the dining room and I'd the pleasure of Lady Octavia's company. She was charming, but rather inclined to drink too much and become overfamiliar, as I was later to discover. Melancholy clouded her, and from time to time a pang of bitterness would flash out toward Sir Guy and his pressing commitments. It saddened me, but he seemed indifferent to her mood.

During lunch I learned Sir Guy would return to London in a week's time, but that his cousin Lord Alba was invited to dinner the very next night.

'You'll like him,' he said. 'He's quite the scientist. He'll be interested in your marine studies.'

'That's encouraging,' I replied. 'I also have it in mind to visit Campbeltown and study the waters there. I hear it has become a busy place in recent years. Perhaps the Duke of Argyll might also be interested in my work?'

I glanced up in time to see Sir Guy's face harden. After an uncomfortable silence Lady Octavia spoke.

'Oh he's a very difficult man, Doctor Lyon. Impossible, you might say. Poor Guy raised the question of the men's wages in the

Duke's new pottery at Campbeltown. A pottery which the Duke set up in order to steal skilled workers from our own pottery here in Greenock. And do you know what that man said?'

I confessed that I did not.

'Well,' said Lady Octavia growing flustered. 'He told Guy, he told him, told him that he was to, to . . .'

'. . . damn well mind my own business,' her husband finished.

Lady Octavia reached for the claret jug. 'You see, Doctor, not an easy man to deal with at all.'

I sensed more was coming. Sure enough Sir Guy didn't disappoint. 'No, never trust a Campbell,' he muttered. He raised his glass to his lips. 'Nothing but peasants on horses. When the Stewarts arrived from France all those centuries ago, the Campbells were still painting themselves blue and hiding in bog water!'

It was an uncomfortable outburst to hear. They were quite oblivious, however, and hacked away at their lamb chops.

After lunch Sir Guy took me on a tour of the grounds and I'd the chance to admire the Manor House. It also gave me the opportunity to study the town below. Smoke rose from factories surrounded by tenements. The wind snatched the smoke and carried it over the east end, where the pattern of industry continued. To the west, upwind of the smoke, grand houses were laid out in a grid, the clop of carriage horses drifting up from tree lined boulevards.

The circuit complete we returned indoors and I passed the remainder of the afternoon taking tea in the drawing room and conversing about life in Edinburgh. As the clock chimed six Sir Guy retreated to his study. Lady Octavia and I remained, she with her embroidery and I with a book by the fire. But while at first it was pleasant to be idle, my mind soon slid back to my mission, each time more insistent than the last.

When the clock chimed half past seven I rose from my chair, bowed to Lady Octavia and took my leave. I declined the invitation to dinner which she pressed, even taking my hand at one point, but I wasn't to be swayed. I left her side, crossed the hall and tapped at Sir Guy's study door. He called me in.

'I'll bid you good evening, sir,' I said, and thanked him again for his hospitality. 'And oh, I almost forgot . . . my work with Commander Birkmyre. I'm sure you understand, sir, only it might keep me away till late. Naturally, I wouldn't want to wake the household, and so I wondered whether, ehm . . .'

I ran my hand through my hair as I sought how to put it, but Sir Guy was already reaching into a drawer.

'Take this,' he said, pressing a key into my palm. 'As long as you're a guest in my house you must be free to come and go as you please.'

Just for a moment I caught his eye, but he smiled, every inch the genial host. So I thanked him, closed the door and slipped it into my pocket.

15

Darkness fell over the mountains in the west. A light wind rose, breaking up the clouds, and the moon was a perfect crescent. The house was silent. It was time to slip out and explore.

Earlier in the day I'd spotted the *Anchor Inn* on the waterfront where, according to Birkmyre, Tom Hamilton had been spotted. I thought it as good a place to start as any.

I lifted my bag onto the bed and emptied my pockets. There was the key to the house, just over four hundred guineas and some loose change, my pipe and tobacco, my notes on the sign of the Double Eagle and my watch.

I changed back into my battered tweeds and boots, pocketed fifty guineas and hunted for a place to hide the rest. After a brief search I found a loose floorboard and slipped the banknotes underneath. Then I crept down the back staircase and out into the cold night. An owl hooted. It felt good to be on the move.

I strode to the end of the drive then downhill toward the town. I passed a lamplighter with his ladder and a fisherwoman with an empty basket. Otherwise there was no one.

Toward the shore song and raucous laughter began to fill the air, with sailors and their girls crowding the tavern doors. A rush of warm sweet air greeted me as one swung open. An urchin in rags dashed barefoot across the cobbles.

'Huv ye a penny, mister?' he whined. 'Hey mister, huv ye a penny?' He tugged at my jacket and trotted alongside until I handed one over. He turned it in his fingers for a moment, then raced back into the tavern.

After several wrong turns I found the waterfront and followed the harbour wall until I reached the *Anchor Inn*. It was a grand old building with three floors facing the water and three stone urns along the roof. Its lower windows glowed. The sounds of laughter and a fiddler's jig grew louder. A crew outside stared as I approached. A sign above the door read 'Kitty Malone, licensee', and mustering my confidence I sidled in.

It was thick with smoke. Dark beams criss-crossed a low ceiling and hay matted the floor. A black log smouldered in a stone hearth. Behind the counter was Kitty Malone, for so I took her to be. She was pale and thin lipped, with coal eyes and hair pulled tight. The only departure from her severe look was some rouge and a violet dress, more colourful than anything else in that drab room, and she was picking at its shoulder as I made my entrance.

The place was neither full nor empty. Cards, music and conversation ceased as eyes turned in from every corner. I searched in vain for the fiddle player, or anything to distract from my arrival, but there was nothing. I crossed to the counter, ignoring my rising fear, and asked for beer.

Kitty filled a pewter mug from a barrel and set it down with a thud. It looked flat as a millpond.

'Halfpence,' she snipped, and with an attempt at a winning smile I handed over the coin and raised the mug to my lips, only to discover that it tasted every bit as bad as it looked. Kitty pock-eted the coin and ran a wet cloth along the counter, ignoring me. I tried not to look at four characters staring up from a nearby table.

'Whit ship did ye come in on?' barked one. He had a scar across his left eye.

The silence grew.

'Eh, the *Strathspey*, this morning from Glasgow,' I replied and regretted it, feeling I'd somehow betrayed Archie's kindness.

'Glasgow,' he sneered, and spat on the ground.

'Ye dinnae sound like you're frae Glasgow,' came a shrill voice. I turned to see who spoke, but all I found were mean faces.

'Eh, no. No, I'm not.'

I thought to say more but silence seemed the lesser risk, and they gradually returned to their hushed conversations. After a while I stopped looking round me and stared into my beer, but not before I noticed a figure in the corner slip out.

I was on the point of putting the visit down to experience and leaving with what remained of my dignity, when from somewhere I found the courage to say what I'd come to ask. I drained the beer and called to Kitty again, but for whisky this time – a drink I'd never taken before in my life. Raising her eyebrows, she lifted a jug, poured me a large dram and set it down with a clatter.

'That's thrippence,' she muttered, holding one hand toward me, the other on her hip. I pretended to fish for the coin.

'Good stuff this whisky, or so I've heard. Is it Irish or Scotch?'

Her eyes narrowed. 'It's all the same to me.'

I handed her a guinea. 'I'm looking for a man who might know a bit about Irish whisky. Tom Hamilton's his name. You wouldn't happen to know where to find him?'

Well, the mention of that name had an effect like gunshot. All conversation ceased and Kitty, who'd been staring at the guinea in her hand, gave me a sharp look. My question drifted in the smoke.

'Drink up and get out.'

'Well now,' I retorted, trying to bluff it out, 'there's no need to be like this. Will you not just . . .' but a hand closed round my neck.

'That's enough laddie,' whispered the man with the scar, his breath hot in my ear. 'Ye heard the guid lady. Now drink your dram and there's the door.' And with that he gave my neck such a squeeze I nearly passed out.

I drained the whisky. It burned all the way down and started me in a fit of coughing. Kitty snatched the glass from my hand.

'Please Miss Malone,' I wheezed. 'I need to find him.'

But my new friend wasn't having it. 'Out,' he growled, dragging me away like a dog.

'Get your hands off me!' I shouted, twisting myself free. He stepped back, raised his hands, then punched me full on the chin. All I remember after that was being dragged by the collar and hurled onto the pavement.

'Good riddance!' And to the background of laughter the fiddler returned to his bow.

Sprawled on the ground with blood on my lips I hauled myself to my feet, my face hot against the chill of the night air. But then I smiled.

I may have been young and no expert on human nature, but when I'd made that last plea to Kitty her face had softened and such a hesitation came over her that I knew two things as sure as my own name.

She cared for Tom Hamilton and she knew where he was.

16

I hurried along the dock to a row of brick storerooms. They were all locked except one and I crept inside. Cramped and musty, it was filled with crates and netting, and closing the door I left a sliver to observe the *Anchor Inn*.

As time went by people passed in various states of drunkenness. One amorous pair even made liberal use of the side wall. Eventually a dozen or so came tumbling from the *Anchor* and made off into the night. One by one the lights on the ground floor went out. A light flickered in a window above as if someone were pacing. Then all was dark.

I waited on, my fingers gripping the crumbling brickwork round the doorframe. Just when I'd decided nothing would happen, out stepped Kitty Malone. Hooded in a shawl she carried a basket in the crook of her arm. She hurried past and I slipped out in time to see her disappear down an alley.

I went after her, but at the far end of the alley she turned a corner. I followed as closely as I dared only to see her disappear round another corner, and all the time the alleys grew narrower and darker. For a moment I lost sight of her. Then I glimpsed a figure ahead and gave chase, only to find myself back at the water's edge but in a different harbour, and not a soul in sight.

I turned back in an effort to retrace my steps and wound up lost in a maze of alleys. Cursing in frustration I slipped on the cobbles and fell heavily. I slithered painfully back to my feet. A solitary lamp gleamed. Which way now, forward or back?

Footsteps.

'Who's there?' I cried into the yawning dark.

A rat scampered past and I caught the gleam of water trickling down the rough walls, barely a coffin's width apart. My heart thumped in my chest and I stood stock still. Then stepping from the gloom came Twisted Lip. He lunged forward, the blade of a knife glinting in his right hand. I brought my left arm up. What I felt next was like a red-hot poker, as he slashed me from elbow to shoulder. Roaring in pain I shoved him back and toppled him to the ground.

'Who are you?' I bellowed. Other hands grabbed me from behind and I was fixed in a head lock.

I flailed with my fists behind me and somehow connected. But by now Twisted Lip was getting to his feet again and stealing toward me, his blade outstretched.

This was it. Mustering all my strength I spun round and launched my second attacker at Twisted Lip. The three of us collapsed to the ground with me on top. The grip round my neck slackened and I struggled free, shooting off like a rabbit.

I reached a side street and clattered along the middle, dodging passing carts. Passers-by stared open mouthed. I crossed the main square and, without slacking my pace, sprinted uphill toward the Mansion House, my lungs bursting. Once I reached the driveway

I slowed. My left arm felt heavy, like a dead weight. I touched the sleeve. It was saturated with blood.

By now my head was light. I fumbled the key in the lock, praying I wouldn't drop it. Eventually it clicked open and I locked it behind me, terrified my attackers were near at hand.

By the time I staggered into my bedroom I was close to fainting. Before leaving I'd trimmed the wick of my bedside lamp to keep it burning. With trembling fingers I turned the screw, breathing so hard it fogged the glass. The flame rose, casting an orange glow. My heart pounded. Sweat trickled down my neck. Weak as I was, I had to dress my wound.

I looked to the copper bath, still with a few inches of water. It would have to serve. I eased the jacket from my shoulders with my right arm, the pain almost unbearable. Then I slipped the sleeve down. Blood oozed, revealing the deep wound. But just as I lifted my head to undo the first button, I froze.

A shadow man was sitting in the window bay, a small table drawn to his side. I watched him lift a glass and raise it to his lips.

'Who the hell are you?' I breathed, my shoulders heaving.

He returned the now empty glass to the table with a long sigh of satisfaction. Leaning forward he spoke, the lamplight catching his face.

'Well, Doctor Lyon,' he said in an Ulster drawl. 'I'll say one thing for old Sir Guy. He keeps a few decent bottles o brandy in that cellar o his, so he does. And you look like you could do wi a nip yerself. Ahm I right?'

I stared at him in shock. The man now sitting in my bedroom

was the last person I expected to see, ever again. I recognised him instantly. How could I forget William Hare, the murderer who'd brought countless corpses to our surgery?

I hesitated, unable to think. Then I fainted flat out.

17

I came to with brandy on my lips. I was propped against the foot of the bed with my shirt off and the lamp at my feet.

A crimson pool gleamed in the bath. My head and shoulders ached but glancing at my left arm I was astonished to see it bound with a cotton bandage.

A fire burned in the grate and William Hare, though I could hardly believe it was he, stood with his sleeves rolled and drying his hands. He had a pipe clenched between his teeth and a look of satisfaction at his handiwork. Clearly, as was suspected but never proved, Hare was highly adept at basic surgery.

'Feelin' a little better are we, Doc?' he said, his shock of red hair glinting in the firelight. 'I'm just after putting seven wee butterfly stitches in that arm o yours, and I figure ye'll be right as rain in a day or two, so ye will.'

He nodded towards my medical kit.

'That's quite a useful bag o tricks ye've got there.'

'What on earth are you doing here?' I cried.

'Shhh!' he warned, raising a finger to his lips. 'D'ye want to wake the whole house?'

He stooped over me.

'C'mere closer to the heat now, and let's get a shirt on ye.'

I let him help me into a chair by the fire. Then he pulled a shirt over my head as if dressing a doll.

'There, that's better. Now you let your old pal William fetch your pipe and a glass, and we'll have a good catch-up together, shall we?'

He fetched another chair and placed the table between us. Then, good as his word, he handed me my pipe and a brandy. I swallowed it in one gulp. He poured me a second. This time I sipped it and settled into a smoke. As the brandy took effect my pain began to ease.

'Thank you,' I murmured. I couldn't think what else to say. If the king himself had arrived to treat my wounds I couldn't have been more astonished.

'Ach it's nothing, Doc,' he replied, a gleam in his eye. 'Sure, I always liked ye anyway.'

He lit his pipe and reclined, smoke swirling. Thin lips curled back over jagged brown teeth.

'Aye, ye always struck me as a straight up and down sort o a man if ye know what a mean. Not a bit like the stuffed shirts at the infirmary.'

'And you never struck me as a murderer,' I snapped.

He gave a hollow laugh, eyes flashing. 'Oh c'mon now, Doc. Let's not play the innocent game. Ye all knew fine well what was going on, so ye did. Sure, did youse not all know half the street girls yourselves anyway? What did ye think killed them,' he cackled, leaning forward, 'a bad conscience?'

My colour rose. It was well known my colleague Doctor Fergusson had been a client of one of the victims, Mary Paterson.

He had been with her the very night before Burke and Hare delivered her corpse to Doctor Knox. I decided not to rise to his taunt.

'Speaking of bad consciences, Hare, I'm surprised you can live with yours.'

He raised his hands to his heart with a mock pained expression.

'Oh that hurts, Doc, it really does. But, as ye know, and as I told them all at the trial, the whole thing was Burke's idea. Sure, what was a simple soul like myself to do, just trying to make my way in an unfair world? So c'mon,' he said, extending his palms towards me. 'That's all in the past now. I'm here to lend ye a hand in this new line o work that ye've taken on. And not a moment too soon by the looks o ye.'

My mouth fell open. 'Surely you're not telling me that, that . . .'

'That's exactly what I'm telling you,' he grinned.

He sipped his brandy.

'C'mon, Doc. This is the British government we're talkin' about here. Ye don't think for a minute that they'd just let old William walk off into the sunset as simple as that, do ye?'

I confess it took me some time to catch up.

'So, . . . you're telling me the Crown knew what you were doing? That's ridiculous!'

He laughed and shook his head.

'Aye, Doc, ye're an innocent abroad for sure. No, old Sir John and your man the Lord Advocate knew fine they had me over a barrel wi the resurrection business. But there was a wee problem with their case, so there was.'

'There wasn't the evidence to hang you both,' I said.

'Correct. And so there was a bargain to be struck, at the right price o course. And on the face o things all proper and above board like. They're practical men, Doc, the pair of them. And after all, they knew that a man who's seen what I've seen, and done what I've done, could come in right handy in this line of work.'

He paused to smoke and stared into the flames.

'But you're a marked man,' I protested. 'A known criminal.'

'I'm no criminal!' he cried, and for a moment the mask of the genial Irishman slipped. 'The deal was I walked from that court a free man without a crime to my name. And that's the law, so it is,' he said, jabbing the air with his finger. 'And as for being a marked man well, away from Edinburgh, there's hardly a one would know me from Adam now, is there?'

I had to concede he had a point. During the trial the Edinburgh newspapers had carried only rough sketches of Burke and Hare. Among so many of his countrymen in Scotland the chances of him being recognised were low.

He chortled, as pleased with himself as ever. 'And sure, Doc, can a poor, ignorant Irishman not get in anywhere, see anything and hear things all over the place, without anyone paying him the blindest bit o notice?'

I could hardly believe it. Had Sir John and the Lord Advocate really done a deal with Hare as the price for his freedom?

'So what's their hold over you? You could disappear any time you choose!'

His face grew serious. 'No, Doc, I get money in a Belfast bank every quarter, and I do what I'm asked. Besides, it's light enough work. More than I ever earned digging canals.'

'But how can they trust you?'

'Sir John has fingers in all sorts of pies, Doc,' he said. 'Some o them none too tasty either. Sure that's the way of it, and to be truthful it kind of suits me.'

He was grinning again, the smoke drifting from his nostrils. I couldn't bear it.

'Truth?' I scoffed. 'You don't know the meaning of the word. I watched Burke twist at the end of a rope, Hare, for the sake of your idea of truth.'

Anger flashed in his eyes and he sank into his chair but I held his gaze. I had his measure. I knew he'd held the whip hand in his partnership with Burke.

Burke was no angel, but he was a fool. Hare, on the other hand, was devious as a witch. Like all snitches, he'd played down his own part and claimed the murders were all Burke's idea, when one look at that sad-eyed giant from Cork told a different story.

Hare broke the silence.

'I can see you're tired, Doc, so I'll let that one go. For now, anyway.'

Silence followed. My thoughts returned to Kitty Malone and the *Anchor*. I was curious.

'Do you know where I've been tonight?'

He gave a mischievous grin and relaxed. 'That I do. Sure the *Anchor*'s a regular haunt o mine, and I figured it'd be one of the first places ye tried. Soon as I clapped eyes on ye I slipped out and made my way up here.'

'So that was you?'

He nodded. 'Quite a piece is our Kitty now, don't ye think, Doc?'

'And do you know why I went there?'

'That's easy. You're looking for your man Hamilton 'cos he murdered some lighthouse keeper.'

I stared into the fire. Could Hare really be one of Sir John's informers?

He sighed. 'Look, Doc, I can see you're still wondering if ye can trust me. Of course, I've nothing in writing from Sir John, but . . .'

'Just a moment,' I said, interrupting him. In the midst of everything I'd forgotten about the piece of paper Sir John had shown me.

'The codeword. Tell me the codeword.'

There was a pause during which Hare stared back with a blank expression. For a moment I thought I had him. Then he smiled and repeated the single word Sir John had written down at the outset of it all.

'Unicorn'.

'My God,' I whispered. 'That's it. That's the word he showed me.'

The ticking of the clock filled the room. I felt my own heart pounding.

'So now ye see, Doc,' he said, spreading his arms and bowing. 'I'm truly at your disposal.'

I reached for the decanter and refilled our glasses. My head felt light, as if the very ground I walked on was no longer certain. But I didn't care. Everything I'd been through had altered reality. Down was up and up was down, and I'd no choice but to accept it or walk away, back to the Infirmary and the comfort of Morningside.

I couldn't walk away. Something devilish had entered my soul. There was a smile curling my lips as I raised the brandy in a salute to my curious ally.

'Well Hare,' I said, 'so be it. I only hope this partnership is more successful than your last one.'

We drank deeply, and I recounted some of my adventures since Edinburgh, though I held a good deal back too. I confess it made my heart glad to see him lean forward agog then rear back slapping his thigh as I led him through each twist and turn. More than once I had to rein him in for fear of waking the household.

'My, you're some lad yourself, Doc,' he laughed. 'You've seen more of life these past days than most of your high types see in a lifetime.'

The endpoint of my tale brought me to the nub of things.

'Hare, I need you to follow Kitty Malone. I'm convinced she'll lead us to Hamilton.'

'Not a problem,' he said. 'I'll stick to her like a limpet.'

I relaxed and gazed into the fire, its flames settling to golden embers. I drifted towards sleep. The clock on the mantel showed two. Hare rose and tapped out his pipe.

'Well ye've had enough shocks for one day, Doc, and that arm of yours'll need a rest, so it will.'

'Where are you going?'

'Don't ye fret,' he winked. 'I'll let myself out just as I let myself in. I'll even put Sir Guy's good brandy back on the cabinet. Sure, he'll probably just think it was the wife, helping herself again.'

'So, what happens next?'

'I'll see ye at the gates tomorrow at twelve. There's other things ye need to know too. But it's late now. Pleasant dreams, Doc.'

And with that he was gone.

I wondered how he'd leave the house, or how he'd got in for that matter, but the truth was I was past caring. I stumbled to bed, and as I laid my head on the pillow sleep was already engulfing me.

18

I woke to the blast of a shotgun and crows cawing. It was late morning, and a breakfast tray lay cold at the foot of my bed. There was fresh water in the bath and a new fire had burned out in the grate. My arm throbbed, the soothing effect of the brandy long gone.

By the time I had washed, dressed and eaten the clock had chimed a quarter to twelve.

There was no-one downstairs. Eventually I found a footman in the tack room, cleaning all the boots.

'Good morning sir. I'm sorry I'm late with these, only there was a bit of a disturbance during the night.'

'Oh?'

'Sir Guy was convinced one of the drawing room windows had been forced. Right enough, a dozen silver spoons are missing from the dining room.'

'Shocking,' I said, adding housebreaking to Hare's growing list of skills.

He handed me my boots.

'Sir Guy and Lady Octavia?'

'Both out, sir.' He lifted the next boot and began brushing

away the mud. 'Lady Octavia's visiting in the west end and Sir Guy has estate business at Ardfern. But I've been told to say you're expected for dinner at seven, sir.'

By the time I reached the gateposts it was after twelve. Hare appeared.

'Morning, Doc. How's that arm o yours?'

'On the mend, thanks to you,' I replied. 'Though I'm less impressed with you stealing Sir Guy's spoons.'

He gave an injured look. 'I've got costs, Doc. It's not as if they'll miss them now, is it?'

I thought to take him to task but let it pass. It was a relief to have someone alongside me, even if it was Hare. But I noticed something different about him.

'What have you done to your hair?'

Instead of red it was jet black.

'Simple enough precaution, Doc. A little bit o soot and dubbin is all. No point makin' it too easy for folk now, is there?'

I shook my head, wondering if things could possibly get any stranger.

'Oh, and another thing, Doc. Folk here know me as Jack Dervil, so I'd be obliged if you'd play along, so I would.'

'Very well, Mister Dervil,' I replied. 'Where are we going?'

'You'll see. Follow me.'

We set off into Greenock, but as we crossed the main square Hare veered to the right and plunged down an alley. I had to walk fast to keep pace with him, and I could tell he was a natural runner. I checked if we were followed but there was no one. We emerged onto a wide street. In the distance I caught a glimpse of the Custom House. A thought occurred to me.

'So you're an agent of Sir John,' I called, stopping for a moment. 'But what of officials in Greenock? Do you deal with them?'

He looked to the Custom House and flicked me a glance.

'You mean Birkmyre? Not a chance. I've nothin' to do with him.'

'Why?'

'He's a strange one, Doc, and a fool to boot. The French navy could sail up to Glasgow and he'd miss it from that office of his.'

'You've been in his office, then?'

He ignored me. 'C'mon. We need to move.'

I was about to follow when I caught sight of a man, head down and hurrying into the Custom House. It was Sir Guy.

'The footman said he'd be at Ardfern,' I murmured, as Hare squinted over my shoulder. 'And Sir Guy told me he didn't see Birkmyre much. What's he up to?'

Hare laughed. 'Ah, Doc. Ye sure like to take folk as ye find them. Let me tell ye, I've heard things about Sir Guy that'd fair make your head spin.'

'Like what?'

He grinned. 'Well, to begin with, he has gambling debts and plenty of mistresses all round London, so he does. And then they say he has Birkmyre turn a blind eye whenever one of his ships comes in, and no questions asked.'

'You mean he's not paying duty?'

He tilted his head. 'So they say Doc, so they say. Hurry up now. We haven't all day, ye know.'

We reached the east end. It was a warren of tenements, factories and public houses all running off the main road. A thin film of soot settled on me. There was ash in my mouth and acrid smoke brought tears to my eyes. Dray horses clattered by, hauling carts loaded with barrels, crates and sacks. Toward the shore a jagged mass of cranes rose like a petrified forest. I followed Hare through the gutters, edging past pools of stagnant water.

'C'mon, Doc, keep up,' yelled Hare, as I slipped yet again. Two infant girls darted by, carrying laundry.

In the distance rose the gates of Sir Guy's pottery and a line of kilns belching smoke.

'Not far now.' he said, as yet another cart clattered by.

'What do they make in the pottery?'

'Oh all kinds of stuff. Jars for whisky, jars for whale oil, cups and plates, pretty glazed tiles. Even china vases. They make it all.'

'So, why are we going there?'

He gave a wry smile. 'That's not where we're headed.' He pointed over my shoulder.

A row of workers' cottages ran opposite the pottery. In the midst of them stood a ramshackle building on two levels. It was red brick, as in England, but subsidence had caused a slip which brought to my mind the lop-sided faces of palsy victims. Above the doorway a name was hand painted in curling letters. *The Glue Pot.*

'Another public house,' I sighed. 'I don't have much luck with these places.'

Hare clapped my shoulder. 'Ah, but I think you'll like this one.'

Before I could protest he was across the street.

'C'mon, Doc,' he called. 'D'ye want answers or not?'

19

The front door of *The Glue Pot* led straight into a snug. The floor was covered in a swirling Turkish carpet. There was a table, some chairs and three stools at a corner counter. Everything was bog oak, black and solid as stone.

Whisky jars marked *Argyll* and *Campbeltown* lined the shelves behind the counter. There were gin jars too, labelled *Old Tom* and *Dutch Ginever* and completing the line-up were kegs of Jamaican rum bearing the *Appleton* crest. Three beer barrels rested on the floor.

It was empty. The clock ticked on the mantel and a fire crackled below. The greatest charm, however, was that every inch of space – corners, shelves and walls – was taken up by china. None of it looked particularly valuable, but a pair of exquisite Japanese vases caught my eye on a high shelf. It was an Aladdin's cave. I liked the place immediately.

'Why have you brought us here?' I asked.

A girl appeared behind the counter.

'What would you like?'

'Porter, lass,' said Hare, taking a seat by the fire and rubbing his hands.

The girl drew off two pots from one of the barrels. 'That's tuppence.'

I handed her the money with a halfpenny for herself. She gave me a shy glance. 'Thank you, mister.'

'Is your mammy there, lass?' called Hare.

'She's just upstairs tidying, Mister Dervil. I'll let her know you're here.'

As she disappeared through the back, I set the pots down and pulled up a chair.

'What's this all about, then?'

'You'll see,' he winked. 'There's nothing like a drop of Irish stout, Doc. Your very good health.'

I heard footsteps on the stair, then in she swept. It's a moment I'll never forget. She wore an ivory dress and was untying a blue apron.

I stood up. Hare turned in his chair.

'Good day gentlemen. Give me a moment and I'll be right with you.'

'Ah, sure, just you take your time, Fiona,' said Hare, eyeing her up and down. 'You know I could watch you all day now.'

My blood rose but she was completely undaunted by Hare. She lifted the apron over her head, folded it, and pushed her hair back over her shoulders.

'I've brought someone to meet you, lass.'

I bowed. 'Pleased to meet you, miss. My name is—'

'I know who you are,' she replied curtly, giving me a swift glance from head to toe and back again. 'You're the new one. Doctor Mungo Lyon of Edinburgh.' There was more than a hint of scepticism in her lilting Highland accent.

I hesitated and looked from one to the other. 'How do you know?'

'Pleased to meet you too,' she retorted with a playful smile, clearly enjoying my confusion, 'I'm Fiona Cameron, the landlady here. And don't fret so, Doctor, I know Sir John sent you. Sit yourself down and I'll be right with you.'

She laid her apron behind the counter, crossed to the front door and bolted it.

'How are you, Mister Dervil?'

'Same as ever,' he grunted, lighting his pipe. 'But enough of the pleasantries. He needs to know what you know.'

'Of course he does.'

She took a seat and crossed her hands in her lap. I leaned forward and took a long drink. The porter was thick, with a sweet taste like liquorice.

'Well, Doctor,' she began, 'I'll come straight to the point. You're staying with Sir Guy Stewart, so you'll already know he owns the pottery.'

I nodded.

'A lot of the pottery's work used to be making whisky jars for the new distilleries. But that changed when the Duke of Argyll decided to set up his own pottery in Campbeltown. Sir Guy was furious.'

'Yes, I heard, Miss Cameron.'

She laughed prettily. 'Please, Fiona is fine.'

I blushed, wondering what had brought her into the service.

'Once the Campbeltown pottery was up and running,' she continued, 'Sir Guy had to lay off most of the Greenock workers. There was no choice but to go to Campbeltown, and many did.

But every so often they're back to see family and the like, and some of them are regulars here.'

She paused, twisting her fingers.

'Have you heard something?' I asked.

'Yes,' she said, and her face grew dark. 'It was about a ship. One that foundered out in the Firth.'

'The *Julietta*?'

She nodded. 'When it was towed to Greenock all kinds of rumours went flying.'

'What?'

'Oh that it was a ghost ship,' she said with a wave of her hand. 'Or a failed attempt to land French soldiers. That sort of thing. I didn't pay it much heed, to be honest. Not till later. About a week ago three of my regulars came in. They were just back from six months over in Campbeltown and having a grand time. The place was busy, a good atmosphere. The three of them were sitting up at the stools there and I was behind the counter.'

'Go on.'

She frowned. 'They were arguing about the *Julietta* business. Then one of them piped up and says it was well known that—'

In the sudden pause, I leaned forward. '*What* was well known, Fiona?'

She winced, cleared her throat and spoke calmly. 'He spoke of a long stretch of sand along the shore near Campbeltown, Doctor, where a schooner had been landing at night.'

Sir John's description of the *Julietta* came to mind and I darted a glance at Hare. He merely puffed at his pipe.

'This ship. How often was it seen?'

'He didn't say,' she replied. 'But it had been going on for months.'

'How did he know that?'

She shrugged. 'Just rumours, I thought. There's forever been boats coming and going at night. Usually from Ireland, trying to give Customs the slip.'

'You can't beat a bit of the old mountain dew,' murmured Hare. I remembered my conversation with Birkmyre. But this ship didn't sound like a smuggling brig crossing from Ireland.

'Go on,' I said.

'Well, a boat making landings on the sands is one thing. But then I noticed the other two with him were a bit – I don't know how I'd say exactly.' She searched for the right word.

'Nervous?'

'Yes, nervous, Doctor,' she ageed, giving me an approving glance. 'That's it. They were jeering, saying he was talking nonsense, shaking their heads and rolling their eyes at me. But then they turned sharp and warned him to keep it down, not to be shooting his mouth off. He'd had a few by then and was rising to them. And that's when he said something that made me take notice.'

She paused.

'What did he say?'

'He said they knew lanterns had been seen on the beach the night the *Julietta* was wrecked.'

The clock chimed the quarter hour. I gave a start and Hare laughed.

'Oh dear, Doc. Has that got you a bit spooked?'

I ignored him. 'There were lanterns, but did he say the *Julietta* landed?'

She thought for a moment. 'No. Not that I remember.'

'Or why any of this was happening?'

She shook her head. 'No. I don't think he knew.'

'Is there anything else?'

'Tell him about the pottery,' said Hare, sipping his porter.

'Earlier,' she explained, 'before mention of the beach and lanterns, the three of them talked of folk firing up the pottery kilns at night. They were having to sweep out the ashes in the morning, though they'd cleaned them the day before.'

'Did they think it was connected to the landings?'

'I don't think it occurred to them. They were just grumbling because of the extra work.' She smiled. 'That's all I know, Doctor, but if I hear anything else I'll be sure to get word to you. Now I know you're here.'

I blushed. 'Thank you, eh, Fiona. You've been very helpful. I'll be sure to tell Sir John.'

'Oh, he knows I always do what I can,' she said. 'He's a good man. He's done more for me than anyone will ever know.'

Whatever lay behind her involvement in the Service, she was loyal to Sir John. I nodded to Hare who finished his drink. The discussion was over. Fiona lifted the pots then unbolted the door.

'Bye, Fiona,' said Hare with a wink. 'And that was a lovely drop of your porter so it was. But sure, everything's lovely about you.'

She smiled. 'You're too kind, Mister Dervil. Now off you go, I've things to be getting on with.'

'It was a pleasure to meet you,' I said, bowing.

'Goodbye, Doctor,' she replied. 'And God be with you.'

20

A drizzle started as we hurried away.

'She's quite a lass, isn't she, Doc?' cackled Hare. 'Sure your eyes were near poppin' out your head when you saw her, so they were!'

I shot him an irritated glance. 'Aye,' continued Hare, grinning. 'Take it from me, she can more than look after herself that one, what with everything she's been—'

I thrust my arm across his chest, almost knocking him backwards.

'Hey, what the—' Then he saw them too, on the far side of the road.

The one with the darting eyes saw us first and called to Twisted Lip. I thanked God for the horses and carts clattering by. Then my stomach turned: they had pistols.

'Run!' I cried, and we sprinted back toward the pottery. Hare streaked ahead.

'I'll be seeing ye, Doc!' he called over his shoulder. 'And don't worry, I'll find you!'

He veered to the right, jumped a fence and disappeared.

I kept on through the gates of the pottery. As I crossed the front yard, I heard a dull crack followed by the low whistle of a passing bullet and realised – with a strange sense of calm – that once again I was being shot at.

Crates filled with crockery stood all around. Two older workers moved among them checking the contents and tacking on lids. At the gunshot they'd looked up and now they stared open mouthed as I sprinted past.

'Hey, what ye playing at son! This is private property!'

A second crack and the shot smashed into a box, shattering its contents. I ducked through a doorway and into the pottery.

The noise was deafening. I was in a vast hall with rows of workers. Each sat at a potter's wheel, concentrating on the wet clay as it gyrated between their fingers. A doorway stood open on the far side and I lurched between two rows towards it.

'Hey, watch where you're going!' went the cry as I blundered through. A trail of destruction formed behind me as one worker after another rose up from his careful labours, the ruined clay slipping like sandcastles in the tide. Eventually I reached the far side and was almost through the doorway when an overseer tackled me round the waist.

'Guns, they've got guns!'

In the midst of our struggle I glanced back. They had followed me in. Uproar turned to panic and there was a rush in my direction. As mob fever took hold I narrowly avoided a trampling and was swept through the door.

I landed out in a courtyard with kilns in rows like giant beehives. I weaved through, heat radiating from them. Just as I was out the other side I clattered to a halt, arms waving in mid-air.

I was teetering on the edge of a pier with a crane at my side, its boom extending over the water. A chain hung from the boom. Below it a barge had just finished loading, its propeller raising a thick churn as it started away. I leapt and caught the chain. It swung out at first, then back towards the pier and I kicked against it with everything I had. This time it swung further out and I let go.

One more swing and I'd have been too late. As it was, I landed on the deck and cracked my head. Staggering to my feet I caught sight of my pursuers staring after me as the barge steamed away onto the river.

The rain was pelting down in windless pellets. It bounced on the deck and pattered on my jacket. My hair hung like rats' tails, my arm throbbed and a red blush was creeping over my shirt. A barge hand came running. He was so shocked he didn't know what to say.

'What – what the – how?' he stuttered, before finally settling for: 'Here, ye cannae just come leaping on board like that! Ye could've got yourself killed!'

I breathed heavily, clutching my arm, unable to speak. He looked back at the pier and grinned.

'That wis some jump though, I have to say!'

The skipper approached. He looked me up and down.

'I don't know what you think you're playing at, son, but ye cannae stay on board.'

I straightened up. 'I have to get back on shore, captain. Can you let me off again?'

'Let ye off?' he replied, his face livid. 'I should just chuck ye over the side, that's what I should do!'

I fished in my pocket, pulled out a five guinea note and held it out. His eyes widened.

'What did ye do? Rob a bank?'

'Look,' I sighed, 'I swear I've done nothing wrong.'

We were no more than a hundred yards out from the shoreline, passing one harbour mouth after another.

'Please, captain, anywhere will do.'

The rain continued to fall and the engine clattered. Eventually he shook his head and turned away.

'Keep your money son,' he called over his shoulder. He returned to the wheelhouse. 'And you, Danny, get back tae your work!'

Danny gave me another admiring grin.

'Ay, Mister Ritchie.'

The captain cut the engine and moved the barge close to a harbour wall. I made a leap for the rusted rungs of a ladder and, as the barge steamed away, scrambled up.

I was at the mouth of a dock crowded with ships. I made my way towards the shore passing one ship after another, ignored by the many dock hands busy at their work.

Then I saw her.

She was low in the water, sleek like a ballroom slipper, and fashioned from a dark wood not native to these shores. Her three masts rose high into the leaden sky and her elegant prow extended above my head. The rigging was neat, her hatches shipshape and the decks clear. As she rose and fell in the languid water, I made out her wheel and a bell towards the stern. She lay at peace. Along her hull ran curling gold letters. *Julietta*.

If only she could speak, I thought, this mystery could be resolved here and now. I thought to board her, but something held me back. It was a sense of the sacred, that it would be wrong to violate her repose. And so, as if in a dream, I continued on, her outline fading behind me into the gathering mist and rain.

I hailed a carriage to the Mansion House and sank back on the bench as the horse took up the strain. I was drenched and exhausted. My shoulder ached and, with a trembling hand, I felt fever on my brow.

21

When I returned to the Mansion House, bedraggled as an alley cat, a wide-eyed footman informed me Sir Guy and Lady Octavia were yet to return. I called for hot water and retired to my room.

My brow burned and the teeth chittered in my head. I hauled off my sopping wet clothes, sank into the bath and stretched out before the blazing fire. The heat was soothing and, feeling restored, I reflected on what I'd discovered.

Assuming Fiona Cameron's information was true, the *Julietta* had been landing near Campbeltown on its voyages between Jamaica and Greenock. What's more, lanterns on the night she was wrecked suggested her arrival had been expected. But what was the purpose of her landings? Apart from some copper, there hadn't been anything particularly valuable found on board. Was the *Julietta* dropping someone, or something, off? Or picking up? Or both? And was Crawford McCunn's disappearance connected? Then there was the lighthouse keeper, Sandy McLeod. Why had he been murdered? And was it connected?

My best chance of discovering the truth about Sandy's murder, I decided, depended upon finding Tom Hamilton. My only lead was Kitty Malone at the *Anchor Inn,* and I was relying on Hare to tail her. What was this all about? Fiona spoke of a failed French landing, but there was nothing to give credence to that. Could the *Julietta* have been carrying an illicit cargo for Sir Guy, on which he sought to evade Customs duty? Could Birkmyre, after the *Julietta* was recovered, have removed the illicit cargo in order to protect Sir Guy?

There was another possibility: whisky smuggling, on a grand scale. Thinking of the distillation process it would certainly explain the copper, and Campbeltown was the whisky capital of Scotland. As for the unusual activity at the Campbeltown pottery, it could be the smugglers were making extra jars for their illicit whisky.

Whatever was going on the evidence pointed to a major plan, well-resourced and well executed. Everything seemed to connect with Campbeltown, and that was a part of the country dominated by the Duke of Argyll. He owned the pottery and had major investments in the whisky business. His involvement couldn't be ruled out. Yet I could hardly bring myself to believe that so eminent an establishment figure as the Duke – or the Marchioness of Bute, or the Earl of Alba, or Sir Guy – could be involved in smuggling anything. So who could it be? Was Crawford McCunn behind it? Or had he uncovered something and paid for it with his life? Could there be someone else in Campbeltown, some senior figure or employee of the Duke controlling this?

Then there was that strange Double Eagle, its twin heads facing left and right, East and West, fierce and all seeing:

. . . A most ancient device of Europe . . . its rootes are deepe, mysterious and extend far back in tyme . . . it symbolises many things

in many places, and its particular significance is not always clear from first encounter...

The text I had read certainly seemed to be correct on that last point, for despite the many other circumstances in the case, I wasn't a step closer to discovering its true meaning or who it represented. *Order and chaos.* Which was it signalling here? Aside from its presence on the *Julietta's* crew I recalled I'd encountered it above Gabriel Birkmyre's doorway.

I told myself it had to be a coincidence. After all, my research suggested it was used in the Scottish Rites of Freemasonry. Perhaps Birkmyre was a senior mason. It seemed fairly likely. Still, there were other possibilities. Perhaps the nobleman's journal might shed more light, if Margaret succeeded in cracking its code.

My fever eased and I looked to my arm. The wound was inflamed, but Hare's stitching was holding up well and the bleeding had ceased. Still, there was a lingering ache even at rest. I felt the need of a strong drink.

After bathing I shaved, applied liniment and a fresh bandage. By this time it was just after five by the clock on the mantel. I pulled on a crisp white shirt with a high collar to my jaw, a pair of black knee breeches, stockings and buckled leather shoes. Then I donned a matching jacket and waistcoat in green velvet and completed the ensemble with a long white cravat tied loose at the neck. It felt strange to be dressed once again in the manner of polite society.

Standing at the bay windows, fitting my watch chain to my waistcoat, I peered into the mirk. The rain continued to fall. Every now and again a gust of wind drove it against the glass, rattling the frames and whistling through the crevices before dying away, only to rise again a moment later. As it did, the trees in the grounds twisted and bent like worshippers at some pagan Sabbath.

The footman knocked. 'Sorry to disturb, sir. There's a note just arrived by carriage.'

He handed me the paper. It was sealed in red wax with the Crown insignia.

'The driver didn't wait,' he added.

The room had grown gloomy. He heaped fresh coal on the fire, lit the lamp at my bedside and drew the curtains. The sounds of wind and rain died away, leaving the room warm and comfortable. I thanked him.

'No trouble, sir. Sounds like we're in for a night of it.'

He paused at the door. 'Sir Guy sends his compliments and asks you to join him in the sitting room whenever you are ready.'

I broke the seal and read the note.

Custom House, Greenock, Fifteenth April 1829

Doctor Lyon,

Despite the limits on my resources a launch will take us to Campbeltown tomorrow morning. We sail from the Custom House Quay at six. I will send a carriage at five thirty. Be prompt.

Birkmyre

Crossing to the fire I dropped the note on the coals. It browned and began to smoke, and as the wax melted there came a sizzle before the paper burst into flame with a yellow flare. As the flames danced among the coals, I lit my pipe and settled myself. I could still hear the storm through the curtains and wondered, with growing unease, just what sort of crossing we would have in the morning.

22

'Doctor Lyon. Your timing is impeccable,' said Sir Guy. 'Come in. I'm preparing drinks.'

I pulled at my collar, still feeling a little fevered. A chandelier lit portraits and dark furniture. Velvet couches extended either side of a towering marble fireplace. From the nearest couch Lady Octavia turned to me and smiled.

She wore a long satin dress with a pearl choker. An antique tiara crowned her powdered hair and a Chinese fan completed her outfit.

'You look radiant, Lady Octavia.'

She fluttered her eyelids then turned to her husband. 'Guy, just my usual brandy. You know your tonic water doesn't agree with me.'

A gentleman rose from the couch opposite and gripped my hand. He was handsome with a ruddy face, thick auburn hair and mutton chop whiskers.

'Doctor Lyon,' said Lady Octavia, 'allow me to introduce Sir Guy's cousin, Lord Alba.'

'An honour, my lord,' I murmured.

'So, you're the man with a passion for the sea,' he boomed.

'I'm a keen student of the sea, sir, yes. But very much an amateur.'

Sir Guy handed us both a glass of gin and tonic water.

'Oh-ho Robert, now this one's an enthusiast. You must have him over to Arran. You been there, Doctor? Beautiful, quite beautiful, you know.'

Alba beamed with pleasure.

'I can well imagine it is,' I replied. 'The whole west coast has captured my heart, even if the weather's rather unpredictable.'

'Yes,' said Sir Guy, passing a brandy to Lady Octavia. 'Not sure I'd be at ease on the Clyde tonight.'

'Nor tomorrow morning,' I added. 'Commander Birkmyre expects me on the water at first light.'

'Oh, I'm sure things will have calmed by dawn,' said Alba lightly. 'Whatever the weather, it rarely lasts in these parts.' He raised his glass. 'Well then. Allow me to propose a toast to your exploits, Doctor. I wish you every success!'

We drank to that and once again I'd the sharp taste of quinine, but the gin mix was stronger.

Lady Octavia beckoned me to sit by her, while Sir Guy and Alba moved to the couch opposite. As I relaxed by the fire I tried to make a good fist of it on the subject of the sea, but it soon became clear to me, just as Birkmyre observed, that Alba was well ahead on that score. A light perspiration rose on my forehead and I wiped it away.

'You must pay us a visit over on Arran,' Alba was saying. 'I'm sure you'd be intrigued by the instruments of science I've assembled at Dunearn.'

'That would be interesting,' I replied. 'What instruments do you have, may I ask?'

Lady Octavia rolled her eyes. 'Don't get him started,' she warned.

Sir Guy chuckled. 'I'll wager there's no one in Britain, Lyon, who has more glass tubes, sulphur and boiling pans than Robert here. He's the Prometheus of the modern age.'

The reference made me think of Frankenstein, Mary Shelley's chilling story which had electrified Europe for the past ten years.

'Hardly dear cousin,' replied Alba, enjoying himself. 'Prometheus gave fire to mankind and was punished by the gods. I merely tinker on the edges, searching for answers. For instance,' he began, 'here's one that may interest you. Now, is it possible for a man to walk on the floor of the sea?'

As the question hung in the air Sir Guy clapped his knee and shook his head. 'Robert, what fresh nonsense is this?'

Alba turned to me. 'What do you say, Doctor? Just imagine the creatures to be seen, the seabed opening before you like a book! Wouldn't that be the way to study the unknown depths?'

I paused, absorbing his idea. I was thinking of something I'd read about and seen pictures of at university. A diving bell it was called, in which a man could be lowered into the water and look through a thick glass slot in its side – and that was my answer.

'You're right, Doctor. But the problems with a diving bell are twofold. The limitation of the air supply, and the lack of mobility.'

'Well let me see,' I said. 'For a man to walk on the seabed he would need a diving suit of some kind, and the means to breathe.' It was simple enough to say from the comfort of the fireside, but finding a solution was not. 'It can't be done, sir. The main problem is air supply. No reliable method has been found to provide regular fresh air to someone below the water. There's also the problem of how to deal with the sea's pressure, which grows greater the deeper you go. The temperature also plummets. Then there are currents, often hidden, but strong enough to sweep a man clean off his feet and far away. No sir, the whole endeavour is fraught with difficulty and danger.'

Sir Guy nodded like a sensible politician. 'Quite right, Doctor Lyon. A fool's errand.' He refilled my glass.

Alba seemed lost in thought. I feared I'd trampled on his dreams.

'It's a beautiful idea,' I added encouragingly. 'And who knows? Perhaps one day we'll have the means to make it reality.'

He smiled. 'My friends. What if I were to tell you that I've done this very thing myself, not two weeks ago? And what if I told you that I did it here on the Clyde, in the waters off Dunearn?'

Lady Octavia gasped.

'What? But how?' I stammered.

'It was all exactly as you just said, Doctor. There was first the question of the diving suit. So, I started by trying to create a helmet. I tried wood at first, but it was simply too buoyant. Then I began to try different metals, and after much trial and error discovered copper was best. It's both light and malleable, you see. I found a talented coppersmith in Campbeltown, and he fashioned a prototype. The next issue was how to overcome the body's natural buoyancy. That was more straightforward. All it took was a pair of boots with thick strips of lead attached to the soles.'

'But you'd sink like a stone!' exclaimed Lady Octavia.

He waved a hand. 'Exactly the point of the exercise, my dear lady.'

It all seems so obvious now, years later, in this century of dizzying progress. But at the time, what Alba was describing was quite fantastical.

'The trickiest thing by far,' he continued, 'was the air supply. I just couldn't come up with a solution. Then, one day in my study, it came to me. I took off my jacket and placed it on the back of my chair, simple as that. It was the sleeves, you see. If I could create long sleeves, impervious to water, then I could attach them to the diver's helmet and supply air from above.'

'Ingenious,' murmured Sir Guy.

'But that was only the beginning. The problem was how to make the sleeves. I tried many different materials, wool, cotton and sailcloth, all with poor results. But finally, at great expense mind, I hit upon silk.'

He sank into the couch and scratched his head.

'The benefit of silk, you see, is that it's strong, light and has a very tight weave. All of which is a good start. I then coated the silk in boiling resin which sealed it completely. The final step was to use coils of copper and wood to form ribs, and this gave the silk tubing strength to retain its shape underwater, even when the pressure closes in.'

'My God that's brilliant!' I cried. Lady Octavia turned to me in surprise. I drained my glass. 'So did it work? Did you actually walk on the sea bed? But, but how did you provide the air supply? No, I've got it! You built a pump!'

Alba nodded. 'Correct, Doctor. I had a bellows maker fashion me a giant set operated from on deck. By connecting the silk tubing to the helmet I created a reliable source of air. Naturally I wanted to be the first to test it, and I can assure you all,' he said, pointing to each one of us in turn, 'that it worked like a charm. Why, I spent a full thirty minutes walking the sea bed at a depth of ten yards, as easy as a promenade at Brighton. I used silk and resin for the diving suit too, and it keeps out the cold quite admirably.'

We all clapped. Without question, what he'd just described was an important advancement in marine science.

'However, my next task,' he continued, 'is to obtain a means of better illumination. You see . . ,' but he was interrupted by the call for dinner. Lady Octavia slipped her arm through mine as we made our way to the dining room. Then, as we seated ourselves round the candlelit table, I continued to press Alba on his experiments.

I've rarely enjoyed a dinner quite as much as that one, but as the wine flowed, I grew exuberant, little realising I was drifting into drunkenness. Alba talked of an observatory he'd constructed at Dunearn, and of a new lighthouse he'd financed on Arran built by Robert Stevenson. I cried out at the great man's name, whose towering lighthouse resting on the Bell Rock – eleven miles off the east coast in the wilds of the German Sea – was already a wonder of the modern world.

Towards the end of the meal Lady Octavia, who had insisted on having me at her side all night, rose to retire. As she made to leave, however, she dropped her napkin into my lap and stooping to retrieve it, squeezed my thigh.

'I'll be waiting for you,' she breathed, glassy-eyed.

Sir Guy and Alba, deep in conversation, broke off and stood with me to bid her goodnight. Her eyes followed me all the way out of the room in a manner which neither of them could fail to see. I hardly knew where to look, but they paid scant attention and continued their discussion where they had left off.

I was drunk by this point and recall little of the discussion thereafter. There is, however, a part that stands out in my mind. My appointment with Birkmyre in the morning was referred to. I asked something I'd never have dared sober.

'I can't help wondering, gentlemen, if Birkmyre is a freemason. Is that a fraternity which you share?'

Sir Guy shot me a look of dismay. Alba laughed and rolled his cigar between finger and thumb.

'Oh-ho, Doctor Lyon, now that is a tricky question. I've no truck with it myself, but Guy here is a master of the craft. Aren't you, cousin?'

Sir Guy shifted uncomfortably. 'Freemasonry is an ancient and noble thing. Its fraternity isn't a proper subject for a conversation such as this. But yes,' he added grudgingly. 'Birkmyre and I adhere to the craft of the square and compass.'

'And Argyle?' I pressed. 'Is he a mason too?'

There was an awkward silence.

'Doctor Lyon, that is a most impertinent question as I'm sure you realise, and one I cannot possibly answer.'

'I meant no offence, sir. I just wondered if perhaps freemasonry sought to advance science. If its members shared a common desire to make improvements for the common good.'

He hesitated. 'Well, yes. I suppose we do, in our own way.'

'Oh come, cousin,' said Alba, waving his cigar. 'Where's the harm in the good doctor's question? Why, it's well known in Society that Argyle's the country's most senior mason. What is it you call him? Grand Wizard or some such nonsense?'

Sir Guy shot him an angry look.

'Robert, I'm surprised at you,' he snapped. 'Well known or not, you know the sacred brotherhood has the strictest regard for secrecy.'

'Brotherhood,' sneered Alba. 'A gentleman's club for self-advancement and back scratching. It's hardly the Royal Society. Now there's an institution which genuinely promotes scientific endeavour.' He rapped his knuckles on the table.

'Science isn't the answer to everything,' cut in Sir Guy. 'There are mysteries which it cannot possibly fathom. Hidden things, secrets things even, which reveal the divine order.'

'Preserve your order, you mean!' he scoffed.

At this point, the politician in Sir Guy took over.

'Well if that's your view, Robert, that's your view,' he said mildly, draining the last of his brandy and extinguishing his cigar. 'It's late, gentlemen. It's been a pleasant evening but it's time for me to retire. Feel free to sit longer and take your ease, but I'll bid you goodnight.'

'Ah, I've offended you,' murmured Alba. 'You know how passionate I can be. Forgive me.'

Sir Guy graciously accepted the apology and, goodwill restored, we crossed the hallway to the stairs and parted on the landing. Back in my room the windows rattled as the storm raged.

My tired mind raced, my thoughts dominated by something I'd spied in the hallway above Sir Guy's study door. For there again was the Double Eagle, and it was the last image I held in my mind before passing out of consciousness.

23

I woke with a cry in the midst of an invisible battle with a two-headed eagle, drenched in sweat and with a mouth like desert sand. Someone was pounding at the door. I fumbled in the dark and cracked it open.

'Oh, thank goodness, sir,' whispered the ghostly footman, a lantern to his face. 'Your carriage. The driver's waiting.'

I drained a pitcher of water to slake my thirst. My hands trembled and lacing my boots took an age of fiddling. I'd barely slept three hours.

The storm had blown itself out and, in the grey before dawn, the trees stood stock still. My breath curled as I crossed the gravel to the carriage, and soon we were rumbling past the gateposts, down to the Custom House and my appointment with Birkmyre. I half expected to catch sight of Hare on some street corner, but he was nowhere to be seen.

The carriage jerked to a halt amid the seagulls' harsh chorus. There was Birkmyre, watch in hand. I rubbed my face, realising I'd forgotten to shave.

'I distinctly wrote six o'clock, Doctor Lyon,' he barked. 'It's now seven. Late night, was it?'

I muttered a weak apology.

'Well, no matter,' he sighed, slipping his watch into his waist-coat. 'I know what Sir Guy's table can be like'.

We stood by narrow stairs cut into the quayside. 'Come on,' he called, descending. 'I haven't all day to stand around.'

A squat steam launch puttered below, its funnel belching smoke. Paddle houses bulged mid-ships, their blades idling in the water. She was the *Comet*, the same that first went to the *Julietta* and towed her to harbour, and I liked the look of her immediately.

There was the vigorous scrape of coal being shovelled below. Then her mooring rope was thrown and, with a toot from her whistle, the *Comet* beat away from the quay. She was no swan but her movement was every bit as graceful and her hull trembled in time with the engine. Ripples spread from her sides as we steamed onto the river, the paddles flopping into water smooth as glass. Despite my pounding head I marvelled at the transformation from last night's storm.

The ship's engineer tipped me a wink and passed out some tea with water drawn from the boiler. Once we were under way and out of earshot of the crew Birkmyre turned to me.

'What have you discovered?'

The hot tea worked wonders.

'Well,' I began, 'I picked up a rumour . . .' Seeing his expression, I went on, 'from a reliable source, that a schooner was making secret landings on the Mull of Kintyre, somewhere near Campbeltown. Now it might be nothing. But it could be what we're looking for.'

'There are places the length of Kintyre where a ship could make a landing. This hardly narrows our search.'

'True, Commander. But we know something else. These landings were witnessed by pottery workers. So it seems reasonable to assume we're looking for somewhere close to a pottery.'

Birkmyre frowned but at least he wasn't dismissive.

'These landings,' he asked. 'Did your source know when?'

'Not exactly. But it looks as if the last landing was supposed to happen around the time the *Julietta* was wrecked, Sandy McLeod was murdered, and—'

'—and Mister McCunn disappeared from Campbeltown,' he said, finishing my sentence.

'Exactly so.'

'But what happened to McCunn? That's the question that bothers me. Was he involved in some wrongdoing? Or did he discover something and come to harm before he could report it? Or . . . ?'

'Or perhaps he decided to leave Campbeltown for reasons that have nothing to do with this case.'

Birkmyre stared at me. 'Debts you mean? Or a woman?'

'Who knows.'

'Very well, when we reach Campbeltown we'll make our way to the Custom House. I'll square matters with Inspector Mackay and see if we can't get a few of his men to join us making sandcastles.'

'Agreed,' I replied, ignoring his jibe.

'Tell me this, Doctor. The last time we met you seemed to think that illegal whisky making could be involved. Is that still what you think?' He shook his head. 'Because, I have to say, I've come across many smuggling operations in my time, but nothing as elaborate as this. Put it this way. Do you think I'd have alerted the Treasury if I thought I was dealing with a common case of whisky smuggling?'

I must admit I blushed at his words. But I also had a sense he knew more than he was telling me. 'And you, Commander?' I said. 'Have you any news?'

But he shook his head and we tailed off into silence. I couldn't help wondering about Sir Guy's visit to the Custom House and I'd half a mind to ask him straight out. But I thought better of it.

We were far downriver now, and a breeze rose as the *Comet* rounded the Tail O' The Bank toward the open sea. The green hills and mountains on either side grew distant, the water choppier, and soon we were out in the estuary, butting south through the waves. Cargo ships in full sail glided upriver and down and Birkmyre, pointing out the Cloch Lighthouse's lonely promontory on the mainland, explained that the next lighthouse would be Cumbrae Island.

As the *Comet* steamed on we drew close to Bute, and I thought again of the Marchioness. Just then, however, a dark speck appeared on the horizon. Closer and closer it loomed, like a bell tower flocked by gulls. It was the lighthouse on Cumbrae Island, and its lantern room glittered in the sunshine, the light glancing off its diamond patterned glass.

The hair on my neck rose to see where Sandy had been murdered. I tried to imagine it during a storm, its beam flashing over the boiling sea. For the hundredth time I asked myself what happened that terrible night, and I thought of Tom Hamilton, of Kitty Malone and finally of Hare, hoping he would lead me to the answers I sought.

Birkmyre interrupted my thoughts.

'There is something new, now that I think of it,' he said. 'It's about Hugh O'Neill.'

I recalled Tom Hamilton's partner from his trading days between Scotland and the Irish coast. 'He's dead. Lost overboard from his ship. It happened over there, off Bute.'

'Do you think it's connected?' I asked.

'Who can say. I don't like it though. I don't like it at all.'

After Cumbrae came Arran, and a distant glimpse of the bay at Dunearn. On the hillside above stood the castle and I smiled to think of Alba marching down to make his underwater promenade. Rounding the south coast of Arran we sailed west towards Kintyre, the waves growing large in the wide open sea. The *Comet* powered on, its paddles turning full tilt but rolling now, and I began to feel quite ill.

'Keep your eye on the horizon and breathe,' said Birkmyre as he watched me turn green and hang my head over the side. 'Looking down just makes it worse.'

I took his advice and fixed my gaze on the coast of Kintyre until the mouth of Campbeltown Loch yawned before us. Soon we were paddling along its length, surrounded by fishing smacks and cargo steamers. The feel of the place was different from the teeming river at Greenock, the boats smaller, the overall impression more rural and unspoiled by the hand of man. Sheep and cattle dotted the fields and closer to the head of the loch the town with its sober steeples hove into view, cuddling into the lee of the surrounding hills.

It took time to jostle through the harbour traffic and I saw countless puffers similar to Archie MacGregor's *Strathspey*, their decks heaped with barrels destined for the Broomielaw. We were close enough to the shore to see deckhands grappling with nets as they swung them up, over and onto the pier in one graceful sweep. A glittering cascade followed as the hard-won herring, the silver darlings of the sea, spilled onto dry land.

Then came the fisherwomen, flicking the fish into creels on their backs before hurrying to the shore-side factories where, knives flashing in their palms, they filleted the herring and pickled them in barrels, ready for the sea once more. Smoke rose from the town and drifted toward us.

'That's from the distilleries,' said Birkmyre, and for the first time I saw him smile. 'It's a grand smell they give off, is it not?'

It was certainly powerful, nutty and caramel sweet. It brought the spices of India to my mind.

When we came ashore Birkmyre strode ahead, his black clothes and eyepatch giving him the air of some terrible storm crow. Fisherwomen, sailors and even harbour officials melted away, some removing their caps. It struck me just how powerful Birkmyre was and that to be Collector at Greenock was to hold an important office.

The Campbeltown Custom House overlooked the pier, the Red Ensign fluttering above. A boy had run on ahead at the sight of Birkmyre. As we approached a portly gentleman hurried out to meet us.

'Commander Birkmyre!' he puffed, wide-eyed. 'What a pleasant surprise. I'd no idea that you would be paying us a visit. Really, had I known—' He patted the pockets of his waistcoat, as if searching for words.

'My apologies for this intrusion, Mackay, but there's really no need for fuss. This gentleman and I,' he hesitated. 'Sorry. Allow me to introduce Doctor Mungo Lyon of Edinburgh. Doctor, this is Hector Mackay, Inspector of Customs at Campbeltown.'

'Well, well, delighted to meet you,' said Mackay as I took his fleshy hand. He had the slow speech and sing-song accent of the Highlands. 'Honoured, honoured indeed. Please, come along inside gentlemen and I'll fetch you up some luncheon. Is it Greenock, then, that you're just after coming from?'

'It is, Mackay, it is,' murmured Birkmyre, glancing at the band of onlookers.

'Let's step inside, shall we?'

The Inspector's office lay on the ground floor and in we filed, Mackay giving Birkmyre his chair. Birkmyre waved away the cold mutton chops carried in on a tin ashet by the office boy, but accepted the whisky which Mackay spirited from a cabinet. I did the opposite, for while the sea air had made me hungry, I couldn't face a dram after my late night with Sir Guy.

We exchanged pleasantries and Mister Mackay talked of the comings and goings at Campbeltown. Then, drawing out tobacco and pipes, we settled into silence. The smoke lingered and Mackay, watching Birkmyre over his glass, waited for him to speak.

'I'll come to the point,' said Birkmyre. 'We're here, Mackay, on a matter of some sensitivity.'

'I see. Just a wee moment, Commander,' and stepping to the door he called out that we weren't to be disturbed.

'Now,' he said, closing the door and sitting back down. 'You were after saying, Commander, that you're here on a matter of some sensitivity.'

Birkmyre nodded. 'Doctor Lyon and I are tasked with an investigation. And it touches upon the recent disappearance.'

'Indeed,' he murmured, shaking his head. 'Mister McCunn. Most unfortunate, so it is. Just failed to turn up one morning and that was it. Gone. A good officer, very able, very able indeed. As was his father before him.'

'But there's something else,' added Birkmyre, and he hesitated as if unsure how to put it.

'What it comes to is this,' I interjected, ignoring Birkmyre's scowl. 'We have information a ship has been landing somewhere near Campbeltown. In a place that may be connected with a pottery.'

Mackay turned to me in surprise. 'A ship? Near Campbeltown?'

'Yes, during the night, on a beach. Now, Inspector, have you heard of anything like that?'

He puffed out his cheeks. 'Well, Doctor Lyon,' he replied. 'That's quite a surprising thing you're asking. But no, my answer is no. Not in recent times anyway. Not since the distilleries dried up all the contraband from Ireland. Granted there's still the occasional brig, but . . .'

'This would be a three-masted schooner,' added Birkmyre.

Mackay absorbed his words.

'Not at all,' he said with a firm shake of his head. 'Gentlemen, I appreciate your saying this is a sensitive matter but, well, may I ask what this is all about?'

Birkmyre and I exchanged a glance. 'May we see a map, Inspector?' I asked, avoiding his question.

'Of course, of course, the Admiralty chart,' he replied, and in a moment we had it on the desk. The Mull of Kintyre stretched north to south in a long finger of land, with Campbeltown and its loch marked on the south east.

'Where is the pottery?' I asked.

Birkmyre pointed to some grey squares drawn on the map just a couple of miles west of Campbeltown.

'There, that's the pottery. If I remember rightly, Mackay, the Duke and the Campbeltown guild had a battle over its location. The Duke wasn't best pleased, so I heard, but finally agreed to build it well away from the town.'

'Just as you say, Commander,' said Mackay. 'Many people in the town think the distilleries quite enough of an imposition, but a pottery was thought to be a step too far.'

I drew back from the desk and tried to remember what Fiona Cameron had told me.

Lanterns had been seen on the beach.

But what beach? I looked again at the map. There were a number of good, sheltered beaches on the east.

Just a couple of miles to the west, however, on the side of the ocean, a lonely stretch of sand formed a wide inviting bay. As Birkmyre had just confirmed, the collection of buildings marked at its southern extremity formed the pottery. It looked a perfect place for a ship to drop anchor and send a rowing boat ashore.

I pointed it out. 'This stretch here. What's it called?'

'That's Machrihanish Bay,' said Mackay at once. 'But its waters can be treacherous. Not an easy place to make a landing.'

'But not impossible?'

'No, I'd accept that,' he replied. 'Not impossible, if the waters were calm and the tide just about right.'

There was one more thing it occurred to me to ask. 'Inspector, I take it you have Watchers in case of smuggling?'

'Of course. I divide the labour among my junior officers.'

'And who's responsible for Machrihanish?'

He shifted at that question, but when the answer came it fell like a stone. 'Well, that was Mister McCunn's responsibility.'

There was a pause.

'Mister Mackay,' I said. 'We'll need two or three good men to search that bay immediately.'

He looked to Birkmyre, who had an air of resignation.

'If you can spare them, Mister Mackay.'

24

Within an hour a team of six of us stood on the sands at Machrihanish.

The Atlantic waves rolled in and the surf crashed against an expanse of sky and ocean. It was a desolate spot for sure, and our clothes and hair tugged in the stiff breeze. The beach stretched a good two miles north, giving way on the landward side to dunes, links and then fields, while to the south some kilns and cottages huddled together to form the Duke's pottery.

We spread out and I headed for the dunes. The firm turf rose and fell in great bumps and hollows. Occasionally a sheep strayed ahead and from time to time a startled corncrake erupted from its cover. Birkmyre followed behind taking little interest, instead looking out to sea and back toward the pottery. When we'd covered about a mile a cry went up from one of the men and we hurried to his side. He held a hurricane lantern, its glass broken, the iron casing showing the first bloom of rust.

'It was lyin' on its side in the grass, sir,' he said, addressing himself to Mackay. 'And there's marks on the ground too, like ruts frae a cart's wheels.' Sure enough, there were tracks about six feet apart leading away from the beach.

Mackay took the lantern and turned it. Brown water spilled from the canister and he raised it to his nose.

'You can just about smell the oil,' he said, rubbing the wick between his finger and thumb. 'I doubt it's been here long.'

We continued our search, the beach gradually narrowing to rocks and a cliff beyond. Mackay came puffing to my side as I peered ahead, shading my eyes against the bright sky. There were elongated black streaks in the cliff face, widening in ragged triangles to the ground.

'Caves,' I murmured.

Mackay pursed his lips. 'It's more than a year since I was up there, Doctor Lyon. Kintyre folk steer clear of those caves, the *uamhan dhubha* – black caves – they cry them, and the wind sings in their mouths.'

'What took you there last?'

'Ah, always a favourite for the Irish boats they were,' he said with a wink, 'good and dry, and just beyond the reach of even the fullest tide. Sure I passed them on my way to speak with Seamus Ben and just put my head round. But there was nothing at all.'

'Seamus Ben?'

'A beachcomber,' he told me. 'Seamus has had a hut by the headland these past forty years. No one minds him, and he minds nobody, but over the years we've come to have an understanding, him and me.'

He chuckled.

'What do you mean?' I asked.

He raised a finger.

'Now the way it goes you see, Doctor, is that I bring Seamus a bottle or two of the *craitur* and we sit and pass the time of day together in conversation about this and about that over a few drams and looking out over the sea and such. Now Seamus is himself from Ireland, Doctor, and would never dream of giving anyone away, you understand. But just by way of example, I might be saying to Seamus something like, oh, "How's the weather been these past few days Seamus?" And Seamus might take a while, sip at his dram, scratch his beard and then be saying to me, "Oh, well now Mister Mackay, there was quite a big storm there a few days ago now, quite a big storm indeed and rather a lot of rain all at once so there was." You see, Doctor?'

There was a pause while I grasped his meaning. 'Yes, I do, Mister Mackay. He sounds like a man worth speaking to.'

'Perhaps, perhaps,' he replied cautiously. 'Though I hardly see him these days now that things are so very busy in Campbeltown, what with all the new distilleries. And besides, I've not a dram on me to be offering him.'

He squinted up at the caves. 'But we'll see, we'll see. Well, now. Shall we take a look up there?'

From the firm sands we picked our way up through the rocks, then ankle deep through a scree of pebbles. The caves were dead ahead, three of them side by side. Sure enough, the wind played over them like a mournful call from the underworld.

'Let's split up,' I said, and headed for the one on the right.

I stepped in over the bleached bones of a long dead gull, a few last feathers still clinging on against the tugging breeze. One of Mackay's men followed. It was dark and dry, with a musty scent of the sea. The pebbles gave way to sand and earth, then widened so we could stand side by side. The crashing tide grew muffled.

'Deep,' observed my companion, with a sniff. 'This one goes back fifty yards or more. There's even cavemen pictures on the walls, further in.'

As my eyes adjusted I looked down and gave a cry. There was a mess of footprints clear as day, and something heavy had been dragged back and forth.

I ran to the cave mouth and called on the others.

'These are recent,' said Mackay looking at the prints, and he delved further in.

Birkmyre frowned. 'I don't like the look of this.'

In my mind's eye I pictured the *Julietta* anchored in the bay beneath a starbright sky, while its rowboat glided toward a lantern. I imagined a cargo dragged up the strand, over the pebbles and all the way here. I sensed Birkmyre was thinking the same.

'Anything?' I called to Mackay.

After a moment he re-emerged, his face puce from exertion.

'There's nothing there,' he breathed. 'Though I'll warrant there was plenty to see at some point. One thing's for sure, though. He held out his palm to reveal a smattering of black dust. 'Whatever they were up to, there was gunpowder.'

Birkmyre's eye widened. 'How much?'

'Couldn't say,' replied Mackay, clapping it from his hands. 'Just loose it was, on the ground.'

'Anything in the other caves?' I asked, but they both shook their heads. There was an awkward silence, then Birkmyre spoke.

'Well, Doctor Lyon, smuggling of some sort, perhaps. Maybe a pistol or two on hand for security. But not a great deal to go on, I'm sure you agree.'

He was right of course. But if nothing else, the cave, lantern and cart tracks convinced me that this was where the *Julietta* had been landing. But why?

'What I want to know,' said Birkmyre, 'is whether this has anything to do with Mister McCunn. I take it, Mackay, he kept a log of his watches?'

'Of course. It's at the Custom House.'

'Good,' Birkmyre nodded. 'I'll need to see it.' He looked again at the footprints. 'Mister McCunn may have stumbled on something and paid for it with his life.'

I turned to Mackay.

'What about Seamus Ben?'

Mackay quickly explained, and we agreed to visit the beachcomber while Birkmyre returned to the Customs House.

I followed Mackay round the headland, the beach thinning as the ground rose at the base of a cliff. There stood Seamus Ben's hut, the wind snatching the smoke from its chimney.

'It's a pity I've nothing with me,' muttered Mackay to himself. 'But it can't be helped.'

The door edged open on our approach and I caught my first glimpse of Seamus Ben stooping in the doorway. There was something of the heron about him, the same solitary patience and unblinking eye.

'It's yourself, Mister Mackay,' he called raising a hand, which he quickly dropped to catch a young collie straining at his side. 'C'mon, Ben, back ye go.'

'Och I'll not stay, Seamus,' said Mackay. 'I'm just after bringing this gentleman to say hello to you. Doctor Lyon it is, from Edinburgh.'

Seamus made an o of his mouth. 'Is that right, now,' he said.

There was a long pause filled only by the wind and the sea.

'It's a fine wee house you have,' I said at last. I meant it too. It was built from layers of tough driftwood.

'Aye. Well. It suits us fine,' said Seamus. He measured every word like a weight in his hand.

I turned to Mackay for a lead in the conversation, but he was busy staring at an area of open ground to the right of the hut, which Seamus appeared to be fencing off.

'What are you planning for there, Seamus?'

He turned and contemplated the endeavour.

'Oh, I was thinking of a few chickens, Mister Mackay. You know. For the eggs. But it's taking an age to find the wood.'

Mackay frowned. 'So I see, so I see. Well anyway, Seamus, I'll come straight to the point, for I can see you're busy. We're just after coming from the caves, and I wondered whether you might have noticed anything on the water these past few months? Anything out of the ordinary, Seamus, if you take my meaning?'

Seamus slowly raised a hand over his mouth and knitted his shaggy brow. Then, at last, he gave his answer with a long shake of the head, but even so I caught a twinkle in his eye.

'Well I couldn't rightly say, Mister Mackay. No, I couldn't rightly say.'

'I doubt he'd tell me anyway,' said Mackay as we marched back down and regained the beach, 'but I'm afraid your being there sealed him up like an oyster.'

I plucked a pebble from the sand and hurled it into the tide. The cry of the gulls rang in my ears like laughter.

'I'm sorry, Mister Mackay. I've wasted your time.'

He cleared his throat. 'Oh I wouldn't say that now, Doctor Lyon. No, I wouldn't say that at all.'

'Why? You mean the gunpowder?'

'Oh there's that all right,' he replied. 'There's certainly that. But no, I was thinking more about Seamus' half-built chicken yard.'

'I don't understand.'

He smiled like sunshine between clouds. 'Dear me, young sir,' he murmured. 'And here's me thinking surgeons must have eyes like hawks.'

He came to a halt.

'Those pieces of wood,' he said, spreading his hands. 'He finds them here in the tide, see? And the pieces he's used for his fences,' he shook his head. 'Well, they weren't there last time I visited him. I'll lay my life on it.'

I was puzzled. 'So he's found some wood on the beach. What of it?'

He fixed me with a stare, then turned and strode away.

'Come on, Doctor Lyon,' he called back. 'We shouldn't keep the Commander.'

'Wait!' I shouted, hurrying after him. 'Tell me! What is it?'

25

'*K*etland?'
Birkmyre was the picture of confusion. 'Are you sure it was *Ketland*, Mister Mackay?'

'As I live and breathe, Commander.'

We were back in his office and once again Mackay spirited the whisky from his cabinet. He poured three drams and handed them round.

'There's not a shadow of doubt about it. It was scorched into the wood. *Thomas Ketland & Company* of Birmingham. Plain as day. And on three separate pieces too. Your very good health, gentlemen.'

He drained his glass.

'And eh, these pieces of wood, Mackay,' asked Birkmyre. 'How long would you say they were?'

'About five feet. The right length anyway.'

Birkmyre's one good eye widened. He slowly raised the whisky to his lips. 'What in God's name have they got themselves involved in?'

I looked from one to the other and back again. 'And five feet would be the right length for what, exactly?'

They exchanged a glance.

'For packing rifles,' replied Birkmyre, perching himself on the edge of Mackay's desk. 'And Ketland make the best flintlock rifles there are.'

'Just a moment,' I said. 'Do you mean to say, that the wood from Seamus' yard came from the packing cases for, for rifles?'

Birkmyre did not reply, but Mackay gave me a nod.

'I've seen cases like that before, Doctor Lyon. At the Revenue men's stores in Glasgow. And there's six rifles to a case.'

'But the Revenue doesn't use Ketlands,' said Birkmyre. 'Too expensive. No. John Bull prefers to stick with the Brown Bess musket.'

Mackay refilled his glass. 'Aye, just so. A serious business.'

My head spun as I tried to catch up with what this meant. Not only had the *Julietta* been landing in secret, but its cargo may have included firearms.

The late afternoon sun cast a sickly ray of light across the office. Dust motes hung in the air. It was getting late for our return voyage to Greenock.

'I think we need more time,' I said.

Instead of answering Birkmyre lifted an open ledger from Mackay's desk and turned it toward us.

'Look here,' he said. 'The watcher's log for Machrihanish.'

We both craned forward to examine the pages. They were blank.

'I can't believe it,' stammered Mackay, 'the Regulations. He knew to follow the Regulations.'

'Damn it, Mackay!' thundered Birkmyre, the sudden change in his temper causing us both to start. 'Is there anything that's as it should be? Why wasn't this checked?'

As the Inspector stumbled out an apology about the pressures of dealing with the new distilleries, I couldn't help reflecting on Birkmyre's hypocrisy. Only that morning he'd been questioning coming to Campbeltown at all. Now that we'd actually discovered something, he was furious.

'Arguing will get us nowhere,' I said, gaining another black look from Birkmyre for my trouble. 'Let's take some time and find out what we can. Now, did McCunn have an office?'

Mackay led us in single file to a room on the top floor.

Shelves lined the walls from floor to ceiling, each packed with duty tables, tide tables, journals of inspection, shipping registers, committee reports, books of accounts, Treasury memoranda, Government updates and other such material of the driest kind. Bundles tied with white ribbon covered the floor. Standing in their midst was an oak desk carved with woodland scenes. I ran my hand along its worn leather inlay. Mackay came to my side.

'It belonged to his father Hamish, God rest his soul.' He quickly crossed himself in the Roman way.

'This could take hours,' grumbled Birkmyre gazing over the jumble.

'Mister Mackay,' I asked. 'Have you gone through any of this?'

He glanced nervously at Birkmyre.

'Well, not exactly now,' he faltered. 'In the first few days after Mister McCunn disappeared things were just a bit, a bit out of order I suppose you'd say. And em, well . . .' He scratched his head and gazed at the floor. 'These past weeks the place has become a store room, really.' He tutted. 'I'll have another word with that boy. This is no way to leave things, just lying about the place in no order at all.'

I lifted one bundle after another, then turned my attention to the shelves. I didn't know exactly what I was looking for. I scanned the rows of books, but there was nothing, and as I continued my search around the room, time and again my eyes returned to that desk until eventually I marched over and tried the drawers. They were all locked.

'Do you have the key, Mister Mackay?'

'Of course, of course,' he replied. 'Just give me a moment.' He fished a great bunch from his pocket and fumbled through them one by one. After an age of trial and error, during which Birkmyre stood with his arms folded, Mackay finally located the correct one and clicked open the top drawers. The mechanism was such that by unlocking them, the drawers below also came free. Mackay and I crouched and pulled them out.

They were all empty.

'I did this before,' wheezed Mackay, rising from his knees and dusting himself. 'And they were empty that time too.'

I remained on the floor, staring at the desk and empty drawers.

'You see, Commander,' Mackay added, turning towards him. 'I don't tolerate my officers leaving private papers about the place. Anything of a sensitive nature, a sensitive nature, mind, must go in the safe in my office at the end of every working day.'

'I follow you, Mackay,' Birkmyre replied with a nod. 'Very proper.' His manner seemed almost friendly, but I wasn't paying much attention to their exchange.

I clambered to my feet. I hardly know why, sheer frustration or instinct perhaps, but I gripped the side of the desk and tried to lift it. Even empty it was a ton weight, but I raised it a few inches.

'What on earth,' began Birkmyre, but just as he spoke there came a noise from inside. Something slid, then halted with a knock.

'There must be a hidden compartment,' I said.

'Well I'll be,' said Mackay. He lifted the opposite end and the sound repeated.

We searched every inch of the desk and in the end it was Birkmyre who found it: an iron button, hidden among carved berries. He pressed it and a drawer shot out. Our three heads came together, staring down, but it proved to be only an empty whisky jar.

The rest of that day I trawled through every item in McCunn's office. I even lifted a couple of floorboards but failed to turn up so much as a scrap of paper. Birkmyre and Mackay had disappeared to search the main office. Later, when I rejoined them, some scattered ledgers and their downcast faces told their own story. It was a sore experience for Mackay. He seemed to be struggling with the change from the old ways, based upon relationships, to the new religion of bureaucracy. Birkmyre, in fact, happened to be loudly lecturing him on that point as I re-joined them.

It was night now and the rain came. It was that heavy, quiet, west coast rain that falls straight as a builder's yardstick. Hitching my jacket over my head I swung a lantern at Mackay's side while he locked and bolted the Custom House door. Then, tucking away the keys, we hurried along the harbour to the sign of the *Black Sheep* where, despite the hour, Mackay charmed the landlady and secured us a room apiece above the public bar.

We slipped round a corner table by the ingle and mopped rain from our brows. Mackay called for ham and hot punch. The place was lively and good natured, but we took our seats amid some stares, whispers and even one hurried exit by a thin, nervous looking man in a long coat and spectacles.

It was late and I was tired. Too tired to make any sense of Crawford McCunn and besides, it was hardly the place for the kind of discussion we needed to have. Mackay half turned from us, exchanging a nod here and there round the room and watching for the punch. Birkmyre frowned at the fire with his thumbs tucked high in his waistcoat. I leaned an elbow on the table, head in hand.

The ham and punch arrived, rousing our interest, and Mackay lifted the jug.

'Don't look,' he whispered as our heads came together. 'But there's a friend of McCunn's by the name of Alex Cunninghame at the bar, and he's got a good drink in him I'd say.'

I busied myself cutting the ham then glanced over. Sure enough, Cunninghame was slumped over the counter, head down. A handful of others stood near. One of them, catching sight of us, leaned toward Cunninghame and whispered.

Mackay sighed.

'Aye, well. He never passes a chance to collar me about McCunn's disappearance, so I doubt tonight will be any different.'

Cunninghame turned from his whisky, glanced at Mackay then stared at Birkmyre. I prepared for a scene, but to my surprise there was no anger in his face. What there was, however, was unmistakable.

It was fear.

Without a word to those around him or even finishing his whisky, Cunninghame made straight for the door. Mackay gazed after him, then glanced at Birkmyre. 'What's his hurry?'

I'd half a mind to follow and see if I could question him, but Mackay laid a hand on my arm.

'I wouldn't, Doctor,' he urged. 'Best just leave him, I'd say.'

As I hesitated between sitting and standing, Birkmyre glowered at me.

'Sit down, Doctor,' he hissed. 'There's no time for you to be off chasing drunks and making a scene. We need to talk about tomorrow. Now, Mackay, tell us the plan.'

Being tired didn't help, but my anger rose. 'How dare you speak to me like that,' I growled.

'Doctor Lyon, please,' Mackay whispered. 'For pity's sake. I'm sure all the Commander was meaning was that he'll be wanting me to suggest the next line of inquiry. Isn't that right, sir?'

But instead of answering him Birkmyre drained his punch and got to his feet.

'I'll leave you to explain things, Mackay,' he said. 'I've had as much as I can take of this one. Good night.'

There was an awkward silence while we watched him pick his way through the crowded room.

I sighed, dog tired.

'I'm sorry about that, Mister Mackay. The Commander and I just don't seem to get on. But enough. What's your suggestion for tomorrow?'

He leaned forward, the fire glinting in his eyes.

'Well, Doctor. Today we searched the bay at Machrihanish and the Custom House. But it occurred to me earlier that there's another place we haven't looked, and that's the distillery.'

'The distillery?'

'The distillery where Mister McCunn worked.'

Mackay quickly explained that dozens of junior Customs officers were assigned to the new distilleries springing up in Campbeltown. Each distillery was required to have a locked office for their use. Here, using the latest Treasury equipment, officers checked both the volume of whisky and its alcohol content. Officers then calculated the excise duty which the distillery had to pay. Given the tremendous value of the tax receipts, the new regime was strictly regulated. The system was based on trust, but every Customs officer had a deed of appointment signed by the Chancellor of the Exchequer, granting unrivalled powers of search anywhere in the Kingdom. No door was barred to a Customs officer. The distillery owners, knowing this, went out of their way to please officers and sometimes played on their weakness. Mackay explained that he'd recently had to relocate a couple of officers who'd found themselves in difficulty.

'Aye, it's a constant battle,' he said, refilling his punch glass, 'but we usually find them a place in Glasgow's tobacco warehouses, where at least they're away from the drink.'

'So which distillery was McCunn's?'

Mackay sipped his punch.

'Springburn,' he replied, 'and a lovely whisky it is too, now. I'll take you there first thing. I think you'll find it interesting.'

26

Campbeltown Loch shone as I stepped from the Black Sheep the following morning. But the picture was quickly marred by half a dozen men gathered at the harbour's edge. Twenty feet below a corpse lay face down in the water, a rope now round its waist. As they hauled the rope the body turned, and I saw it was Alex Cunninghame.

They soon had his swollen body on the ground and, calling for space, I knelt alongside. I closed his eyes, which even in death were fixed in fear, and wiped the tell-tale foam from his lips and nose. He'd drowned for sure. There were no signs of a struggle on his face or hands, but he'd suffered a blow to the back of his head. Whether this had happened before or after he'd entered the water it was impossible to tell. Word was spreading, but nobody, it seemed, had seen or heard him go in.

The Burgh police officer arrived and the body was taken off to the Minister. I joined Mackay and Birkmyre beside the pier. I must admit I was shaken.

'Aye, a terrible shame now, so it is,' said Mackay as I came up. He drew out his watch and began to wind it. 'I've no wish to speak ill of the dead, so, but still, when a man flies close to the wind from time to time, well . . .' but as he searched for how to put it Birkmyre murmured a line from Burns:

'. . . *She prophesied that late or soon,*
Thou would be found deep drown'd in Doon . . .'

'Exactly so, Commander,' answered Mackay. 'To be blunt, I was surprised Mister McCunn associated with him at all.'

Their lack of concern troubled me almost as much as the death itself, but for once I held my tongue. Cunninghame's life certainly seemed cheap.

'Well, gentlemen,' said Mackay. 'Shall we?'

Turning from the pier we followed him along a vennel between the Burgh Court and the Custom House into a warren of ancient passages. The last thing I expected to come across was a distillery. Yet crossing the cobbles and under an archway a wide space opened up and we landed in what, at first glance, could pass for a college quadrangle. In the far corner two dray horses waited with a cartload of barrels in front of a warehouse.

'Here we are,' said Mackay with a sweep of his hand. 'Springburn Distillery. Just opened last year.'

I can never forget the smell of the place. It was an unusual mixture of malty beer, peat smoke and a hint of whitewash. Mackay briefly explained the functions of the neat buildings in different architectural styles around the square. There were two barley lofts and three malt barns all with low pitched roofs; twin kilns for roasting the malted grain, their chimneys billowing grey smoke; the stone Mash House forming the distillery's kettle; the Tun Room with its ranks of beer filled Wash Backs; and finally the Still House, complete with fluted copper stills and Spirit Safe, into which the trickle-born whisky arrived before being barrelled and left to slumber in the warehouse.

There were a hundred questions I wanted to ask Mackay about the process, but we were interrupted by the arrival of the proprietor, Aaron Colville.

'Good m-morning gentlemen good morning!' he called. 'I received your m-message, Mister Mackay. You're most welcome, m-most welcome indeed.'

After I was introduced, he turned to Birkmyre. 'As for you c-commander,' he added, holding out his hand and practically bowing, 'it's an honour to see you again so soon after, now let me think, the w-winter dinner in Ayr, wasn't it?'

Birkmyre gave a tight smile and shook his hand. It struck me that a stiff breeze could easily carry Mister Colville off, and yet there was something sprightly about him, making it difficult to place his age. A green velvet jacket drooped across his shoulders. He had a thin tortoise-like neck, a neat black beard and gold pince-nez. There was a definite resemblance, I thought, to Aeneas McGarvie, Edinburgh's renowned professor of Greek, who once succeeded in setting fire to his own hat during a public lecture.

Despite Mister Colville's pleasant greeting, and aside from his obvious stutter, he seemed distracted, anxious even. While he spoke to Mackay his fingers drifted to a watch chain across his waistcoat and a pendant in the shape of a set square and compass.

'So M-mister Mackay,' said Colville adjusting his pince-nez and looking to each of us in turn. 'Your note gave little indication of your p-purpose. How c-can I help?'

'Oh it's nothing at all sir,' replied Mackay blandly. 'I just wanted to show the Commander and Doctor Lyon our procedures.'

Mackay produced a list and peered at it.

'Now then, so many young customs officers these days,' he said, running a finger down its length. 'Let me see. Ah yes, our new officer from Cornwall. Mister Talland. Is he here?'

'Certainly,' smiled Colville, 'he's in the warehouse. I'll have someone bring you to him.' He called one of the men.

'You'll f-forgive me if I d-don't join you', he added, 'but I've an ap-ppointment with the parish m-minister. Every Sunday, you see, he p-preaches the evils of drink to his terrified parishioners, while all the while I quietly provide the money for his new steeple, not to mention the annual outing.'

I grinned. 'An interesting arrangement.'

Colville pulled on a pair of gloves. He glanced at my companions then gave me a wry look.

'The Lord m-moves in mysterious ways, Doctor Lyon, his wonders to perform, but his good minister sometimes seems to think I own a g-goldmine rather than a distillery.' He headed for the archway. 'Good day, gentlemen, and my c-compliments to His Majesty.'

We found Mister Talland seated at a desk with rows of barrels behind him. He was peering into a large beaker which, drawing closer, revealed itself to be almost brim full of whisky. He lifted what looked like a golden wand with a bulge in the middle and dropped it in. It disappeared, resurfaced, then bobbed to a standstill. He took a measurement.

'That's nine inches depth, at fifteen ounces gives . . . let me see . . ,' he murmured in a soft Cornish accent, writing all the while in a long columned ledger. He was oblivious to us until the last moment.

'Mister Mackay sir,' he exclaimed, dropping his pen and standing. 'How can I assist?'

He looked to each of us, recognised Birkmyre and swallowed hard. But Mackay put him at ease and explained the purpose of our visit.

'We just need to search the place for anything that McCunn might have left behind,' he said. 'But not a word now, Talland, ye hear? I don't want this getting about.'

Talland nodded. Just then a workman approached to lift away the whisky sample. Mackay slipped into character.

'Yes, Doctor, quite the latest marvel now, so it is,' he boomed, retrieving Talland's instrument from the bucket and passing it to me. 'A hydrometer they call it, and with one of these in his hand, so, and with a good head for arithmetic, an officer can calculate duty in the blink of an eye.'

The brass hydrometer gleamed in my hands. It was still wet with whisky that stung my nostrils.

'And now that Talland here has calculated the degree proof of the alcohol,' continued Mackay, 'you'll see the sample is returned to the barrel, the volume of which at three shillings a gallon proof gives a duty figure of . . . ?'

Talland consulted his ledger then closed his eyes to do the arithmetic in his head.

'Sixteen pounds, four shillings and ninepence, sir. And mind and tip it all back into the barrel!' hollered Talland after the retreating workman. 'I caught that one yesterday – he'd drunk away three pints raw spirit from the barrel in the time it took him to walk fifty yards.' He shook his head. 'Three pints it was sir, Lord preserve me,' but my companions hardly batted an eyelid.

'Now Talland,' said Mackay when the workman was out of earshot. 'Did McCunn leave anything behind? Anything at all?'

Talland took a moment. 'Well there were the ledgers sir, same as this one I'm using now. He'd left the duty ledgers in the Customs office. Is that what you mean?'

Mackay waved his hand. 'Yes, yes, we'll get to them. But what I mean is, did he leave anything personal, or out of the ordinary?'

Talland slowly scratched his ear and frowned.

'Not that I can recall, sir. Though . . . half a moment, yes, now that I think about it there was sommat – or talk of sommat at least. Because I never saw it myself.'

'What didn't you see?'

'His hydrometer set.'

'What?'

'Yes sir,' said Talland, his eyes darting to each of us. 'Well, we've each been issued with our own set . . .'

'Yes, yes,' interrupted Mackay.

'Of course, sir. Sorry, sir. Well, when I first arrived at Springburn I unlocked the Customs office and laid by all my equipment and other items. Now I'm firm, sir, that any distillery workers, they ain't allowed in the office, except an officer invites 'em in I suppose, sir. But that morning a workman puts his head round the door and says to me, laughing like, that he hoped I was a tidier man than Mister McCunn and what a job they'd had sorting out the office.

'Well, that puzzled me, for I couldn't rightly say how they came to be in it, sir, except perhaps it was left unlocked when 'e disappeared or sommat. So I told him he'd no business being in there what with no customs officer present and as how it was against the regulations. But he only laughed again, and away he went.'

'So what did you do?'

'Well, sir, I 'ad a look round me and saw right enough the office was clean as a whistle except for all the ledgers piled in a drawer, and I got to wondering about what it was they'd tidied away or tidied up. So out I went to find the feller but strange, from that day to this I've never seen him again.'

'But the hydrometer, Talland. You were saying about McCunn's hydrometer.'

'Oh my goodness, yes sir. Well, that was another story you see, on account of I was in the Still House one day a while back and looking to take a proof measure of the whisky flowin' out the still. I was about to unlock the Spirit Safe when I realised my hydrometer set, in its box 'an all, was back in the office. So I says to a feller there that I was away to get it when he says to me that there's no need and Mister McCunn's hydrometer was at the back of a cabinet just there, where the men keep tools and spare parts and the like.

'Well I was surprised to hear it of course, sir, being a handsome piece 'an all, that to my way of thinking should've been in the office if any place, as opposed to hidden away in the Still House.'

'So, what did you find?'

'Well, sir. Next thing was the cabinet was locked and no key to be found in the distillery or the office. And of course I wasn't best pleased about that seeing as how, as Customs man, I'm to have a key for every place. So in the end I took a bar and forced it. But there was no hydrometer there to be found, sir.'

There was silence once he'd finished his account. Mackay and Birkmyre exchanged a glance.

'Mister Talland,' I asked. 'Did you raise any of this with the owner, Mister Colville?'

'Well no,' he faltered. 'I didn't really think it was my, my place, sir, to . . .'

'Of course it was your place, sir,' barked Birkmyre. 'You're an officer of the Crown, are you not?'

Talland, taken aback, managed a subdued 'yessir' and stared at the floor.

Thereafter, for the sake of form as much as anything else, Mackay announced that we would search every corner of the distillery. So we proceeded from room to room, building to building, following the entire cycle of the distilling process from grain to glass. It took more than three hours from beginning to end, but emerging back into the courtyard from the Still House we hadn't a single thing to show for our trouble. By this time it was close to noon and Birkmyre was beginning to grumble about catching the tide for Greenock.

'Very well,' sighed Mackay. 'Mister Talland, let's just have a quick look in your office before we go.'

The Customs office was every bit as interesting as it sounds. It had little to recommend it but a large desk, a few chairs and a shelf crammed with ledgers revealing nothing about what, if anything, Mister McCunn had been doing besides his duty to the Crown. We were on the verge of bringing the search to a close when an idea struck me. On the wall behind the desk was a hook board with row upon row of keys, each with a handwritten label. As I ran my eye along them I checked off every place we'd searched, except one. At the bottom, dusty and unused, hung a key labelled 'Mister Colville's Office.' But when I proposed searching it, Birkmyre and Mackay surprised me with the force of their resistance.

'We can't possibly do that,' said Birkmyre. 'It's his private office.'

'The Commander's right,' added Mackay. 'It would be a gross breach of trust.'

I reflected on how little I'd discovered since arriving in Campbeltown. I'd shortly be returning to Greenock, and who knew if I might ever have the chance to return. I thought back to the Lord Advocate, and the day I'd received my mission in Edinburgh. This was too important, and I decided not to back down.

I turned to Birkmyre.

'Commander,' I began, 'only last night Mister Mackay told me that a Customs officer holds the King's Warrant to search any property in the realm. You know my mission and who sent me, so I take it you'll respect my request that you—'

Birkmyre raised a hand. 'Enough,' he said. 'I see what you want to do. Very well. On your own head be it. Talland, the key if you please.'

'But Commander,' stammered Mackay, 'if we wait just a wee while Mister Colville might—'

'No, Mackay. Our young friend here has made up his mind.'

Talland went to hand Birkmyre the key, but he nodded at me. 'Give it to him,' he said.

I crossed the courtyard to Colville's office. A workman called to a colleague, and by the time I unlocked the door a crowd was gathering. I pushed it open. There was no going back.

My companions followed me in, then stopped.

A Persian carpet covered a room filled with all manner of objects. Portraits lined panelled walls with a bay window onto the courtyard. Two tigers' heads stared out above a desk littered with candles, papers, glass jars, a telescope and a magnifying glass. A pharaoh's coffin leaned against a bookcase. Twin globes of the Earth and heavens stood either side of a longcase clock, its tick resounding like a warning, and in that moment it struck the quarter hour.

My heart raced. Every which way I turned there was more to see, all bearing testimony to Colville's eclectic mind. I began to despair of conducting a search. Colville could return at any moment, and the thought of explaining began to overwhelm me. But I took a breath and began.

By the time two more quarters had chimed the sweat was pouring from my brow. I'd rifled through papers, emptied every drawer, scattered every volume, upended tables and even disturbed the pharaoh's slumber. My companions watched in horror, no doubt awaiting as I did too, the wrath of Aaron Colville.

At the bay window I pulled back a curtain, revealing a bench heaped with cloth, books, paintings and other curios. The curtain caught, triggering a cascade onto the floor, and I stopped for a moment contemplating the chaos.

It was at this point that Mister Talland, God bless his sharp eyes, spoke up.

'That's odd,' he murmured, pointing to a corner of the bench newly revealed. 'What in the world is that doing there?'

They gathered at my shoulder.

It was a perfectly ordinary hinged mahogany box, partly covered by a red silk shawl, which I gently shifted to reveal an equally ordinary looking brass plate. But the engraving on its surface was unique.

Sykes Hydrometer, No. 47
Property of Mister Crawford McCunn, Officer
His Majesty's Customs and Excise

There was a long pause during which we were all too stunned to speak. From somewhere behind me I heard Birkmyre murmur, 'Please wait outside now, Mister Talland, there's a good fellow. Make sure no one else comes in. We'll call if we need you.'

I eased aside the box's twin catches and lifted the lid to reveal McCunn's hydrometer. It was laid out on blue velvet and surrounded by the disc weights essential to its use.

Mackay lifted it gently and turned it in his hands.

'Seems in order,' he said.

I began to lift the individual weights and passed them to Birkmyre. One in particular, however, was stuck fast in its place. As I tugged in an effort to free it, the velvet base came away to reveal a void below.

'There's something in here,' I said.

It was a solid metal block, heavy as a brick.

'There's a notebook in there too,' I heard Mackay say, but I was still examining the block. Looking closer, it was split in two pieces lengthwise. The top part slotted neatly into the piece below, with a moulded dimple at each corner.

I removed the top piece and turned it over. Then I laid the two pieces side by side. There were six circles in a row along the inside of both pieces, and despite the black surface of the metal I began to see that each circle was engraved with words and images which confused me until, with a sudden rush of realisation, everything became clear.

In one piece, beautifully picked out in reverse, were six images of Saint George astride his horse, sword in hand and cape billowing, while his famous adversary the dragon lay flailing below. On the other piece the six circles repeated the familiar image of the King's late father George the Third, his brow crowned with a laurel wreath.

'Why I'll be damned,' I cried. 'It's a mould for minting coins!'

It could hardly be any clearer. A narrow channel had been cut into both pieces which, when joined, linked one circle to the next and led to a perfect little hole at one end. 'Look,' I said, pressing the pieces together again and upending them. 'The molten metal must be poured in here to fill the mouldings one by one. Presumably the pieces are wedged together while it's done.'

Mackay fumbled for his spectacles and squinted at the mouldings. Birkmyre, meanwhile, was scanning through the notebook.

'You're right,' said Mackay, his voice barely a whisper. 'Someone could make a lot of coins with this, that's for sure.'

He scraped his fingernail against the moulding and frowned.

'And not just any coins,' he added, straightening himself and removing his spectacles. 'There's only one coin in the realm with that design.'

Birkmyre glanced up from the notebook.

'Sovereigns,' whispered Mackay. 'This is for minting gold sovereigns.'

27

The sun was setting over the Firth of Clyde.

Birkmyre, alongside me on the deck of the *Comet*, was a shadow against a purple sky, and all was silent save the rhythm of the engine and flop of the paddles. We'd hardly spoken from the moment we left Campbeltown.

Birkmyre had gone below, saying he needed time to think, but in the last few moments he'd returned on deck. I spoke first.

'The notebook. May I see it?'

He'd kept hold of it himself. Now he reached into his jacket and handed it to me.

I flicked through the first few pages. At the top of each was a date, with a column of figures and a total. I added them together. Whatever it was came to just over two hundred and twenty thousand.

The dates were as follows.

Arr: 7th December 1827
Dep: 12th December 1827
Arr: 15th March 1828
Dep: 21st March 1828

Arr: 24th June 1828
Dep: 29th June 1828
Arr: 30th September 1828
Dep: 4th October 1828

I recalled Sir John telling me the *Julietta* averaged three months for round trips. There was almost exactly three months between departure and arrival each time. Between each arrival and departure there were usually just a few days. On the last marked page there was the heading '*Arr.*' but nothing else, and the remaining pages were blank. At the back of the notebook there were tell-tale jagged strips.

'There are pages missing.'

Birkmyre frowned and stared out to sea. 'Are there? I hadn't noticed.' He cleared his throat. 'So, what do you make of the dates then, Doctor?'

There was something different in his tone.

'Well,' I replied. 'It looks as though the dates are a record of the *Julietta*'s landings at Machrihanish. The arrivals must be inbound, from Jamaica to Greenock, and the departures outbound going the opposite way – so two landings in quick succession, dropping and collecting every time. On the last occasion she failed to arrive, meaning the drop off from Jamaica didn't happen, presumably because of the crew's fever.'

He gazed over the side without replying.

'So the two questions I ask myself,' I continued, 'are first, what cargo was the *Julietta* to drop at Machrihanish the night she failed to make her *rendez-vous*? And second, since that cargo wasn't dropped off, what happened to it? Because nothing was found except sugar – and some copper, of course.'

He turned to me, arms folded. 'Ah yes. The copper. You'll recall your theory about the copper, Doctor Lyon.'

'Well, I did think it could be connected with making pot stills but,'

'But you were clearly wrong. Your theory was naïve.'

'Why so?'

There was a pause before he replied.

'I've been a Customs and Naval officer for many years, Doctor, and seen a few things in my time. And one thing I can tell you, there's more than just gold in a gold sovereign. They're minted with what's called Crown Gold, Doctor, which is an alloy of eleven parts gold to every one-part copper. The copper gives them strength. Now, that,' he concluded, 'is why there was copper on the *Julietta*, Doctor Lyon. Nothing to do with pot stills.'

He was right, of course, though I was embarrassed to admit it.

'So you think this has nothing to do with whisky?'

He shook his head. 'I fear not.'

Darkness grew as the sun dipped below the horizon. A crewman lit lanterns fore and aft and the shore lights twinkled as we approached Custom House Quay. As the *Comet's* engine slowed Birkmyre placed a hand on my shoulder.

'Now look here, Mungo.' It was the first time he'd used my Christian name. 'Let me speak plainly.'

I waited for him to continue.

'You're out of your depth. You've discovered some things, I grant you, and done well for a young civilian. But you leap to conclusions.'

I tried to interrupt but he wouldn't yield.

'Let me finish please. You turned up drunk, an hour late, and when we did reach Campbeltown your conduct was erratic. As for that performance at the distillery, well, it'll take years to rebuild Aaron Colville's trust.'

'But—'

'No, Doctor.' He raised a finger. 'It's time for me to take a decision. I'm discharging you. This is a Customs matter now, and as Collector of Customs I must have control.'

I forced myself to stay calm. Yes, I'd made mistakes. But I'd got other things right. Things Birkmyre had overlooked. Despite the power of Birkmyre's argument, Sir John's reasons for recruiting me still echoed in my ears. I was an outsider, but my mission was the Crown's mission. It wasn't mine to relinquish. Not without a fight.

'You know who's behind this, Commander, don't you?'

I searched his face.

'What makes you say that?' His eyes darkened and he gripped my shoulder. He didn't deny it.

'You're a mason,' I said, committing myself. 'And it's a strange coincidence that the Double Eagle in your office matches those from the crew of the *Julietta*. Too much of a coincidence, perhaps?'

He stepped back, releasing me. The *Comet* was edging closer to the quay. A crewman stood ready with a noose.

'Go on.'

'It seems to me, Commander, that this mission troubles you, as does my involvement. There are masons bound up in this. And that puts you in a difficult position. Particularly here, under the shadow of Argyll.'

'And tell me, what significance do you attach to that particular fact?'

'I had it from Alba that the Duke is your senior man – a fraternity you share with Sir Guy, and Colville too, unless I'm much mistaken.'

Anger swept his face. 'That was a very unfortunate thing for his Lordship to say.'

The *Comet* drew up at the quay.

'Very well, Doctor Lyon.' He snatched McCunn's notebook from my hand. 'You've made your views clear, ludicrous as they are, and my patience is past its limit.'

He seized a lantern and stepped ashore.

'Is that all you have to say?' I shouted after him.

He turned, glaring.

'Your involvement in this matter is at an end, Doctor. Go back to your patients.'

'Commander, wait—'

'But I warn you,' he barked, cutting me off. 'If I find you lingering on and attempting to interfere in my jurisdiction, then I'll have you arrested. Understand?'

He left me standing, my mouth agape like a landed herring.

28

The mantel clock chimed midnight and I slumped before the fire. The remains of a cold supper lay beside me and the last of a bottle of claret in my glass. On my return to the Mansion House I'd learned my hosts were on Bute calling on the Marchioness, on one of her rare visits north.

'Oh, and there's that,' the footman had added, pointing to the hall table. 'It came this morning. From Edinburgh.'

Carefully checking the seal, which seemed intact, I prised open the letter. It was from Margaret, encoded in our usual way.

Dearest Mungo,

I pray this letter finds you safe and well.

As soon as you left I set to work, though I knew nothing of this mission of yours. That only came later, with your letter from the barge.

Mungo. I sense much danger in your task. You must be careful.

You flatter me by asking my advice, so here it is. You're a Lyon, which means you always do what's right. But I know you better than anyone, dear brother, so forgive me when I say you can be prideful.

I see our father in you. Some years ago, as I nursed him, he confided in me. When mother died his world came apart. He wanted to come with us to Edinburgh, but he believed grandpapa would think it unmanly, so he sent us away and stayed on in India.

He regretted those years and confessed it was pride had kept him from us. Learn from this, Mungo. Never let pride keep you from admitting a mistake. That is my only advice. But enough. You are likely in the midst of things, so I'll come to the point.

Success.

The code is made up of three Spanish texts, one running forward, the other two running backward. My breakthrough was discovering every third word, running forward, formed the Lord's Prayer. That was the first text.

Two discoveries then led to the solution.

With the prayer deleted, every line contained ten words.

The first two lines both ended with 'en', a common way to begin a sentence in Spanish.

The hidden message is wound round a second text, in pairs of lines, like this:

servidor	*nombre*	**vuestro**	*de*	**amen**	*la*	**de**	*lugar*	**el**	*en*
no	**humilde**	*cuyo*	**yo**	*mancha*	**dios**	*de*	**nombre**	*un*	**en**

The second text is Don Quixote. He must have committed it to memory – which is all the more surprising considering his native tongue was French, as you will see.

Be very careful Mungo. Lizzy tells me there's a man on the corner she hasn't seen before. I've sent this via Thomas, the grocer's boy, after he called on her this afternoon. True love has its uses.

Your loving sister,

Margaret

I laid the letter aside and gazed at Margaret's solution which I hadn't yet deciphered. A day earlier and I'd have set to work in a heartbeat. But Birkmyre's warning and Margaret's letter made me want to summon a carriage and head home. I'd had enough. I lit my pipe and gazed into the flames.

Margaret was right. My father would die rather than have his father-in-law think less of him. But there was more to the story. There had been other things to consider. Father didn't have the means to come home after mother died. He had worked to build capital to buy our home. It was a difficult decision, I could see that, and those years had been hard. But there was no gain without sacrifice. Whatever my father had said I felt sure he'd acted for the best.

Then I thought about pride and had to concede Margaret was right. I'd be ashamed to fail. But was it a mistake to soldier on? After all, the Lord Advocate and Sir John had chosen me for this mission. They wanted an outsider, and that instinct seemed right given my discoveries in Campbeltown and Birkmyre's parting words.

The battle in my weary mind continued to and fro while Margaret's translation lay untouched. As the clock struck one I reached a decision. I would decipher it, turn it over to Birkmyre and end my mission. I was about to start when what sounded like a handful of gravel ricocheted off the bay windows. Then it happened again.

I drew back the curtains and lifted the sash.

'Hare!' I called softly. 'Is that you?'

'The very same, Doc.' He sounded agitated. 'Now will ye do's a favour and open the back door, quick like.'

Lifting a lamp I descended and let him in. But as I turned to lead him he disappeared for a moment only to return with the decanter of Sir Guy's good brandy. His hands were trembling and caked with blood. There was a gash across his cheek.

I reached towards him but he turned away.

'Just ran in tae a couple o your friends on the way, Doc.'

'Let's get you upstairs. Were you followed?'

'Can't be sure. Think I gave them the slip.'

In my room he darted to the window and scanned the grounds, before coming back to pour himself a large brandy. His wound stretched from lip to ear.

'You better drink that,' I said, diving into my bag. 'That needs stitching.'

Hare swallowed the brandy while I fished a line of catgut through a half-moon needle. The cut was deep and had the clean sides of a knife wound.

'This will sting,' I murmured, applying iodine. I'd known it to cause grown men to cry out, but he didn't even blink.

'Never seen that stuff before,' he muttered. 'Stinks don't it?'

I quickly made four neat stitches, but again he made no sound.

'There, that's you,' I said, pouring him another brandy, and he stepped to the mirror.

'Thank'ee, Doc. Not bad. Not bad at all.'

It felt good to be useful.

'Last time I saw you was after our visit to *The Glue Pot*,' I said.

He sipped the brandy and winced, raising a finger to the stitches.

'Och, but I knew ye'd be fine, Doc, a smart man like you. Whit a commotion ye caused in that pottery though, eh?'

Laughter hissed through his teeth, followed by a convulsion of coughing.

'Well anyway, ye'll be pleased when you hear what I've got to tell you.'

'Why's that then?'

''Cause I've been busy this last while doing exactly what you asked o me.'

'You followed Kitty?'

'That I did, Doc. And she takes a fair bit o following that one. Twice I tried and failed, but tonight I stuck to her. It was late on, after closing time at the *Anchor*, and just then I sees the bonny Kitty hurrying with a bundle in her shawl.'

'Tom Hamilton,' I whispered.

'Could be, Doc, could be,' he said with a sly glance. He took another sip of brandy.

'So where did she go?'

'Well, I follows Kitty for the best part of a mile up one lane and down another, all the time movin' east along the shore. It's an auld and crumbling part of town along there, so it is, but eventually out she turns at the front of a right queer lookin' place with five gables facing the river, each one with a light glowing from a wee window high up.'

He raised a leg and began to rub the sole of his foot.

'I'd never seen the place before but I recognised it from what I've heard in the taverns round the harbour. It's a sailors' rest they say, but with a name for smugglers in days gone by, when the lights from the wee windows would signal to ships on the water.

'Well, as I'm watching from behind a heap of barrels, Kitty stops at the door and gives it a few raps. A moment later, I hears a bolt sliding back and a key turning, and next thing she's away in and the door locked at her back. Well, she was in there over an hour, though what she was doing I couldn't say. But at one point, clear as a bell, I heard a man cry out like he was in awful pain.

'It stopped quick as it started, and everything went quiet as the grave. But not long after, I hears the door again and out comes Kitty, this time without the bundle and looking terrible. I waited on a wee while till the coast was clear and then came here thinking to fetch you over. It was on the way that I ran into bother, but I doubt they'll know where I followed Kitty, and that's that.'

He drained his glass.

'C'mon, Doc. What are we waiting for? Kitty was fair upset, and I don't doubt that if Hamilton's there right enough, he's not a well man.'

I shook my head.

'You've done well, Hare,' I sighed, 'but it's over for me now,' and I told him of Birkmyre's threat.

'Arrest you?' cried Hare, when I'd finished. 'Now why would that good for nothing auld woman make a threat like that?'

I poured a brandy. 'I wish I could tell you that, Hare, I really do.'

'But ye don't trust me,' he whispered, and sat down.

'No, it's not that,' I lied. 'It's just that, well—'

'It's just that I'm William Hare, nothing but an ignorant Irish murderer, while you're all gentlemen, so you are.'

He drew out his pipe and tobacco.

'I wouldn't put it like that.'

'Course ye wouldn't, Doc. But ye need to wake up, so ye do.' He lit his pipe, blue smoke curling above his head. 'After all, nothings quite what it seems now, is it? Something stinks about this whole business, and I know enough to say that if Birmyre's threatened to arrest you then ye must be on to something big.'

He leaned forward.

'Now, he's not going tae help ye no more, Doc, but I can and I will if you'll only tell me what this is all about. See I told ye, I like this line of work, and I've always liked you too. And I meant it.'

My head spun.

'Well what's it to be? Will ye share with your partner what ye know?'

I thought back to the beginning of it all. 'If I share with you what I know, I'll be disobeying Sir John's orders.'

'And did you not just tell me that you were told Birkmyre was to do your bidding? And did Birkmyre not disobey that order? No, Doc. Sir John's not here. But if he was, I'm thinking he'd want you to use the wit God gave you to get the job done, and Birkmyre be damned.'

I made my decision. By the time the clock struck two I'd told Hare everything. He listened, face unmoved, until I reached the end and Margaret's work.

'I was just about to decipher it when you arrived. I've decided to hand it to Birkmyre then return to Edinburgh.' I sighed. 'But now, well, I'm not so sure about anything. Except I'm dog tired, and that's a fact.'

He gave me a wild look. 'Tired is it? Tired! The things I've seen and done in my time, Doc, I don't sleep and that's a fact. No. Men like you and me, Doc, we'll sleep when we're dead and not before.'

He poured me the last of the brandy. 'Drink,' he said harshly. 'Then to work. You've no time to be tired.' He held out the glass. 'Go on,' he urged, calmer now. 'I'll wait while you do it.'

I drained the glass and reached for Margaret's translation.

29

With the energy of a dervish I deciphered Margaret's work on the journal and by the time the clock struck four the task was done. My hands trembled as I reached the final few words, the enormity of the *Julietta*'s fate opening before me.

I looked across at Hare, smoking quietly by the fire.

'You have to hear this.'

In the name of God Amen I, your humble servant at Spanish Town, once again make this report to you, most illustrious and righteous guardian of the lofty honours of the Double Eagle, and so record in this journal of yours the voyage of the schooner Julietta from Kingston Harbour in Jamaica to the port of Greenock on the western coast of England.

Three days before the feast of the Immaculate Conception of the Blessed Virgin, and loaded with five hundred tonnes of cane sugar, we sailed east across the Caribbean Sea. Five leagues out of Kingston, as arranged, we met the brig Méduse at anchor. The transfer of our additional cargo was then made. One thousand pounds weight Spanish gold, one hundred pounds copper.

We continued eastward with light winds, then tacked north through the treacherous Windward Passage (mercifully calm, God be praised), then north east past Turks to the Ocean. We are fourteen in total including myself, Captain Estrego, Mister Walker the first mate and an indentured crew of eleven, all enlisted to serve our cause in secrecy. Two new recruits from Panama are acquitting themselves well.

As I make this entry on our ninth day out of Kingston we are under full sails two hundred leagues into the Atlantic and beginning to pick up the Trade Winds north to Bermuda. Captain Estrego wisely takes the slow but steady route. From Bermuda we follow the breezes of the Horse Latitudes to the Azores. From there it will be east to the Portuguese coast, then north to England.

May the Almighty look down with his all-seeing eye and grant us safe passage.

Day fifteen. We have passed Bermuda and Estrego has begun the slow turn north east to the Azores. We have avoided hurricanes, though the tropics were stormy. The Trade Winds have fallen to nothing, however, and we idle in a bank of fog. A swarm of mosquitoes bedevils us night and day. There is an eerie calm save for a pod of whales lazing in the water off our starboard side. I pray the morning will herald a breeze.

Day thirty-two. What a joy, Inspector General, to hear this morning the watchman's call of land! After seven hundred leagues of ocean we are nearing the Azores. This, the longest leg of our crossing, has proven unfortunate.

Two days ago, one of the Panamanians staggered on deck like a drunk. Just as Walker went to remonstrate with him he collapsed and vomited black bile. According to the crew he'd kept his distance for some days. His face was jaundiced. Blood seeped from his eyes and gums. He has yellow fever.

Panic spread. There and then Captain Estrego ordered him lifted with a boat hook and dropped overboard without ceremony.

Shocked by this inhumanity, I challenged Estrego afterwards in his cabin. He flew into a rage, blamed me for bringing him on board, and hinted the other Panamanian should fear for his life. That evening the crew lit a bonfire on deck. Carrying torches, they went through the ship smoking out the fever. The other Panamanian was shunned like a Jonah, and the following day came the predictable news that he'd disappeared in the night. I'm appalled by his murder but, as always, sailors follow their own code, devoid of morals. Estrego is nervous, fearful that the fever has spread. The ship is gripped by a great unease.

The captain is duty bound to raise the Yellow Jack. He should alert the harbourmaster when we reach the Azores. But the crew are refusing to drink the ship's water, so at the risk of mutiny we must make landfall and replenish. I pray God will spare us any recurrence, but only time will tell.

Day thirty-three. I take up my pen, Inspector General, to relate a terrible turn of events. Shortly before noon we dropped anchor at the Azores. We waited for permission from the Portuguese authorities to come ashore and replenish. The harbourmaster eventually rowed out in a tender together with a complement of soldiers and, coming on board, exchanged pleasantries with Estrego. Despite the captain's attempts at concealment the harbourmaster sensed something was amiss.

He asked why we were undermanned. The captain, sweating profusely and trembling, attempted to make light of it. But the wily harbourmaster demanded to inspect the crew.

Estrego had no choice. The men assembled, and I groaned to see what no one could admit. Three of the men showed clear signs of fever.

A heated exchange followed. The harbourmaster and his men disembarked, shouting that anyone attempting to come ashore would be shot. Estrego had no choice but to set sail. With the men in the blackest of moods, the Julietta lifted anchor and slunk away.

Chaos followed. In full view of the frightened crew, Walker and Estrego bellowed at one another. The captain stormed off to his cabin, ordering Walker to take the night watch. I fear some calamity by morning. I write this by candlelight and pray the Blessed Virgin will deliver us from this terror.

Day thirty-four. Dawn reveals Walker and three of the crew have taken the dinghy in the night. They must intend to return to the Azores rather than risk death on the Julietta. We are eight of us now, and I must relate what I've dreaded to record thus far. Estrego is fevered.

There is a distant and defiant look in his eye. Swallowing rum in great gulps he muttered to himself that he will not abandon the Julietta to the vagaries of the sea. He has trimmed the sails and set a course for England.

Day thirty-nine. We are the ship of the damned, Inspector General. God has surely abandoned us. I hear the cries of Estrego and the crew as they battle the waves. I'm sick too, now, and crawled from my cabin in thirst. There is nothing for it but to drink from the butt in the galley. I found a fellow dying there, his lips cracked and swollen.

I barely recognised him for the hearty soul he once was, a strong lad of twenty from Havana. I doubt he will last the night. Leaving him I crawled back to my reeking cabin, green seawater slopping over the floor. My mind wanders. Pain and exhaustion grow. I will die here on this bed. God, the Virgin and all the saints help me. I have tried to live a good life.

Jours perdus. Je m'éveille pour le tangage du navire violente, pas de mot a partir du pont. Biscay? Estrego? J'ai besoin de . . .

Un cri. Nous passons Kintyre mais j'ai besoin de . . . je suis ci-dessous . . . la cloche sonne . . . si . . .

I finished speaking. The terrors endured by the *Julietta*'s crew were awful, but the revelation of her cargo was astonishing.

'Good God,' I whispered. 'A thousand pounds of gold. That's nearly half a ton. What happened to it?'

Hare gave a low whistle.

'I don't know, Doc, but men will do anything where treasure's involved. All the more reason you need to find Hamilton. And quick.'

I lifted Margaret's letter and translation.

'Let's go.'

'Just a minute,' replied Hare. He grabbed my medical bag. 'I've a feeling you'll need this.'

30

The moon gleamed in a star bright sky, and nothing stirred save a fox scampering across our path as we hurried towards the harbour. Hare was cautious, keeping to the shadows and stopping at every corner to listen for anyone on the road, but not a soul did we encounter. Soon I was lost, trusting to his sense of direction as we looped down one lane and then another, before emerging at last on the riverbank, the water black as tar. Hare turned to the right, keeping back from the harbour's edge, and I followed on for a few hundred yards until he dived behind a pile of barrels.

'There,' he pointed. 'The House of the Five Gables.'

Hare was right in his description. Long and low, it was a strange building from a different time, forgotten and left to stand when all about had been demolished to make way for the modern age. Its whitewashed stone walls were rough and uncut, the doorway and double row of windows cramped and small. Five crow-stepped gables rose above the upper windows, each gable tapered to form a chimney. Beneath every peak a light glowed from a round glass.

'What now?' I said, crouching beside Hare. 'Should we wait?'

He pointed to one of the upper windows on the corner. 'I reckon he's up there. After Kitty went in I saw a light just for a moment, and then the curtain was drawn.'

I looked from the dark window to the ground fifteen feet below and then along to the heavy front door.

'So how do we get in?'

'That's easy, Doc. Just march right up to the door, knock, and tell whoever answers you're the doctor Kitty sent for to see the man upstairs. If you bluff it out I reckon that'll get ye in. And then it's up to you.'

I swallowed hard and gripped the handle of my bag. 'What about you?'

'I'll wait here and keep an eye out. First sign of trouble and I'll give you a signal by flinging a stone at the window. Now off ye go, and I'll see ye right back here after.'

I clapped him on the shoulder. 'Wish me luck.'

I walked towards the door feeling none too confident about my reception. The gables loomed above me closer and closer, and glancing back I saw Hare behind the barrels give me an encouraging wave. I took a deep breath and rapped.

Silence.

For what seemed an age I stood on the threshold, thinking whoever was inside must be sound in their bed. I rapped again, then glanced back in Hare's direction. There was no sign of him.

Just as I was about to knock a third time a woman answered.

'Who's that at this hour! That better nae be you, Jock. You're getting nae drink here!'

'Open up, it's the doctor! I was sent for by Miss Malone and I've no time to stand about.'

'Doctor? What doctor?' came the suspicious reply. 'Kitty never mentioned a doctor to me. Whit's your name?'

'Doctor Robert Knox,' I replied, my disgraced mentor's being the first that came to mind. 'Now look here, madam, I was home in bed when I got this call. Miss Malone promised me a guinea to come, but it's all the same to me whether you let me in or not. Which is it to be?'

There was a pause followed by the clacking of bolt and key. The door swung back revealing an old woman in a shawl, carrying a lamp. 'Well ye'd better come in,' she muttered. 'But naebody telt me aboot nae doctor.'

I stepped over the threshold. 'Now, where's the patient?'

She lifted the lamp and gave me a narrow look. 'Ye dinnae sound like you're frae round here,' she rasped. 'I've never seen you. How long have you been in Greenock?'

'Not long. I'm from Edinburgh. I've just returned from five years in India.'

I held her gaze, inwardly cursing my foolish mention of Edinburgh and India. Eventually she glanced at my bag and seemed satisfied.

'Aye well, it's probably for the best anyway,' she muttered. She turned to the stairs. 'You'd better follow me.'

I stooped after her and followed her along the upstairs corridor to a door.

'Wait here.'

My heart thumped as the old woman opened it. Lamplight traced the outline of a bed. She shuffled in. Then, as she stepped aside, I saw a ghastly sight. It was the waxy face of a man beaded with sweat, mouth open, eyes fixed.

'Tam, Tam,' she whispered, shaking his shoulder. 'There's a doctor here tae see ye. Kitty sent him.'

He gave a low moan, pitiful to hear. So this, at last, was Tom Hamilton. And not long for this world, by the look of him.

'Hush, Tam, hush,' she said. 'Rest easy.'

I stepped towards the bed and immediately raised my hand to cover the stench. Gangrene.

'How long's he been like this?' I gasped.

'Two weeks,' she said. 'When he came ower a month ago he'd a broken leg. It'd healed aw crookit, so there was nothing fur it but tae break it again and set it right.'

A grubby sheet covered him and I recoiled at the thought of what lay beneath.

'And did you break it?'

'Och, it wis horrible,' she sighed. 'He was shoutin' that it had tae be done, tho' Kitty didnae want tae dae it. So he drank a bottle o rum and I put a strip o leather 'tween his teeth. He telt Kitty tae break it and then haul it straight wi everything she had.'

She glanced toward him.

'He passed out cauld afterwards, and we tied his leg. At first it seemed a wee bit better. But then, well, then it didnae.' Her voice trailed off.

She looked away as I lifted the sheet. A swollen, putrid mass met my eye. Two greasy splints were tied either side.

'Open that window.'

'But he disnae want—'

'The window. Now!' I barked, cutting her off, and she hurried across. Cold, clean air drifted in. 'He needs something for the pain.' I removed my jacket and rolled up my sleeves. 'Go and boil a pail of water. Do it, now.'

I drew a pint beaker from my bag and filled it with three-quarters rum and one-quarter tincture of laudanum. I raised his lips to its edge.

'Tom,' I called. 'Drink this. It'll help.'

He sipped the mixture until I'd managed to get half of it down him, then drew out my watch and waited. After ten minutes his breathing and colour improved. A few minutes later his eyelids flickered. He turned his head.

'More,' he whispered. When I'd finished pouring the rest into him, his head flopped onto the pillow and he heaved a sigh.

'Did Kitty send for you?' he croaked.

'She did, Tom, she did. And I want to help you if you'll let me.'

He blinked and swallowed hard.

'She's a good girl, Kitty. I should've married her years ago.' He turned to the wall. 'Too late now though. All too late.'

'Listen to me, Tom.' I placed my hand on his shoulder. 'I can help you, but there isn't much time. You were at the lighthouse when Sandy was killed. What happened that night?'

He closed his eyes and shook his head. 'I dinnae want tae, I dinnae.'

I took out my tobacco pouch, filled my pipe and lit it.

'How about a smoke Tom, eh? I can't imagine a lighthouse man that doesn't enjoy a pipe.'

At the smell of the smoke he half turned and I lowered the pipe to his lips. He inhaled deeply, savouring the flavour.

'Why not tell me the whole tale, Tom.'

He relaxed as the rum, laudanum and tobacco began to take effect. 'I dinnae think you'll believe me if I do.'

'Well let me get you started. You're from Greenock. A fisherman to trade. You entered the lighthouse life at Oban a few years ago. Am I right?'

He nodded, dreamily. 'I wis happy in Oban.'

'You knew a man called Hugh O'Neill?'

'That wis before the lighthouse. We used tae sail the routes frae Ireland fur a few years. Good times.' He frowned. 'Here, whit kind o a doctor ur ye anyway, askin' aw these questions?'

'One that wants to help you,' I said. I passed him my pipe again. 'Why were you transferred to Cumbrae?'

He drew on the pipe, relaxed and closed his eyes. Smoke drifted from his lips.

'I wis at Oban two year when the order came frae the Board saying I was to go and join Mister McLeod on Cumbrae. That's all I know.'

'Who gave the order?'

He shrugged. 'There was just the letter. I left the next day.'

'So how was life on Cumbrae?'

He frowned. 'Och, Sandy was a right bad tempered so-an-so. Nothing was ever good enough, and everything I did had to be done again.'

'Is that why you killed him?'

He shot me a look of fury. I could see his fists clenching under the bed sheet, and he strained his neck toward me.

'As God is my witness,' he said through gritted teeth, 'I didnae kill Sandy McLeod.'

I gazed into his eyes searching for a lie, until eventually he sank back onto his pillow. The old woman returned and I moved to the doorway.

'That's the water boiled,' she said, squinting past me at Tom. 'Are ye coming doon fur it?'

I said I would.

'He looks a wee bittie better.'

'He does,' I murmured. 'But I need some time with him now. I have to cut his leg off, you see.'

She nodded, agape. I began to close the door.

'So long as I dinnae have to be here fur that,' she muttered, turning away.

When I went back to his side he glanced at my bag.

'What's going tae happen tae mah leg?'

'I'll take care of it. But you've got to help me first. I'm prepared to believe you didn't kill Sandy. But you must tell me everything. Can you do that?'

There was fear in his eyes as he wrestled with the burden of his untold truth. But, after a long pause, he heaved a sigh.

'Gie me another draw o that tobacco,' he whispered.

And then he began.

'I wis on the lighthoose at Cumbrae nae mair than a few weeks, when one day a Customs Officer stopped by in a steam launch. He was friendly like, just said he happened tae be passing. Well, I could tell Sandy didnae like the look o him frae the start. But then, Sandy didnae seem tae like anyone.

'A couple o days later he was back again, and this time we'd a chat ootside away frae Sandy. He asked if I'd like tae earn a wee bit on the side. Nothing dangerous. Just fur helping him oot was all. He telt me he wis 'on the level', an when we shook hands I knew he was a brother mason. Well I didnae see any harm, so I asked him what he was after.

'He telt me there'd be a ship coming up and doon the Firth sometimes, and that he'd arrange tae make sure I was on watch when it did. He said I might see it coming and going frae over Campbeltown way, and that I wis tae pay it nae heed and make nae entries in the log aboot it.'

He squinted at the pipe. 'Here, this is oot.'

I took it from his hand and refilled it.

'So what did you say?'

'Suits me, I telt him. And that's exactly how it was. He sent word whenever the ship was expected, and I made sure tae be on watch. Twenty-five pound he gie'd me every time,' he added, tapping the bed sheet with his fingers.

I relit the pipe. 'This Customs officer,' I said, puffing quickly and passing it to him, 'what was his name?'

He took a draw and shook his head. Smoke shrouded his face.

'Naw. I dinnae want tae say.'

'So what happened next?'

He closed his eyes.

'Well it was back in January. Word came frae this officer to expect the ship again during the day, same as before. But my shift passed withoot sae much as a glimpse of her. There was a storm brewin' that afternoon mind, and after dark, aboot an hour afore Sandy took his shift, who should arrive but yon officer again, in a launch.

'I was surprised tae see him I can tell ye, and right away I knew there was somethin' badly wrang. He was anxious. Telt me the ship was drifting up intae the firth, and hadnae landed at Campbeltown as it was supposed tae.'

'So what did you do?'

'I telt him there was nothing I could dae, that Sandy would shortly be on watch and would raise the alarm if he saw her drifting. But yon officer, he didnae like that one bit. He was beside himself. Said we hid tae get oot tae her soon as she appeared and no alert anyone.

'Well, I knew Sandy would hae nothing tae dae wi it, and so eventually I persuaded him tae wait. I said that maybe the ship wouldnae appear 'til after Sandy's shift anyway. So we waited, me in my bunk and him waiting doon below.'

He stopped to take a sip of water and another smoke. 'The storm grew and grew that night. I didnae sleep a wink what wi thinking aboot Sandy, the ship and himself below. The wind fair howled roon the lighthoose, and I even felt it shifting. It wis like a blade o grass bending in a breeze.'

He raised a hand to cover his eyes, his fingers trembling.

'As I lay there listening tae the storm I heard it. Distant at first, hardly anything really, then louder and louder, clearer and clearer. It was the pealing of a ship's bell, and a dinnae know why, but there was something desperate, terrifying aboot the sound of it.'

'What happened, Tom?'

He glanced at me through his fingers.

'Sandy heard it too. Next thing I heard him shouting on me tae wake up. I was oot my bunk in the blink of an eye, but when I got tae the door, Sandy was already way below and heading fur the beacon.'

His eyes gleamed in the glow of the lamp, tears welling.

'He had tae light it, ye see. That's your duty when there's a ship in distress.' He shook his head. 'Sandy was only doing his duty.'

There was a long pause while Tom Hamilton gave way to his emotion, and the pipe slipped from his fingers. I placed a hand on his shoulder. He heaved a long sigh.

'How did it come tae this,' he mumbled, rubbing his eyes.

He was a pitiable sight.

'Did you see it happen?'

He nodded. 'By the time I was ootside Sandy was already climbing tae the beacon. It was pitch dark and raining fierce. The lighthouse beam came round, and right then I seen him behind Sandy, wi – wi—' He raised his hands. 'Wi an axe ower his heid,' he stuttered.

A sudden gust made the window creak on its hinges.

'The windae!' he shrieked, recoiling like a scalded cat. 'Close the windae, naebody's tae know I'm here!'

I closed it, leaving an inch for the badly needed air. The room had grown cold by now and I glanced at the empty hearth.

'I'll have her build a fire,' I muttered, thinking of the amput-ation I'd soon have to perform, and returned to his side. He'd grown unsettled again. I prepared more rum and laudanum, but this time a half measure. Something was still puzzling me.

'So, the officer killed Sandy to prevent him raising the alarm,' I said, lifting the beaker to his lips. 'But what difference did it make?'

He drank off the mixture in gulps then lay back with a long sigh.

'Ach, but that wisnae the end o, it, you see,' he said eventually, giving me a sly glance. 'Because something else happened that night that I think you'll hardly believe. You see, he took the steam launch out intae that storm, wi me on board on the promise o a thousand pound, and we drew right up to that ship.'

My mouth fell open. 'In that storm? Impossible!'

'Possible or no,' he replied, 'I'm tellin' ye that's what happened. We lashed the steam launch to the side o that ship and up on deck we both went.

'He was like a man possessed as he burst intae the cargo hold, and I helped him lift out every bag he wanted. Together we hauled them doon ower the side.'

He leant toward me, his finger raised. 'And every wan o them full o gold, as God's my witness.'

'Go on,' I breathed.

A shadow crossed his face.

'As soon as everything was safe aboard the launch, that snake-in-the-grass pulled a pistol on me and fired. I was lucky though, 'cause he missed. But I fell and broke my leg goin' ower the side and intae the water. I swear to this day I've nae idea how I did it, but I woke up on the sands at Prestwick wi a crowd o bairns roon me. And that's the whole truth.'

He sank back, exhausted.

31

A grey dawn loomed to seagulls' cries.

It was time to amputate Tom Hamilton's leg.

I unrolled my scalpels and laid down my hacksaw. With Tom strapped down I could amputate in under a minute, but the stump would need cauterising. I looked to the hearth. There was a poker which would serve, once red hot. I needed to tie him down though. I hurried downstairs.

The old woman sat alone, none too pleased to be kept waiting. A kettle hung in the fireplace and swinging it out she sloshed boiling water into a pail.

'He needs tying,' I said, lifting the water.

She shuffled away and reappeared with a coil of ship's rope.

'Here. That'll have tae dae.'

It was strong stuff.

I nodded towards the hearth. 'Can you bring hot coals and set a fire?'

'Coal costs money,' she snapped.

I fished sixpence from my pocket. 'Here, then. I'll go on ahead.'

I was racing upstairs, thinking only of the operation, when suddenly a crash resounded.

With three strides I was through the door, then the blood froze in my veins. I dropped the pail and the rope slipped from my hands. Tom Hamilton's throat was split side to side. His jaw worked with fading force and blood oozed in a thickening bloom. One of my scalpels lay beside an upended chair and the window was open, its frame broken.

With a cry of rage I ran and looked out onto the deserted waterfront, then spun around in fear that the murderer might yet be in the room – but there was no-one save Tom, his life slipping away. I rushed to his side calling his name, thrusting my hands over the gaping wound in my desperation to staunch the bleeding, but to no avail. The last beats of his heart fluttered through his blood-soaked chest, and then he was dead.

I didn't appreciate the danger of the situation until the old woman hurried in.

'What's aw the clatter,' she began before she too froze in her steps, staring from me to Tom's corpse and back again. As I turned to plead with her she shrank back from my bloodied hands, and a low gargling rose in her dry old throat. Her breath brought her shoulders heaving, her noise growing and growing into a scream so awful that I sunk to the wall with my hands at my ears.

'Murderer!' she bellowed. 'Help! Save me! You, you, stay back, get away frae me!'

She ran clamouring from the room and without a moment's thought I made for the window.

Clambering onto the ledge I looked in vain for any sign of Hare, all the time asking myself why he'd failed to alert me to any danger. Lowering myself by my fingertips I dropped to the ground and sprinted for all I was worth along the water's edge.

But the old woman was through the front door screaming murder, and faces started appearing.

One man saw me, took up the cry and gave chase. Others joined, and in no time there was a mob roaring for my capture.

'Stop him! Murderer!' went the cry, and as I passed others, they stood amazed for a moment, then joined the pursuit. At any moment I might be overpowered and brought to the ground, so I juked down an alley, their shouts fading.

It was a dead end surrounded by tenements and I dived into the open stairwell of the nearest one, the echo of my steps ricocheting off the walls.

Through and out onto the back green I went, where two char women were spreading sheets on rows of washing line. Dodging to the back wall I made a leap and hauled myself up as cries once more rose from behind. I gashed my calf on scattered glass along the ridge, then I was down the other side and into a stonemason's yard. Twisting through half-finished blocks I reached a railing and vaulting the spikes, landed, at last, back in a street.

Men walking to work stared as I clattered out in front of a horse then disappeared round the next corner. On and on I went from one street to the next until I emerged onto a teeming harbour and stopped, bent double, gasping for breath.

Steam cargo ships were drawn up in a row, their funnels belching and cattle pouring down their gangways. Steam rose from their backs as the frightened animals disembarked to the cries of drovers whipping them on. Farmers were gathering for a market day, dogs barking at their sides. No one paid me any heed as I pressed forward. The air was thick with the stench of wet hay and fresh manure.

Holding pens surrounded a ring, and the auctioneer called out one animal after another then rattled off the bids. A blackboard stretched behind him and two clerks chalked up each lot as it came through. I edged closer, surrounded by country folk.

'. . . fine heifers yon, good land over by . . .'

'. . . aye, auld Mackay rears grand beasts ower on Arran . . .'

'. . . this next lot's frae Kilcreggan. Awful damp there this year though. The slaughterhoose buyers dinnae seem too taken wi them . . .'

Cattle were arriving from all around the Firth of Clyde for this flesh market, and many of the animals were destined for Greenock's slaughterhouse, into which a steady line of the poor creatures was already streaming.

In the front row of the ring stood tight lipped buyers who indicated their interest to the auctioneer with the slightest nod, shake of the head or curl of the lip. Around them thronged country gentlemen, farmhands and drovers. Some leaned on staffs or against fences, puffing on pipes. Others stood upright with arms folded, a blade of grass between their teeth and an obedient sheepdog at their side. But all were dressed in the simple country clothes which marked them for the hillside rather than here, amid the bustle of Greenock. A ruddy farmer in tweed cap and jacket half-turned to me with a nod, then returned to contemplate the latest animal in the ring. Glancing down at my battered tweeds and boots I sensed an opportunity.

I fetched the pipe from my pocket and clenched it between my teeth. Then I turned up the collar of my jacket and buried my head down a little, copying the shy country manner of many around me. It was a start, but I cursed my fair hair which singled me out.

Just then, however, a cow slipped in the mud and lay bellowing on the ground. A small crowd gathered round the pen while the drover, laying staff and cap aside, vaulted the fence and struggled to get the animal back on its feet. He was joined by another, and as the onlookers watched and called good humoured advice I sidled past and lifted the staff and cap. Then I made my way to the far side of the ring. There, at the foot of the auctioneer's steps, I slipped on the cap and leant on the staff, for all the world a countryman come to town.

I hadn't been standing long when, sure enough, four men jostled through the crowd. They pointed here and there and questioned everyone as they passed. Word soon spread that a murderer was on the run, and within two minutes I'd overheard three descriptions, all different, but all making mention of the culprit's fair hair.

'... bear of a man, hands like shovels, jumped clean ower an eight-foot wall ...'

'... dartin' rat's eyes ...'

'... pretended tae be a doctor then murdered the poor soul in his bed ...'

'... well, it widnae be market day in Greenock without something to stir the crowd!'

While the ripples of interest spread, I kept my head low. The men moved from the square toward the slaughterhouse, their search continuing, and little by little the conversations around me returned to the ring.

For the moment I was in the clear, and I began to reflect on what I should do next.

Of one thing I was certain: Greenock was too hot to hold me. I couldn't return to the Mansion House or the Custom House.

I'd no idea where Hare was, and while I thought of Fiona Cameron and *The Glue Pot*, the chances of my getting there safely seemed remote. Besides, I couldn't bear the idea of bringing trouble to her door. I considered taking a boat to Glasgow but felt certain they'd all be watched. In any event, I'd no idea from which harbour the Glasgow boat left. Just then, however, my thoughts were interrupted as the auctioneer brought down his hammer and moved to the next bid.

'Lot one hundred and twelve gentlemen, and this is the first of two dozen heifers born on Arran and raised by Mister Alistair McTaggart of Kames Farm on the Alba Estate. I'll start the bidding at fifteen shillings – now who'll give me fifteen shillings for this fine beast?'

A healthy young animal with shaggy red hair trotted into the ring and stopped. On the far side Mister McTaggart, beaming with pride, received the praise of those nearby. The bidding started.

'Thank you, fifteen, twenty now, twenty-five, thirty, thirty-five, thirty-five, thirty-five . . . forty, thank you, with you at forty, forty-five now, thank you, sir, forty-five, forty-five, all done at forty-five . . .'

A final nod from one of the stony-faced bidders.

'. . . thank you, with you at fifty, sir, fifty, any advance on fifty? Sold, fifty shillings, to Mister McAllister of Greenock. The next lot, gentlemen—' It was an excellent price and the proud farmer was shaking hands with those nearby when a large hand came clapping down on his shoulder.

'Well done Alistair!' boomed Alba, his words carrying across the ring. 'I wouldn't be surprised if that's the best price of the day. You've done us proud as usual!'

The earl was dressed in country style and turning from McTaggart he walked and talked among the farmers, shaking a hand here, clapping a dog's back there and sharing a joke with the drovers. Then he strolled from the crowd to a stand where he chose one of the hot pies on offer, turned and began chomping, steam rising in the cold air.

I walked to him.

'Good morning, sir. What a pleasant surprise to find you here.'

He turned mid-bite and for a moment didn't recognise me.

'Why, Doctor Lyon! This is a surprise.' He took a final bite, threw the crust to a passing dog and wiped his hands. 'Enjoying the market?'

I tried to nod and smile while he rattled on about farmers and their modern husbandry.

'But what brings you here?' he asked, squinting at me. 'You look rather worn out, Doctor. Are you quite well?'

I felt fever growing in me again and with trembling hands I rubbed my forehead.

'I hardly know where to begin, sir. But the fact is, well—' I hesitated, glanced left and right then looked him square in the eye.

'I'm in trouble. Serious trouble.'

He raised his eyebrows. 'Trouble? You? What kind of trouble exactly?'

A passing drover turned his head but carried on.

'I can't say just now,' I whispered. 'But I swear, on my honour, I've done nothing wrong.'

Beads of sweat trickled from my brow.

'Look, Doctor Lyon,' he frowned. 'Whatever this is, it's serious, I can see that. But if you've done nothing wrong as you say, well, shouldn't you go to the authorities?'

'There's no one,' I said. 'No one in Greenock I can trust. All I can say is my presence here isn't–' I closed my eyes. 'There's more to it than studying water.'

He gave me a puzzled look.

'But how can I help you?'

I thought back to our dinner together at the Mansion House.

'Because the other night when we dined together, I confess I was . . .' I tried to find the words. 'Impressed by your appeal to science, I suppose. By the courage of your convictions.'

He shook his head, yet there was a twinkle in his eye.

'Doctor Lyon, either you're very smart or very stupid.' He gave me a knowing look. 'This wouldn't have anything to do with your questions the other night about the masons, would it?'

I swallowed hard. 'In a way.'

He folded his arms. 'Well, I've never been a friend of theirs, but I've never been their enemy either. What do you want?'

'I have to get out of Greenock, sir, and catching sight of you I recalled . . . that is – you were kind enough to suggest—' My voice trailed off.

'Ah, I see,' he replied. 'I follow you now. What you want to know is would this be a suitable time to pay me that visit at Dunearn?'

I nodded.

He glanced at my head. 'As I recall, Doctor, under that cap you've a head of fair hair. Am I right?'

I realised what he was thinking. 'You know I do. And I repeat, I swear—'

'Upon your honour, yes, I heard you the first time,' he interrupted with a wave of his hand.

Just then a farmer approached and I lingered on one side while they chatted. At last the farmer moved away and Alba turned back, irritated. 'Really Doctor,' he said, 'you put me in a difficult position.' He sighed. 'You swear you're innocent?'

I nodded.

He ran a finger across his jaw and looked to the ground. 'Well you've given me your word, Doctor, and from what I've seen of you, that's worth something.'

He brushed aside my thanks and looked me over. 'When was the last time you slept?'

It had been two nights ago.

'Right,' he said firmly. 'Follow me.'

He produced a hipflask as we walked. 'Have a dram. You look like you could use it.'

The whisky warmed my throat and I passed it back, murmuring my appreciation.

'Don't mention it.' He moved toward one of the steamers. 'Just keep your head down.'

A crew member saluted as we stepped aboard. Alba led the way up some stairs then across to the starboard side which had a view over the river. We passed several cabins until he reached the forward end.

'Here,' he said, 'in you go. Help yourself to anything, but for pity's sake stay out of sight.'

Thanking him I hurried in.

'I'll return at four,' he winked, 'when we sail for Arran.'

I closed the door.

Two armchairs stood before a fireplace. Through an adjoining door lay a bedroom. But at that moment I only had eyes for a side table with a flagon of wine, a platter of bread and cheese and a bowl of apples. I ate and drank my fill, then chewing on an apple I crossed the room and sank into one of the chairs. My eye drifted back to the fireplace. It was surrounded by white marble with dolphins carved on either side. Fighting off sleep I stumbled to my feet, for something else had caught my attention. It was a full-length portrait above the fireplace: the figure of an aged widow. Though her countenance was severe the echo remained of a once great beauty. She stood side on, glancing over her shoulder, her hands resting on a broken pillar. Pomegranate trees, colourful birds and distant hills filled the background, as though she lingered in a garden of remembrance.

The image blurred and I blinked several times. There was something unsettling about her, about the scene. Something cruel, some hint of danger in her dark eyes and the turn of her lip. Italian perhaps, but not French. Or was it Spanish? Yes, Spanish, I decided, definitely Spanish. I stumbled back a step, my eyes drifting to her delicate fingers curling around a rosary, then down to the pillar. Was that a monkey peeping from behind?

I leaned closer now, towards that broken pillar on which her hands rested, and peered between the vines which twisted round its plinth. There was something on its lichen spotted surface, something . . . could that be . . . ?

The remains of the apple slipped from my hand.

How was it possible?

How was it possible that there, carved in the very heart of that plinth – that there, the exact image from the dossier I had once held in my hands in Edinburgh – that there, of all places, was the Double Eagle? And how was it possible that running below was the same Latin legend *sine unitate nihil sumus*?

I grasped the cold marble, too late to realise I'd been drugged, too late to react to my three hunters as they entered with triumph in their eyes. But before I fainted to the floor there was one final image. It was a single word, a single name, its curling letters at the foot of the frame.

Julietta.

32

Darkness. Darkness and pain were all I registered, then the gallop of steam engines.

I was conscious of lying flat on a floor which shuddered in time to piston strokes. I tasted iron and swirled my tongue, hardly recognising the wreckage of my own mouth. There was a gap in my jaw where I'd lost a tooth. I tried and failed to open my eyes. When I raised a hand there was the clink of chains at my wrist, followed by a sponge-like sensation where I'd expected to find my face.

I sat upright. With every breath came a dull ache and I added broken ribs to the tally of my injuries. At that moment the floor pitched heavily and a rush of slack water sloshed over me. I pressed some of the water to my face, clearing the crusts of dried blood from my eyelids, and slowly managed to open one eye.

Grey light from a porthole revealed an iron-clad cell. There was a door to my right, but as I shuffled towards it my chains pulled tight. I slammed my hands against the wall, shouting until I was hoarse. But answer came there none, only the incessant pounding of the engines. I checked my pockets and found them empty. For some reason they'd overlooked my watch and I quickly drew it out, only to discover it had stopped. I wound it, soothed by its ticking, and marked the passing of the next few hours while the ship rolled and tossed, the light from the porthole growing gradually dimmer until stars appeared and I drifted to sleep.

The door slammed, jolting me awake, and a bucket of cold water was poured over my head.

'Wake up, scum.'

Someone kicked me full in the stomach and I slouched forward, coughing and retching. A hand grabbed my hair and I was thrown back against the wall. It was Twisted Lip.

'Someone here to see you,' he sneered, throwing a bowl on the ground, the contents of which I couldn't begin to describe. Most of it appeared to be moving.

The engines stopped, and low voices murmured in the corridor. Then a lantern appeared in the doorway.

'Good evening, Doctor Lyon. Goodness, this place does smell. Forgive me if I open this.'

Alba unscrewed the porthole and hung up the lantern.

'There, that's better,' he said, and began to remove his gloves. His red hair glinted and every trace of his bluff manner disappeared. Where once I saw humour there was now only cruelty.

'I expect you're wondering why you're not dead, Doctor.'

I stared at him, my arms cradled across my chest. 'You killed everyone else that got in your way. Sandy McLeod, Tom Hamilton, Hugh O'Neill.'

He smiled. 'Hugh O'Neill's death had nothing to do with me, I'm afraid. It really was just one of those things that can happen at sea, from time to time.'

He reached into his jacket pocket. With a sinking heart I realised he had Margaret's letter and her translation of the journal.

'You know, I really must congratulate you,' he said, turning the pages in his hands, 'and that sister of yours.'

'Leave Margaret out of this,' I growled, 'this is between you and me, no one else.'

'I hardly think so,' he replied. 'The only thing between you and me is that chain, Doctor. And that's the way it will stay for the rest of your short life.'

He leaned forward. 'I could have you killed right now, but it amuses me to think of you on my plantation, where you'll work and sleep with the rest of the slaves, until you're dead. Confused? You needn't be. You see, this ship isn't just crossing the Clyde to Arran. It's going a little further. As a matter of fact we're out in the Atlantic headed for Kingston, and making good time.'

'This is madness.'

'Far from it, I can assure you. You know, it's a shame you'll never make that report back to your masters in Edinburgh. Though I promise you, you'll live to see my plan come to fruition. Sadly, however, your view will be from a sugar cane field, with a basket in your hand and a whip on your back. Now, I'd very much like to stay and continue this chat, but I'm sure you'll forgive me if I return to my own quarters, basic as they are. Pleasant dreams.'

'Who's the guardian of the Double Eagle?' I cried after him. 'It's you, isn't it? You're the Inspector General! What are you planning?'

'Dear me, Doctor,' he replied, closing the door and leaving me in darkness. 'And you think I'm mad?'

33

There were times I was inclined to agree with Alba, that I was indeed mad. The fever, growing in me since Greenock, now seized control and I shivered for days and nights on end, my forehead burning, my mind raving. But every day I ate the disgusting scraps which they threw down, though at first they made me vomit until nothing remained inside.

My conditions were no better than a slave on a slave ship, and I was left to lie in my own filth. Every night a bucket of water was tipped over my head, and I became grateful for the small mercy of a drainage hole in the far corner which cleared the worst of it. After a week I hardly cared. My fever slowly passed and even the swelling round my eyes diminished.

If there's one thing I fear though, it's rats, and the ship was plagued with them. By day I'd see them scuttling round the room, up and down the drain hole. At night I'd lie awake with them scratching and squealing, even scampering across my chest.

Sometimes the engines pounded all day and the going was smooth. Other days they saved the engines, and to the sailors' cries they'd hoist sails to catch a breeze. More than once the ship ran into storms, and I hollered and pulled at my chains until my wrists bled to the bone. I was terrified we'd sink and I'd be dragged to the ocean floor. But the storm lifted every time, and with each passing day the air grew warmer, the circle of sky through the porthole a deeper shade of blue.

The thought of reaching Jamaica brought me no comfort, knowing the fate Alba had in store for me. But I prayed an opportunity to escape would somehow present itself. I thought of Margaret and cursed myself for involving her, but there was nothing for it but to wait and hope for better times. I tried to gauge how long it would take the ship to reach Jamaica. Relying on sails and good weather, I remembered the *Julietta* could make the round trip in three months, or just over six weeks in each direction. But this ship, with the benefit of steam as well as sails, could do it in less.

I woke one morning to the ship steaming through calm waters. The sky was deep blue and from time to time I heard a gull's cry. By midday the heat was so intense that I lay panting and sweating, thinking of Indian summers. I told myself that we must have reached the Caribbean.

As the blue sky faded to black the engines stopped, and I sighed at the respite from their racket. There followed the usual routine with the bucket of water and my crawling bowl of slops, then sleep.

I woke bathed in moonlight and looked for the rat I assumed had roused me. But there was nothing save the ship's rocking. A bell high above tolled three. I felt a great unease without knowing why, and my heart pounded in my chest. Somehow it was too quiet. There came the merest whisper of a footstep outside. Perhaps they mean to kill me after all, I thought, and with my hair prickling I watched the door creep open.

I scuttled against the wall, chains rattling.

'Sshh!'

The intruder closed the door and turned to face me.

'Hare!' I cried. 'What the – where – ?'

'Quiet, Doc!' he whispered. 'Here, have a proper drink, for God's sake.'

He passed me a bottle and I took a thirsty swig. It was port, sweet thick port wine and it tasted like heaven.

'Careful now,' he said, wrestling it back. 'Not too much. We've a long night ahead of us, you and me.'

I was too confused to ask what he meant. 'How the hell did you get here?'

'Long story,' he replied, 'but I'll give you the gist of it, from the last ye saw of me.'

He crouched down.

'Back in Greenock, I spied the three of them that's been hounding you outside the Five Gables, and one of them climbed up to the window. There was nothing I could do to warn you, so I went round to the other side and started to climb up. Then I heard that daft woman hollering murder, and by the time I got back round ye'd taken off like a rabbit, so ye had.

'Some pair of legs you have when you want to, eh? Well, I followed the crowd as best I could, and ended up in one place after another. Then I saw ye wi that cap on your head talking to some grand feller, but I kept my distance. I followed ye to the shore, so I did, and when ye went aboard, I waited. Then I saw those three devils going up the gangway after you and I knew it was bad, so I snuck aboard.

'Well, I've been a stowaway in the cargo hold the whole time, wi plenty tae eat and drink, so I have, though I've done a fair bit o sneaking about after dark and all.'

He gave me a strange look.

'Doc, ye'll hardly believe the stuff that's down there.'

'What like?'

'Gold for a start,' he whispered. 'Boxes and boxes of it. But that's not all.' His voice grew lower. 'They've hundreds of rifles, barrels full of pellets, and sack after sack of gunpowder.'

I was stunned.

'That must be why all the gold,' I said at last, 'why he's been—'

'Who?' interrupted Hare, 'Who is he, anyway?'

'Lord Alba, Sir Guy's cousin.'

And then it hit me. It was a realisation both simple and yet astonishing.

'But he can't be,' I whispered. 'It's . . . it's unthinkable.'

'What d'ye mean?' said Hare.

'Alba,' I replied, looking him in the eye. 'It's Alba. He's, he's . . . he's planning a revolution!'

My mind returned to the Double Eagle, and the words of warning I'd read but failed to understand in the library at Glasgow University.

. . . It symbolises many things in many places, and its particular significance is not always clear from first encounter . . .

If it was the symbol of one secret order, couldn't it be the symbol of another? An order equally, or perhaps even more powerful? I thought again of the widow *Julietta* standing alone. A solitary figure in a foreign garden.

'My God,' I whispered, picturing the West Indies. 'It's alone. Jamaica's alone, hemmed in by Spanish Cuba and French Haiti in the midst of the Caribbean . . . I think he's determined to overthrow British rule in Jamaica.'

I could hardly believe what I was saying.

'He's what?'

'There's some ancestral connection, some ancient birth right behind this,' and I recalled Sir Guy's words about his bloodline. He had spoken of his noble lineage, of Scotland's kings and queens before the coming of the Hanoverians.

'He's being helped by very powerful people,' I said, 'very powerful indeed. And Jamaica may be just the beginning.'

Suddenly there were footsteps and Hare pressed himself into a corner. The door opened and in came Twisted Lip.

'What's yer noise,' he barked, kicking my legs. 'I keep hearing yer chains rattling.'

He drew a blade and pressed it to my face, sadistic pleasure gleaming in his eyes. 'Now you keep it doon or I swear tae God I'll—' There was a sound like paper ripping. His eyes stretched wide in surprise as he hung in the air, then crumpled to the ground. Hare had slit his throat.

Hare was on him in a flash, rifling his pockets.

'Keys, keys' he muttered, followed by a look of triumph.

'Time for us to get out of here, Doc.'

Hare set to work on the manacles, trying key after key until the right one clicked home. The chill of the night air felt strange against my wrists.

'But we're still at sea,' I said, clambering to my feet. 'Where can we go?'

'Aha, that's where ye're wrong, Doc, and that's why I came to get you. We're no more than a mile out, but they won't risk entering the harbour until morning.

'I heard them drop anchor a good few hours ago, and then a rowing boat came out from the shore not long after. There's a few of them up above having a right good drink and a chat, judging by the sound of it, and I reckon if we're quick, we can climb down the anchor chain, and get away in their boat.'

I hesitated. For weeks I had been incarcerated, barely able to move. 'Are you sure about this?'

Hare looked to the corpse. A thick pool of blood was spreading across the floor.

'Have you a better idea?' he shrugged. 'C'mon, Doc. It won't be long before someone comes looking for him.'

He was right.

'Let's get out of here,' I said.

34

We raced along corridors, sneaked past cabins and finally emerged on deck on the port side. Across the water lights gleamed round a bay.

Hare suddenly dragged me flat up against the wall, the pair of us frozen in the moonlight. He put a finger to his lips and pointed left. No more than thirty yards away a guard was pacing with a rifle over his shoulder. He kept on away from us until he passed out of sight.

'Time to show what you're made of,' whispered Hare, and he slipped his knife into my hand. Then he nodded in the opposite direction.

'Do what you have to, and I'll get you along there.'

Before I could say a word Hare scampered away, a shadow against the wall. I gripped the knife and swallowed hard, thinking back to the man on the roof of Davie Wellburn's farmhouse. I'd reacted in anger when it was kill or be killed, but this was different. This was cold-blooded murder.

I slipped along that deck as if in a dream, the guard coming into sight as he leaned over the deck rail. Something had his attention down the side of the ship and for a moment he paused, relaxed and unafraid. I closed the distance between us, blood pounding in my ears, and brought the knife up in front of me. He was no more than three feet away when laughter resounded from the deck above and a fist slammed on a table. And just in that terrible moment, a moment which haunts me still, he turned.

There was surprise in his young eyes as I plunged the knife through his chest, and then he sighed. His hands came up round my neck but there was no power in his grip, and his eyes rolled back in his head. I pulled the knife out, wet to the hilt with blood, and with the frenzy of a madman plunged it back into him again and again, until he slipped and fell dead to the ground.

I stared down, appalled by what I'd done. Reacting to some instinct I closed his eyelids, then ran.

Hare was waiting beside the anchor winch, a massive chain extending over the side. I handed him the bloodied knife.

'I knew ye had it in ye,' he whispered grimly.

I felt sick and numb, angry even, that I'd taken a young life so easily. But deeper inside me there was something else which I shudder to admit. It was elation.

A cry came from inside.

'Your man below, they've found him,' said Hare. He clambered over the rail. 'C'mon, Doc. Quick now!'

The chain swayed in mid-air as I picked my way down and glanced to the water thirty feet below.

'Where's the boat?' I shouted, little caring who heard me now.

'Along the side,' he replied, 'ye'll have to swim and get it, Doc. Ye see I, I can't.'

I could hardly believe what he was saying.

'My God, Hare. You can't swim?'

'Well I thought . . . I thought I could maybe wait, and ye could come back for me,' he stammered.

Voices called, followed by figures at the rail. We were only a few feet now above the water.

'There's no time for that! Jump!'

Hare hesitated, still clinging to the chain, then finally let go and landed on his back with a splash. I followed into the warm water.

My clothes were like a lead weight, and it took a great effort to stay afloat while dragging Hare. The ship towered above as we flailed our way towards the rowing boat.

Shots rang out and bullets thudded into the water all around me. The boat was just yards away now and I kicked hard, fighting to stay afloat until eventually we reached its side and I hauled Hare up and in. Exhaustion overwhelmed me, cramps spread through my legs and I began to sink. But just as panic set in, Hare grabbed my arm and, with amazing strength, heaved me up.

I lay gasping while Hare slipped the mooring, ran out the oars and pushed us away.

'C'mon, Doc, get rowing!' he shouted, and grabbing an oar, I hauled for all I was worth. More shots rang out and bullets crashed into the sides, sending splinters spinning. But we picked up speed and with every stroke the ship grew more distant, the shots more haphazard, until we were clear and rowing in the Caribbean beneath a canopy of a thousand stars.

I collapsed onto my back, the oar slipping from my grip.

'Haha! We made it Doc! That was something else, so it was!'

He bent over and hauled me up.

'And we even managed to get you a wash and all!'

35

When I think back now, all these years later, to that triumphant moment in the rowing boat (and Hare who, by some miracle, produced the remains of his bottle of port), it seems incredible to think that he and I were there, in the middle of the Caribbean off the south-east coast of Jamaica, four and a half thousand miles from Edinburgh. Though the exact date has long since escaped me, it was May 1829. Prior to that journey, the beach at Machrihanish was the furthest west I'd ever been.

While the island of Jamaica was known to me from childhood tales of pirates and buccaneers like Sir Henry Morgan, Blackbeard and Calico Jack Rackham, I knew nothing about the place itself; and as the exhilaration of our escape settled to weary uncertainty, its hills and valleys loomed before us, dark and forbidding.

Trailing his hand in the still water, Hare turned and asked me the one question I dreaded.

'Well, Doc, what do we do now?'

I drained the last of the port and heaved the bottle into the night air, hearing it land at some distance with a plop. The boat rocked in the still sea, and for a long time I stared across to the harbour lights.

'I don't know,' I replied. 'But we have to stop him, whatever it takes.'

'You only *think* ye know his plans though. What if you're wrong, Doc?'

I considered it. 'I admit I've made mistakes, but I know I'm not wrong about this.'

I peered towards the shore. 'Now I don't know this place,' I began, 'but I reckon . . .'

The crack of a pistol shattered our tranquillity, and we spun round to see a second vessel emerging from the gloom.

'Raise your hands the pair of you, and no sudden moves!'

We complied at once. At first I feared it was Alba's men, come to recapture us. But as the boat moved closer, I was almost relieved to see it was a patrol boat, bristling with redcoats. At the prow stood their captain, a white band across his chest and a pistol in his hand.

'Who are you? What business do you have out in the bay at this hour?'

Four rifles pointed at our heads.

'My name, sir, is Doctor Mungo Lyon, surgeon of Edinburgh.'

Hare shot me a nervous glance.

'And this is my associate, Mister Dervil. Jack Dervil.'

The captain frowned. We didn't appear to be their usual customers.

'I'm afraid we're rather lost,' I stammered.

'Lost is it?' He barked. 'Well? Have you a permit from the harbourmaster?'

I glanced to Hare, then shook my head.

'Very well, I'll have to take you both into custody. You've no business being this far out, what with over two dozen ships waiting in these waters. It's against regulations.'

He gave a nod and four of his men boarded.

'Wait,' I began, as they shackled our arms and jostled us into the patrol boat. 'Look I'm sure I can explain if only you'll—'

'Tie that boat astern, Jenkins, and we'll pull it to shore,' he said, ignoring me. He proceeded to give our rowing boat a long hard look, and my heart sank as he called for a lantern. Its glow revealed first the gunshot damage and then the Jamaican colonial crest, painted across the transom.

'Are you going to explain this?' he asked, wide-eyed.

There was an uncomfortable silence and I looked to the ground.

'Say nothing,' muttered Hare.

'Well this is a harbour launch,' said the captain. 'And whatever else you've been up to – and I will find out – stealing one of these is a felony. You'll both be up before the magistrate. Tomorrow.'

36

The following morning at dawn, I blinked awake to a riot of trills, whistles and screeches. Hare lay on the straw across from me, hands clasped behind his head, snoring like a lord. I glanced at our cell door, a pail of water resting at its side. It may have been a prison, but it was a palace compared to what I'd endured.

As I lay puzzling over the colourful sounds, I thought of India and the monkeys chattering in the trees. These sounds were different and accompanied by sudden bursts of fluttering.

I stretched in a wide yawn and crept to the window. A scent of spice came wafting off the rose-tinted bay, and a low mist hung on the water. Unlike the wilds of Scotland, this land looked rich and fertile. A row of forest domes extended from the mainland, each one smaller than the last, like sugar lumps melting into the sea. The cause of all the commotion was a company of parrots I could just glimpse by peering down onto a tree clinging to the cliff face. Far below the surf boomed.

Kingston and its harbour were sheltered by a finger of land which all but sealed the bay. At the very tip of this finger, jealously guarding the channel in and out of the bay, stood Port Royal, the fort in which we were now imprisoned.

Port Royal had been Jamaica's principal settlement from its earliest days as a Spanish colony founded by Columbus himself. Under British rule it became a pirates' lair, crowded with inn houses and brothels, its rents once equalling those of London. But following an earthquake its fortunes had dwindled, while those of Kingston across the bay had risen. The sole function of Port Royal was now military. Rows of cannons bristled from the walls, pointing left to the sea, dead ahead across the channel and right over the bay.

As the sun rose it burned away the mist until every ship was revealed in the bay. I counted over two hundred. There was a grubby Nantucket whaler belching smoke and flying the Stars and Stripes; two and three-masted schooners everywhere, all flying the Red Ensign; stately Spanish galleons and nimble French corvettes, all captured and pressed to the King's Service; brigs and coasting sloops from neighbouring colonies; steam tugs chugging here and there; and finally, making its way through the channel and into the bay, a three-masted paddle steamer. It was the ship that had brought me from Greenock.

With the sight of it my thoughts returned to Alba; and I confess, as I took in all the industry of Kingston bay, the idea of a revolution by the hand of one man seemed absurd. How could he possibly hope to achieve it? But just as that doubt grew within me, I recalled his words during our last conversation.

I promise you, you'll live to see my plans come to fruition.

Watching his ship grow closer I made a vow to stop him.

To the rattling of keys, the cell door opened and in stepped an infantryman carrying bowls of porridge and a lump of bread. Hare stirred and opened an eye.

'Grub's up, lads,' he said in a north England accent. He laid them down with a clatter. 'You've half an hour and then it's over to Kingston for your hearing before the Beak.'

I made a start on the porridge.

'This isn't bad,' I said, tearing the bread and tossing half to Hare.

He sniffed, leaned over and lifted his bowl.

'Seen worse,' he grunted. 'I tell ye though, Doc. What I wouldn't give fur a smoke.'

I nodded at that, thinking of my lost pipe and tobacco pouch. We ate in silence, neither wanting to speak first.

'I've been thinking,' I said at last, running my bread around the bowl, 'about when we're called before the magistrate.'

Hare frowned, head down.

'What of it?'

I sensed a change in him.

'I'm going to try and pass him a note.'

He looked up. 'Why would you want to do that?'

'Because I'm going to ask for a meeting with the Governor.'

He gave a hollow laugh.

'Ye think it'll make a blind bit of difference? Trust me, Doc, I've been in front of a lot of beaks in mah time, and they're all the same. They don't give a damn about anything, except their lunch maybe.'

He looked down. 'No, the best we can do is take what's coming to us, get a passage home and forget this place.'

'What? Forget this place?'

He chewed his bread and fixed me with an empty stare.

'It's over, Doc. Your men back in Edinburgh, though. They'll see us right.'

My blood rose. 'But damn it!' I shouted. The bowl and spoon clattered to the ground. 'He's got to be stopped!' I paced about the room like a caged animal. 'This is huge!' I said. 'Don't you get it, Hare? Alba's a traitor!' I pointed to the window. 'All that, out there. The towns, the ships, the trade, and everything that links it to home. It took generations to build. If we don't stop him then, then he's going to just take it, take it all!'

But Hare just stared back with the same vacant look.

'Oh this is a waste of time,' I muttered, turning away. 'I don't know why I'm bothering to explain this to you, of all people.'

I'd no sooner said it than I realised I'd gone too far. There was an uncomfortable silence.

'Fair enough, Doc,' he replied, his voice barely a whisper, 'but I owe my life to your country, and I was treated fairly, so I was.' His lip trembled. 'Oh a gentleman like you, now. Ye can't begin to know the hell I came from in Ireland. I've got to live with what I done, so I do. But I've been given a chance, and I mean to take it.'

There was a long pause, during which we both looked to the ground.

'I spoke out of turn,' I said eventually.

I looked up at his face. The scar on his cheek had healed well, and the stitches had done their work.

'That's all right, Doc,' he replied slowly. 'Ye're a good man, so you are. Even if ye're a bit loose in the head some of the time.'

It was nearer noon before they came and led us in chains to a waiting skiff, then across the bay to Kingston. A mass of merchants and sailors thronged the harbour. Some stood talking and pouring over inventories, while others shouted orders from ship to shore. Teams of men hauled wagons piled high with goods, and everywhere Jamaica's produce was on display, all destined for the Empire's markets.

There were sacks of coffee and ginger piled onto carts, and crates of indigo for dying clothes blue. I saw men lifting boxes packed to the brim with bread-nuts, while others carried bundles of cotton. A ship stood ready, sails hoisted and cargo hold open, while the crew guided in barrels of pickled pimentos and kegs of molasses and rum. Four men passed in front of me in a row carrying slabs of raw mahogany on their shoulders. Then another four passed with blocks of *lignum vitae*, the hardest wood in the world.

The undisputed king, however, and the most valuable crop of all, was sugar. And here in Jamaica, more sugar was produced and exported than anywhere else in the world. It filled warehouses, the names of the plantation owners painted above. *James & Company, Jamaica and Liverpool; Hendersons of Kingston and Glasgow;* and *Crawfurd, Lyle & Robertson of Long Bay, Bristol & Madeira.*

But stepping ashore at Kingston that day, as a prisoner in chains, I came face to face with slavery. There were hundreds of slaves – men, women and even little children – herded in gangs and chained for the monumental crime of the colour of their skin. The horrendous practice had been abolished in Britain more than twenty years earlier, but here in the colonies it continued, underpinning the entire island economy, an evil too great to conceal.

Weaving through the throng our guards led us from the harbour down a lane leading to the courthouse. It was a solid pile, built like a Greek temple. Barristers idled on the front steps, their papers tied with red ribbon. No one spared us so much as a glance as we trudged to the cells below.

'Stealing a rowing boat,' smiled Hare with a shrug. 'What's the worst that can happen?'

37

And so it was I found myself standing in the dock of a Jamaican court with my partner in crime William Hare, if only on a charge of theft of Crown property. The clock struck two, the court rose, and onto the bench stepped the master of our fate.

He had the grey look of a man who'd never laughed in his life, whose time was spent indoors contemplating criminals and the punishments they deserved. He took his seat with a wince and adjusted his spectacles. There was probably little he hadn't heard in his time, and even less he was prepared to believe.

'Call the next case,' he murmured.

The clerk, a red-faced man with the look of a good lunch, rose to his feet. I gripped my note. I'd scribbled it moments ago using paper, pen and ink I'd begged from the well of the court. It set out my allegations against Alba and that I wished to speak with the Governor.

'Call the case of the King and Mungo Lyon and the King and Jack Dervil,' the clerk pronounced. He looked up. 'Are you Mungo Lyon? Are you Jack Dervil?'

We nodded.

The judge wrote something in his papers. 'Read the charge,' he said.

The clerk proceeded to do so, with several squints at the indictment and repetitions here and there. Having reached the final words, which ran something like '. . . *and thus you did wickedly and feloniously steal and damage the King's property,*' the clerk raised his bloodshot eyes.

'How do you plead?'

I can honestly say that until that moment the question of how I would plead hadn't crossed my mind. I hesitated and looked about. The prosecutor, a nervous man in a clean wig and white collar, stared at his papers and made hurried notes. But the defence side of the bar was empty.

The clerk repeated the question.

The judge lifted his eyes from his papers.

'Well? Do you plead guilty or not guilty?'

'Guilty, I suppose,' I replied at last, 'but can I just mention that—'

'The accused Lyon pleads guilty,' said the judge, ignoring me. 'Make a note of that Mister Redfern. Carry on.'

The same question was asked of Hare, who immediately answered the same. Once our pleas were recorded the judge invited the prosecutor to speak.

'No thank you m'lud,' he replied, bobbing his head.

'Very well. Prison, sixty days,' barked the judge. 'If that's all then,' but suddenly the prosecutor jumped to his feet.

'Yes,' sighed the judge. 'What is it now?'

'M'lud. I have here ehm, in the papers, m'lud, ehm, a request from the office of the Attorney General on the Island and it's as regards the, ehm, the first accused, m'lud, that is to say, Mister Lyon.'

The judge frowned. 'What is this request?' He lifted his pen.

'Well, m'lud, ehm, it appears that information has been received just this morning from a reliable source. Highly reliable, m'lud.'

The prosecutor pulled a sheet from his papers and passed it to the clerk, who passed it to the judge. The judge read it and, without a flicker, passed it back.

'Go on.'

'Thank you, m'lud. Well. It would appear from this information available to the Attorney General that Mister, ehm, Mister Lyon is wanted in the town of Greenock, which I am given to understand is a port located on the west coast of Scotland, m'lud, and ehm, that he is wanted on the capital charge of murder, ehm, in respect of a certain Thomas Hamilton.'

The judge stared at me. 'I see.'

'Accordingly, m'lud, my request – that is to say the request of the Attorney General – is that m'lud order the immediate return of Mister Lyon to Scotland to ehm, to face the said charge of murder.'

The prosecutor finished speaking and sat down.

'I'm innocent of that charge!' I shouted.

'Silence,' replied the judge. 'That may very well be, Mister Lyon. But that will be a question for a Scottish jury to decide.'

There was a pause during which he adjusted his spectacles again, formed his hands into a peak and addressed himself to the prosecutor.

'This is a little irregular, is it not, sir? This request doesn't come from the Lord Advocate in Scotland but, as you tell me, from the Attorney General here on the Island.'

The prosecutor rose to his feet again.

'It does, m'lud,' he replied, fiddling with his wig, 'but again I stress the information comes from a highly reliable source. Which of course, I'd rather not, that is to say, in open court, m'lud . . .'

The prosecutor trailed into silence and sat down. There was an anxious pause while the judge made some more notes. Then he put down his pen, called to his clerk for a whispered discussion and finally, to my surprise, addressed himself to me.

'Stand up, Mister Lyon. Your extradition is requested to Scotland as you have heard. However, I have decided, given the circumstances, that I wish to be addressed on this application not only on behalf of the Crown but also by counsel instructed to represent your own interests.

'I will therefore continue this application for a period of seven days, during which I advise you to seek representation from one of the barristers here on the Island. If you cannot pay the Court will provide counsel from the poor roll. Now, do you understand?'

'Yes, sir, but there's something I need to—'

I held my note out for the clerk, but he was too busy writing.

The judge gave me an irritated look.

'Yes, what is it?'

'I have a note that I wish you to read, sir. Please. It's very important.'

The clerk finally looked up and I stretched toward him, my chains rattling. But just as he leaned to take it the judge interrupted.

'Leave it, Mister Redfern, leave it just now,' he muttered. 'If it's important no doubt Mister Lyon's counsel will refer to it next week.'

He removed his spectacles and rubbed his eyes.

'Very well, take the prisoners down.'

The note hung at my fingertips.

'All rise!'

The guards lifted the hatch to the cell below.

'Stop! Wait!' I cried, pushing them away.

The judge gathered his papers and turned, ignoring my protest.

'Your highly reliable source!' I shouted. 'It's Alba! He's planning a revolution! He means to overthrow the government of this Island! Please, you must listen to me!'

The clerk and the prosecutor looked astonished. For a moment the judge stiffened, but he continued off the bench.

'C'mon, sir, there's a good gentleman,' muttered a guard. 'No point makin' a fuss now.'

Halfway down I caught the prosecutor staring after me. I balled the note and threw it.

'Read it!' I shouted, as the hatch thudded shut.

38

The rest of that day I sat dejected in our cell, my arms round my knees, while Hare lay opposite. The sun sank, tinging the sky red.

Hare was right. The judge wasn't interested and my outburst looked like the ravings of a lunatic. Meanwhile Alba advanced with a plan so astonishing that no one would believe me. It occurred to me that perhaps I was mad, and that I'd imagined the encounter with Alba in the course of my fever. It was possible. After all, I'd known patients in the infirmary who would swear to things that couldn't have happened, so vivid were the impressions of their sick minds. In any event, how sure was I of Alba's plans? Had I really seen the Double Eagle in that picture? Was *Julietta* not perhaps just the co-incidence of a name? Had I even read it correctly?

The more I thought, the more hopeless it all seemed. And like Hare, I began to think it best to forget the whole affair and trust the Lord Advocate and Sir John to set things right. I fished out my pocket watch, but even that trusty companion had come to a halt. Salt water had furred its cogs and crusted its springs. My father had given it to me seven years ago, when I became a Fellow of Edinburgh's Royal College of Surgeons. He'd said little at the time, but I knew how proud he was. For the first time I prised open the back plate to reveal its workings and, to my surprise, found an inscription.

To Mungo
because the right time is always now
J L

With a yawn I stretched myself out on the hay and drifted towards sleep. It was typical of my father to hide a message like that, to be discovered by chance someday. And for a moment it was like he was there, encouraging me.

I woke with a start. The door clanked and in marched two guards. One held a lamp while the other hauled me to my feet.

I was led through a warren of dank tunnels. We climbed stairs and passed sentries stifling yawns, their rifles at their side, passed barefoot messenger boys hurrying with orders and passed porters carrying kegs of powder and provisions from the quartermaster's store. We hurried past a row of narrow musket holes, each giving a glimpse of the dark sea below, until we emerged through a raised portcullis onto an open range at the summit of the fort. The sultry air was filled with crickets chirruping. A forest of stars added lustre to the silver moon.

As we crossed to a door at the far side, I stifled a gasp. At least two dozen cannons circled the range taking in Kingston Bay, the channel, the finger of land joining Port Royal to the mainland and finally the open sea. Cannon balls the size of men's heads were piled in pyramids, each capable of bursting a ship's hull.

'What's this about?' I asked one of my guards.

'You'll see soon enough,' he muttered, adjusting the rifle strap on his shoulder.

He knocked, then entered without waiting. It was a candlelit room with a large desk, from behind which a crimson-faced officer raised his eyes in the act of sipping from a wine glass.

'Ah. Our guest Mister Lyon, I presume.'

'Yes, sir. Will that be all, sir?'

He waved a hand. 'Wait outside.'

'Sit down, Mister Lyon,' he ordered. 'Major Crombie.'

'Thank you but I prefer to stand, Major' I replied. 'And it's Doctor. Doctor Mungo Lyon.'

He raised his eyebrows. 'You're a doctor? Blast it, nobody told me you were a doctor.' He slipped his hand across his stomach and narrowed his eyes. 'A surgeon?'

'I am.'

He leaned back in his chair. 'Well I damn well hope you're a better doctor than the useless quacks that infest this island, Doctor Lyon. If it was left to me I'd have the lot o them lined up against a wall and bloody well shot.'

'I'm sorry to hear that, Major,' I replied, 'but I can't think you've summoned me here in the middle of the night just to discuss the state of medics on Jamaica.'

'Don't be insolent!' he barked. 'You'll do well to remember you're a prisoner here.'

'Crombie, can we please get to the point,' spoke a weary voice from the shadows to my left. A figure in a black robe stood by the fireplace.

'What's going on?' I said, shifting my head from one to the other. 'Who are you?'

'I wanted to see you for myself,' he replied. 'You're younger than I thought.'

I glanced to the Major. He frowned, drew a decanter to his side and refilled his glass.

'This gentleman wishes to speak to you,' he said.

From the look of him and from the judge's words earlier, it occurred to me he might be a barrister come to help with my case.

'You're a lawyer?'

He exchanged a glance with the Major. 'I am, Doctor Lyon. But not for hire, I'm afraid.'

I sighed. 'Look, frankly I'm tired and—'

He raised his hand, interrupting me. 'You passed a note to one of my prosecutors today,' he said, 'and he brought it to my attention.'

I then realised who he was. 'You're the Attorney General.'

He nodded.

I shook my head. 'I've nothing to say to you, sir. I want to speak to the Governor. You've already spoken to Alba. On his say-so you want me returned to Scotland for a murder I didn't commit.'

'A murder you claim you didn't commit,' he said, folding his arms. 'Just as you claim to be a doctor. Where exactly did you train?'

Well, I drew myself to my full height at that question. 'I'm proud to say I studied at Edinburgh,' I replied, a little pompously I admit, 'and I've been a Fellow of the Royal College of Surgeons there these past seven years.'

He raised an eyebrow.

'Proud? I'm surprised to hear you say that, what with recent events in that unfortunate city. It doesn't seem to me that you and your colleagues have much to be proud about.'

'Just what are you suggesting?'

He gave a dry laugh. 'Oh word travels, Doctor Lyon. Word travels, even way out here in the wilds. So forgive me if I don't find the accusations of an Edinburgh surgeon particularly convincing right now. Especially when he travels in the company of a low Irishman.'

I shook my head. 'A lesson in reputation from a lawyer. Now that is amusing.'

He took a step towards the desk. 'Incidentally,' he said, feigning a frown, 'whatever happened to the other one after the trial? What was his name again? Hare, wasn't it? Yes, that's right. William Hare.'

The colour rose in my face and I looked away. 'How should I know?'

'I see. Terrible business that, a murderer allowed to walk free. I'm glad to say he'd have hanged in London where our courts don't concern themselves with such petty rules as, what's it called? Corroboration?' He shook his head. 'A pointless principle and a barbarous outcome from a barbarous land.'

I shot him a look of fury and clenched my fists. 'I'm no lawyer,' I growled, leaning towards him, 'but I know this. Any Scot is worth ten Englishmen.'

Well when I said that he stiffened. Out of the corner of my eye I caught Crombie stifling a grin.

'I'm actually Welsh, Doctor Lyon, not that it matters. Though it demonstrates your unfailing ability to get it wrong.' He lifted my note from the desk. 'For instance,' he said. 'You claim Lord Alba's ship is packed with gold, guns and ammunition. That right?'

I nodded.

There was a pause before he continued. 'Earlier this evening, against my better judgment, I obtained a warrant and had it searched. Nothing was found in the hold except tin pots and engine parts.'

He tossed the note down. 'What do you have to say to that?'

I admit for an instant I doubted Hare, but only for an instant.

'Alba obviously had them moved,' I shrugged. 'It only goes to prove how resourceful he is.'

He paced to the fireplace, his hands behind his back.

'I need hardly add the Governor is furious. Lord Alba is a trusted member of this community, Doctor Lyon. His reputation has been besmirched. What's worse, however,' he added, 'is that your baseless accusation has made me look a fool. I won't have that.'

'Well, what about searching his estates?' I snapped, my voice rising. 'Or hasn't that occurred to a legal genius such as yourself?'

'Control yourself Doctor Lyon,' growled the Major.

An uneasy silence followed, and then the Attorney General spoke, his voice trembling with anger.

'You've made cryptic reference to some fanciful organisation, some league or other marked by a Double Eagle. You claim to be acting under the orders of no lesser persons than the Lord Advocate and Sir John Foster of His Majesty's Customs and Excise, and then you casually claim that Alba's involved in a plot to overthrow the government of Jamaica. In support of these

claims you offer not a shred of evidence and, despite the fruitless
search of his ship, you expect me to march a team of men up to
Denholm House and demand the right to ransack his lordship's
property. Madness.'

My mouth fell open. Something had suddenly come to mind.

'Oh yes,' he went on sarcastically. 'I can see the Governor being
thrilled at that idea, what with the Island's May Ball taking place
there in a few—'

'Just a moment,' I interrupted. 'Did you say Denholm House?'
I clutched my head. 'I've heard that before somewhere, but I just
can't—'

'No!' he snapped, waving his hand. 'No, no. This has gone
quite far enough. Now I've seen you for the hot-headed fool you
are, I refuse to listen to any more of your ravings. Crombie,' he
said, 'get him out of here.'

'As you wish, sir.'

He summoned the guards.

'You're making a mistake!' I called over my shoulder as they
removed me. 'You're endangering the lives of everyone on this
island!'

But he remained by the fireside, staring into its embers.

39

I slammed my fists against the cell door and slid to the floor.

Everything I'd worked to achieve, every effort I'd made and, worst of all, the life I'd taken from that young man: all of it came to nothing but one word, looming like a tombstone.

Failure.

Through the darkness I sensed Hare watching. Then he shifted and I knew he'd turned away.

There was nothing more to say.

As I look back at myself in that cell, I shouldn't have been so disappointed by failure. After all, in those days of pioneering surgery, as many as nine out of every ten operations we performed at the infirmary resulted in failure and death. It was a hard lesson, time after time, to see one's efforts come to naught, but my profession was nothing if not persistent.

Every now and again everything would come right. The deep wound would close, the patient's fever pass, and little by little recovery would begin. We learned lessons. But the delicate shoots of success reached deep down through the hard soil of defeat.

This was just another failure, like so many I'd endured. But it was hard to bear.

I slept long that night and far into the following day. There was nothing to do, nothing to rush for, no battles to be fought in my mind. The life of the fort continued as before, with the fifes and drums of flag raising, and the mild civility of British imprisonment. The guards came with fresh hay and fresh water, and our meals were left out precisely on time.

With defeat came acceptance. Naturally I thought of escape but it was hopeless. The bars were solid iron with nothing but the cliff below. The guards worked in teams. Quite simply, the fort was too well run to offer the slightest opportunity. We had nothing, not even the will to try.

Three days passed with the same routine morning, noon and night. Hare managed to scrounge some tobacco and clay pipes from a guard. On the fourth day, as the late afternoon sun was sinking, bringing a cool breeze from the water, Hare and I lit the pipes and sat back like two princes in a palace, smoke curling round our heads.

'So, Doc,' he began. 'What you planning on doing when we get back?'

I closed my eyes for a moment, listening to the crickets and the parrots.

'I've had enough defeats,' I said. 'It's time for something different.'

Hare gave me a keen look. 'Another mission, maybe?'

I smiled. 'I doubt they'd want me after this mess, don't you think? Besides, there are other things.'

I thought of the sea and the world beyond Edinburgh. Then I thought of Margaret, and then Fiona. I'd thought of her often and finally I understood why. It was because I wanted to see her again.

'What about you?' I asked, refilling my pipe. 'What will you do?'

He shrugged. 'I'll pick up where I left off, so I will. Doin' jobs where I'm needed, I suppose.'

I nodded. My mind was still on Fiona, however. I thought of the moment when Hare and I had left *The Glue Pot*.

'Hare,' I said after a while, 'you were once about to tell me something about Fiona, something to do with her past. What was it?'

He frowned. 'Oh that. Word in Greenock is she was in service a good long time ago. A maid so I've been told, in a grand house somewhere. There was a scandal and Fiona, well, she was with child. She was sixteen or so at the time, judging by the age of her wee girl. D'you remember her, Doc, the lassie that served us?'

I nodded.

'Well that was it. Fiona was flung out of that house and left to fend for herself. But she was too proud to go back to her people in the Highlands for help, so she landed in Greenock. Back then Sir John was the Collector, before Birkmyre's time. She came looking for work cleaning at the Custom House. Sir John gave her the job and she worked well for a few years. Then one day he came to her with an opportunity, to be his eyes and ears in the town so he said, and in exchange he'd set her up with a licence. The rest is history, as they say, and that's all I know about it.'

There was a pause while Hare took a long puff of his pipe and blew smoke rings into the air.

'You're sweet on her, aren't you?'

'I just care, that's all,' I mumbled.

Hare nodded. There was nothing more to be said about it and we drifted back to silence, the sounds of nature mixing with the regular comings and goings of the fort. I'd allowed the routine to convince me that whatever Alba's plans were, he'd probably abandoned them. I'd finally remembered where I'd heard mention of Denholm House, whispered by one of Alba's men on the road to Glasgow. But it came to nothing. Hardly enough to prove an armed revolution.

The key rattled in the lock, too early for mealtime and a guard barged in, agitated.

'You've to come at once,' he blurted. 'It's the Major.'

'What's the matter? Is he ill?'

'Please, you must come. He's shouting for you and just threw his piss pot over the head of another doctor, the one who's been treating him this past while.'

I glanced at Hare, who stifled a laugh, and got to my feet. 'Very well,' I sighed. 'But if he's shouting and throwing things, I doubt he can be that ill.'

I followed the guard to the door. Just before I left, Hare called after me.

'Hey, Doc.'

I glanced back.

'Do what you need to do.'

I nodded. 'I doubt I'll be long.' And with a tap of my fingers on the doorframe, I was gone.

40

'Has this come on suddenly?' I asked, as we climbed once again to the summit.

'Very sudden,' he replied. 'He was pulling on his britches for the May Ball this evening when he cried out and started rolling round the floor in agony. That other doctor —Fitzsimmons he's called — well he's been having him swallow all kinds of potions and whatnot. But the Major, he won't have it no longer. Says he wants a proper doctor.'

This sounded more serious than I first thought. My concerns only increased when, as we crossed the range, the Major bellowed in pain. We ran to the door where a chaotic scene met our eyes.

The Major was writhing on the floor in front of his desk, his face purple, his hands clasped in agony over his belly. Stripped to his long johns, he'd kicked his regimental trousers into a heap. Fitzsimmons stood trembling at the far side of the desk, wiping his face with a handkerchief. An array of coloured bottles stood before him, together with a mixing bowl and a spoon. As we rushed in he stuffed the handkerchief away, his free hand flitting from one bottle to the next.

'Get that blasted quack out of here before he bloody well kills me!'

Fitzsimmons frowned, sweat beading his brow. He appeared to reach a decision and grabbed a green bottle.

'A purgative to clear his bowels,' he muttered. 'That's what's needed here.'

I prized free the Major's hands and compressed the area round his swollen navel. It was tight as a drum.

'How does that feel?'

He gritted his teeth, sweat drenching his hair. 'Bloody awful,' he whispered.

With one hand I brushed his forehead to confirm the high fever, while moving the other across his abdomen.

'How about here?' I said, pressing again.

He gave a sharp cry and jerked his leg, his knee colliding with the back of my head.

'What the hell d'you do that for!' he bawled.

Driven on by the Major's cry, Fitzsimmons plucked one bottle after another, all the time spooning into a bowl and stirring.

'You!' I shouted to the guard. 'What's your name?'

He stood watching, wide-eyed. 'Me? It's Jenkins, sir, Corporal Jenkins.'

'Well Jenkins, get round behind the Major and help me turn him.'

'Yes, sir. Right away, sir.'

He dropped to his knees, and together we rolled him onto his left side until I was able to compress his lower back.

'How about now?' I asked.

The Major gave an agonised howl. 'Just the same,' he said, sucking his breath through his teeth. 'Damn it all, if I could only shit it out I'd be—' but before he could finish the thought, he convulsed in another spasm of pain.

'He's right of course,' shouted Fitzsimmons over the Major's cries, a look of triumph on his face. 'All he need do is *expellere stercus*, drive out the blockage from his bowel, and all will be right as rain.'

We laid the Major on his back.

'What have you been giving him?' I asked.

Fitzsimmons flicked me a look of irritation but continued stirring.

'I started yesterday with a *bolus* of mercury and pig fat to grease his fundament and lower passages, with clear instructions *repetatur dosus per noctem*. Then I began this morning, in line with the wisdom of Paracelsus, by applying my mind to the *umores corporis* and the best way to stimulate the—'

'This is madness,' I shouted, interrupting him. 'Don't you see what's wrong with him? Your potions are only making it worse!'

Fitzsimmons dropped his spoon into the mixing bowl and stepped back from the table.

'How dare you?' he retorted. 'I'll have you know I'm a trained apothecary, a physician of many years standing. What right have you, whoever you are, to barge in here and—'

'Enough!' I shouted and gave him a look of such fury that he backed even further away.

I knelt by the Major. His breathing was sharp and shallow, and fear was in his eyes.

'Major Crombie, you have acute appendicitis. Your appendix is swollen, and these purgatives you've been taking are adding to the pressure.'

He gave a low moan.

'I can save you. But I must operate and remove the diseased appendix right away, before it bursts and kills you.'

Fitzsimmons' mouth fell open.

'You can't mean, good God, you don't mean to say that you're going to, to cut him open? You'll kill him!'

'It's the only way,' I said.

There was a pause, then the Major opened his eyes.

'Do it man,' he wheezed, swallowing hard. 'And for God's sake do it quickly.'

'Madness,' Fitzsimmons muttered, 'utter madness. I'll have nothing to do with it.' He began to gather up his bottles.

'Stop!' I cried, 'you can still help here. Can you mix me a sedative? Have you any laudanum? I need something strong to put him out.'

He looked from me to the Major and back again.

'But laudanum will calm him,' he replied fearfully. 'That's not what he needs to force out the—'

'Do it damn you!' bellowed the Major.

Fitzsimmons, chalk white, was torn between staying and leaving. But his fear of disobeying the Major won and he started mixing the dose.

'Jenkins,' I said, turning to the corporal, 'is there a medical room?'

'Yes, sir.'

'Go there and fetch every surgical instrument you can find. I need needle and thread, a pan of hot water and clean linen. Now run.'

'Yes, sir. Right away, sir.'

As Jenkins took off, I cleared the desk. It would serve as an operating table. All the while I thought back to my classes and my Bible, Doctor Bell's *Principles of Surgery*. The most senior man at the Infirmary, Bell was a surgeon without equal, a man with a mind like a razor and a hand like a dove. Though the professors were suspicious of his unorthodox methods, the young medics worshipped him, and I'd assisted while he performed countless operations.

Only once, however, had I stood at his shoulder and watched him carry out an appendectomy on a young boy. His wise words, often repeated in the midst of our shining faces, came back to me like the refrain of a song.

'I regard skill in operating as of the utmost importance. It gives the surgeon perfect self-possession. A bad operator will hesitate. But a skilful operator will avoid difficulties because he will act with courage and conviction. So work hard at becoming good operators. That way, you'll become great surgeons.'

It was time to show what an Edinburgh surgeon could do.

By the time Jenkins returned with supplies, the Major was drinking the last of the laudanum. His breathing gradually relaxed and, as he fell into a deep sleep, we lifted him onto the desk.

The surgical tools were antiquated but in decent military condition. I needed to make an incision through the abdomen and push aside the layers of skin, fat and muscle until I reached the peritoneum. This slippery membrane formed a protective pouch, inside of which were his intestines. I needed to pierce the peritoneum and quickly find the appendix. It lay at the joint where the small intestine became the large intestine. I then had to cut off the appendix and stitch its stump, stitch the peritoneum, then every layer back up until I reached the skin.

While it might sound as simple as peeling an onion, the reality was close to impossible. The opening would bleed like fury from the first cut. The tissues would slip between my fingers like warm butter, and the appendix would hide itself in the mass of twisting intestines. Even if I removed it, closing the peritoneum would be like stitching the skin on a rice pudding. And all of this assuming I didn't make a single slip with the needle or knife.

Fitzsimmons stumbled backwards toward the wall, chalk white, his hands clenched above his head in astonished anticipation. Jenkins stood ready with water, linen and a bowl to receive the appendix. I took a moment to focus on the shining surface of the skin. I rolled my sleeves past my elbows. Then I lifted the sharpest blade and made the incision.

From the moment of that first cut I dived from a rock and plunged below the surface of a crystal sea. All breathing stopped, all sounds became dull, even when Fitzsimmons vomited on the floor. My eyesight narrowed to a single, steady point. The twisting, bleeding innards of the Major became the fronds of delicate sea flowers, which I slipped apart in search of an oyster's glistening pearl. The only voice I heard was in my head, guiding my fingers, telling me where the treasure lay and how to find it. Down I swam, deeper and deeper until there it was, the oyster, open and unsuspecting, just within my grasp.

It was only when I surfaced for a moment to ask Corporal Jenkins to hold out the bowl and receive the Major's appendix, that I realised he'd fainted clean out. I delved back down and began closing him up. I'd no idea of time's passage until, with a final snip of the thread and a hand across my brow, I straightened up and took a deep gulp of air.

The Major's chest rose and fell, his breathing steady.

Fitzsimmons stood at my side holding a branch of three candles.

'What's that for?' I asked.

He stared at me. 'Don't you remember?' he whispered. 'The sun was setting and the room was almost in darkness. You were shouting for more light.'

'Oh.' I glanced around me as if seeing the office for the first time. 'I see. Thank you.'

I began to wash the blood from my arms. Jenkins slumbered on the floor, dead to the world.

'Who *are* you?' asked Fitzsimmons.

I dried my arms and shook his hand.

'Doctor Mungo Lyon, surgeon of Edinburgh. Sorry to give you such a rough time of it earlier. Your laudanum did the trick though, well done.'

He stared from me to the Major and back again, his mouth opening and closing like a fish.

'I've never seen anything like that. What you did, you saved his life.'

'Well, that remains to be seen.'

I sighed, glanced round the room again, and froze.

Do what you need to do.

Fitzsimmons was babbling now, on and on about surgery and techniques he'd heard of being used in France, journals he'd read and other such things.

'Look,' I said, interrupting him, 'it's getting late and you've done a great deal. In fact, I couldn't have done it without you, I really couldn't. I think it's best if I stay a while. But you'll probably want to be going.'

'Oh yes of course, Doctor Lyon. I'll just collect my things.'

He gathered his bottles into his bag, hesitated, and looked down at Corporal Jenkins.

'Will he be? Do you think we should . . . ?'

I grinned, and patted Fitzsimmons on the shoulder. 'Oh, let's let him sleep a while, eh? After all, not everyone's cut out to be a medic!'

'No, I suppose not,' he replied with a twitch of his lips. 'Well, I'll just be going. My bill, I'll—'

'I'm sure it'll be paid in the morning. Goodbye, Doctor Fitzsimmons.'

'Yes, goodbye, Doctor Lyon. Amazing, quite amazing.'

There wasn't a moment to lose. I locked the door and picked up the Major's britches. Then I darted to the far corner where, on a wooden stand, hung the rest of the Major's dress uniform and powdered wig. Draped across his red jacket and white sash was an item that caught my attention. A black Venetian eye mask with a long-hooked nose, exactly the fashion for a society Ball.

As I donned his uniform I thought of my Indian ayah, Ranjita, and a time she'd found me crying.

'What's the matter, little Mungo sahib?' she'd asked, cradling me. A boy had punched me and stolen my kite.

'I hate him,' I'd said, tasting blood on my lips. 'I'll always hate him.'

'Sshh, little sahib,' she'd soothed. 'Hate is a strong thought. Always remember the wisdom of Buddha. Be careful what you think, *because what you think, you become.* Think hate, and you will be hateful. Think love, and you will be loving.'

I'd always remembered that wisdom, but now I had to put it into practice.

You see, it wasn't enough to pretend to be Major Crombie.

If I was to escape the fort and make it to Denholm House, I had to become Major Crombie.

41

The uniform was far from a perfect fit. His britches came up short at the ankles and were three inches too wide at the waist. The short grey wig slipped a little on my head and, even when fully buttoned, I could still fit three fingers between the shirt collar and my neck. What's more, the jacket was a little short at the cuff and the boots pinched as I pulled them on. But where before I'd allowed doubt to overwhelm me, now I saw only opportunity. People expected to see the Major. So I would become him.

Using one of the surgical blades I scraped away my stubble. My hands and face were too pale, but after rubbing them with the blood-soaked linen they darkened to a nutty brown. I rolled my shirt and stuffed it under his tunic. I donned his wig, his cocked hat, his sash and his sword. Finally, I attached the mask.

I tried a few lines until I'd captured his gruff and colourful speech. And for the final effect, I drank three glasses of wine from his decanter.

Just as I was about to leave there was a knock.

'Major Crombie, sir! Are you all right in there?'

'I'm fine dammit,' I barked, marching to the door. 'Perfectly fine.'

I took a deep breath, unlocked the door and slipped out into the gloom.

'Blasted doctors,' I muttered, slamming the door behind me. 'Been on me chamber pot for the last hour.'

I glanced through the mask at the soldier's face and recognised him as one of the guards. He hesitated.

'Are you quite well, sir? Only you don't sound,'

'Course I'm all right, dammit!' I wheezed. 'Swallowing all that quack's poison's just playing havoc with my throat is all.'

He stared back at me, his mouth open.

'Well?' I barked. 'What is it now? Can't you see I'm off to this blasted Ball?'

He gave a start.

'Of course, sir, the carriage is still below. The captain just wasn't sure if, I mean, do you want me to . . .'

'Fine,' I said, putting my hand to his shoulder and turning him away from the door. 'That's fine. Lead on. You can fill me in on the way.'

We passed soldiers at every turn, each drawing themselves to attention as I passed. There were more than a few grins at the sight of the mask, but otherwise not one of them so much as raised an eyebrow. At one point the guard turned to speak to me, but I waved him on.

'In a moment,' I muttered.

With a final salute to the sentries I was through the main gate. The carriage stood waiting, the driver dozing at the reigns.

'Wake up!' I shouted, thumping the side. 'Denholm House, and be quick about it, damn you.'

'Sir, wait, sir,' said the guard as I entered the carriage. 'Isn't the captain to accompany you?'

An idea struck me.

'No,' I replied. 'Tell the captain to gather every man he can spare and follow on. I've a feelin' there might be trouble at this Ball. Every man I say. Understood?'

He stepped back and saluted.

'Yes, sir. Very good, sir.'

I banged the roof.

We sped along the finger of land joining Port Royal to the mainland.

'How long till we get there?' I hollered, holding my hat against the wind.

The driver half turned. 'Not long, sir,' he shouted over his shoulder. 'Road's just a bit rough above Kingston.'

I'd no idea what to expect and all the old doubts came crowding back. What if I was wrong? What if this Ball turned out to be simply that? But no, I told myself, Alba was too cunning to pass up the opportunity. I steadied my resolve.

As Kingston grew closer the driver made a sharp turn up a rutted path. The carriage rocked and I gripped the edge of my seat as we climbed, the moon disappearing behind a canopy of trees. The horses seemed to take forever now, and once or twice the carriage halted while the driver picked his way forward. At last, however, with a tremendous jolt, the wheels crunched onto a gravel drive and we passed between gateposts.

The tension mounted within me as the trees thinned and the moon reappeared. It cast a silken light over fields of sugar cane as far as the eye could see. There were figures among the crops, and

I realised they were slaves who, despite the hour, laboured endlessly. Torches in sconces winked in the passing. Fields turned to pristine lawns. The haunting cry of a peacock echoed, curdling the blood in my veins, and in that dread moment I caught sight of Denholm House. Light blazed from every window.

Never had I seen such a vast mansion. I counted six pillars at the head of a flight of steps. Wings fanned left and right, disappearing into the mirk, and violins, laughter and dancing came drifting in the sultry air. Here it was, Lord Alba's colonial mansion; and any doubt about his wealth and ambition vanished from my mind.

The driver drew the horses to a halt and I stepped out, heart pounding. Two footmen swept wide the front doors and, casting aside his fears, Major Crombie made his entrance at Lord Alba's glorious May Ball.

42

Vienna unfolded before me.

At the foot of a grand staircase the hallway teemed with chattering guests. The older men stood in dress uniform and powdered wigs like my own, red cheeked and smoking cigars. The younger ones sported tailcoats and toyed with their glasses, while their masked eyes followed the society daughters gliding round the room. There were dresses of rich yellow satin, crimson velvet and ivory silk. There was hair sculpted into lush curls, and ears and necks glistening with diamonds, emeralds and sapphires.

Slave boys in brocaded jackets darted through the crowd with trays of champagne, chocolates, candied orange slices and sugared apricots, and the whole scene was lit from the centre by a chandelier blazing with candles.

As I lingered, ignored by everyone, a footman bent forward and cupped his hand to my ear.

'Whom shall I announce sir?'

Waving my hand dismissively as I imagined the Major would, I removed my hat and thrust it towards him.

'No need, sir, no need. Thought that was the whole point of a masked ball, what? Just fetch me a drink, damn you, and be quick about it.'

The footman bowed and disappeared, returning a moment later with a coupe of champagne. I drifted into a corner beside a tall plant and an elderly gentleman in a long wig. The guests' faces were flushed with drink and there was excited talk of the waltzes which had just finished. Off to one side a set of doors opened onto a ballroom. A troupe of musicians were shifting their instruments, but when the violins resumed a young man with sandy hair glanced at me over his shoulder and approached.

'You must be Major Crombie,' he beamed. Blue eyes shone through his mask. He'd a lilting Scottish accent.

I took his hand with a gruff response, somewhere between a cough and clearing my throat.

'And who might you be, sir?'

'McCunn, sir, Crawford McCunn. I'm Lord Alba's secretary.' He grinned. 'He'll be glad to know you've arrived, Major.'

The young man looked to my glass and clicked his fingers. A boy came running.

'Make sure the Major gets plenty champagne.'

With a bow he slipped into the crowd and whispered to a figure in black. Despite the mask I recognised it was Alba. He gazed at me and nodded. Raising my glass I returned the greeting. Then he gave his attention to a striking woman in a blue satin dress. She was tall with long hair, her face covered by a white mask.

My hand trembled as I sipped, but in the next moment I all but dropped the glass. As she tilted her head and smoothed her hair, I realised who she was.

Fiona Cameron.

For the life of me I couldn't believe it. All these thousands of miles from Greenock? What was she doing here? Alba lifted his hand and caressed her neck. He leaned toward her, his lips at her ear for a moment, then swept away.

Without stopping to think I crossed the room to her, our faces still concealed.

'Fiona?'

She turned.

'It's me!' I urged. 'Mungo! What are you doing here?'

She took a moment to comprehend.

'Doctor Lyon? What on earth!' she gasped. 'You should leave before you get hurt!'

'What are you talking about?' I glanced round nervously and stepped closer to her. 'You're the one in danger! Don't you realise what Alba's planning to do?'

'Shush! Not another word, Doctor.' I glanced down to see her nervously twisting a large purse. 'I know what he is and what he's planning,' she murmured, staring after him, 'and I've got to be the one to finish this. Tonight.'

'Finish what?'

'She's just a child,' she added, more to herself than me. 'She can't understand. But perhaps one day she will.'

'You're not making any sense. You need to get out of here and leave this to—'

'No.' She cut me off sharply and turned to face me again. 'You're the one who needs to go, Doctor. This is no place for amateurs.'

With that, she turned and moved away through the crowd. Too astonished to reply I was just about to follow her when a gong sounded and all eyes turned to Alba, halfway up the staircase.

'My lords, ladies and gentlemen! The time has come. Reveal yourselves!'

To the applause and cheers of his guests, Alba swept away his mask with a grin. All around the room others did the same, but as I turned back to look for Fiona she was gone.

'And now,' cried Alba as the laughter subsided, 'I'd like to invite the ladies to adjourn to the Chinese parlour, while the gentlemen join me in the drawing room.'

The guests divided and, though I strained to find Fiona, the crowd pressed me in the opposite direction.

'Here, take that mask off!' shouted an amiable drunk as I passed through the doorway. He began pawing at my face, but I jerked my head back and made light of it.

'It's the damned strings,' I muttered, pretending to struggle with the knot, 'can't seem to untangle the blasted things!'

The drawing room was long and narrow with a row of windows down one side. Spaced between the windows a dozen black footmen waited with silver trays of brandy glasses resting in their arms. I scooped one into my hand as I passed, then made for the far end where I lingered behind a grand piano.

The room began to fill with Jamaica's colonial leaders, most crowding round the fireplace, others flopping onto couches and chairs scattered here and there. Candles flickered in the gloom picking out the gold leaf in the cornicing, the rows of medals on proud chests, the crimson of the curtains. Just as the air of expectancy grew to a head, ripples of applause broke out and in marched Alba accompanied by a kindly looking old gentleman in a pink jacket and blue sash. Spotting the Attorney General a footstep behind I realised this was the Governor.

Those in the centre made way as a chair was fetched and placed between the fireplace and the windows. Alba invited the Governor to take his place of honour. As the Governor stood in front of the chair the footmen at the windows moved forward with their trays. Once everyone had a drink in their hand, the Governor raised his arm and the room grew silent.

'Gentlemen, the King!' he shouted; and every man responded in unison.

With the toast drunk, the Governor took his seat amid ripples of conversation, some producing pipes and cigars. Half a dozen of the footmen circulated with decanters, rather clumsily I thought, and with the glasses recharged Alba called for silence.

'Gentlemen, a toast: to His Majesty's Governor, Sir Henry Barrie!'

'Sir Henry!' came the good-natured response, and once again the brandy was drunk off with gusto.

Then it was the turn of the Attorney General to step forward; and in the same fashion a toast was drunk in honour of their host, Lord Alba. The Attorney General extended his hand and Alba took it, beaming with pleasure. Clearly, the whole embarrassing business of the search had been forgiven and forgotten.

The pleasant hubbub resumed and, once again, I began to fear I'd misjudged the entire evening and that everything would pass off without incident after all. Just then, however, one of the doors at Alba's back opened and closed. McCunn slipped to Alba's side and whispered in his ear.

There was something so sly in McCunn's look that I sensed something wasn't right. Alba stiffened, whispered something back and McCunn signalled for more brandy. The glasses were refilled by the footmen and, as they resumed their places by the windows, the conversations once again faded. All eyes returned to their host.

Alba scanned their expectant faces. Then, drawing himself up to his full height, he thrust out his arm.

'Gentlemen, my toast is this: to the most ancient and revered Order of the Double Eagle!'

43

Someone gave a high-pitched laugh which hung in the air then died, for there was no smile on Alba's lips. The stunned silence which followed was punctuated by two sounds. The first was a soft click from the drawing room doors as McCunn closed and locked them; and the second was a loud crash as the footmen dropped their trays and whipped out rifles from behind the curtains.

As I tore off my mask the door beside the fireplace burst open and in rushed a dozen riflemen. They fanned out and, together with those already in the rear, surrounded the company. One rushed behind me, his rifle digging into my back. They were Maroons, the independent mountain men of Jamaica's interior. They were nervous and fidgeted with their new firearms, but there was no mistaking their looks of triumph.

Sir Henry rose to his feet.

'Alba!' he shouted, his face livid. 'What on earth is the meaning of this farce?'

Alba drained his brandy and gently laid his glass on the mantel.

'Sit down and calm yourself, Sir Henry,' he sneered. 'You're surrounded. The Maroons have joined me in rebellion, and two thousand wait in the hills, armed and ready. On top of that, seven warships lie off Port Royal, awaiting my signal.'

He brushed an invisible speck from his jacket and continued in the same disdainful voice.

'British rule is over, Sir Henry. At dawn Jamaica will awake to a new era.'

Sir Henry stared back, then turned to his anxious countrymen. Slowly he scanned the room, taking in every familiar face, and every one of the fierce Maroons. Lastly, he exchanged a glance with the Attorney General and turned back to face Alba.

'No one is to react,' he shouted. 'Be calm, gentlemen, please.'

With that, the Governor sat down and a long sigh went round the room. Heads were bowed but one spirited soul, a naval officer much the worse for drink, wasn't having it.

'You treacherous swine!' he cried, his face purple. 'By thunder, how can you do this to your own!'

He took a step closer, his fist drawn back to strike. A rifle exploded at point blank range and he fell, dead.

There were loud gasps, shock registering on every man's face, but Alba didn't flinch. Instead, he signalled to two Maroons who proceeded to drag the brave man's body to one side. With a nod to McCunn, a table was fetched up in front of the Governor, together with ink and a quill.

Alba produced a document and laid it down.

'Now if you'd be so kind,' he said, palms flat on the desk and staring into the Governor's eyes, 'these are the articles of surrender which I insist you now sign.'

Sir Henry leaned back in his chair. 'Why on earth would I do that?'

Alba grinned and curled his palms into fists. 'Because if you don't, my dear old Sir Henry, I'll have every man in this room shot, starting with that fool of a nephew of yours.'

He flicked a glance towards a pale young man standing two steps behind his uncle. 'And when I've done that,' he growled, 'I'll start on the women.'

Sir Henry's eyes widened, but he made no reply.

Alba turned his palms face up. 'See reason,' he urged. 'Surrender the island to me without another shot, and I guarantee you all safe passage home.'

'And if I refuse?' replied the Governor.

Alba's eyes narrowed.

'Then I will be a *Dessalines* for Jamaica.'

A ripple of horror went round the room at the mere mention of Jean Jacques Dessalines, the ex-slave leader who had executed thousands of French colonists on Hispaniola during the recent Haitian Revolution.

Sir Henry gazed at the paper. All at once he looked very old and tired, and my heart sank at the realisation he would have to sign. I knew nothing of the Governor's character, but it occurred to me that Alba must have studied him and played out this moment a thousand times. I thought to cry out, to tell him to stop, that the soldiers I'd ordered to follow were on their way from Port Royal. But I'd no idea when or even if they would arrive.

Sir Henry had his hand at his forehead now and leaning forward he gave a sigh.

'So be it,' he whispered. 'But I'll need more light to read this document.' He raised his eyes with a pitiful look. 'And before I sign, Lord Alba, I wish to drink one last glass of rum, as governor.'

Alba stepped back, folded his arms and gave an irritated signal to McCunn. A candelabra was laid on the table together with a decanter of dark Jamaican rum and a single glass.

The Governor lifted himself from his chair, his eyes on Alba's face. He poured from the decanter and, raising the glass to his lips, took a sip. He closed his eyes, savouring the rum's intense sweetness, and for a moment a smile played on his lips.

'Gentlemen,' he called, turning to the astonished company, 'Lord Alba declares British rule at an end, and I stand here, the embodiment of your sovereign lord and King.

'I am ordered, before you all, to surrender this island. It is your King who is ordered. You see the position. And so with a heavy heart, I must call upon you, must call upon you – to fight!'

As he shouted this final word Sir Henry grabbed the decanter and hurled it across the room towards the windows. It smashed onto the floor, the rum splashing everywhere, and he launched the candelabra after it. The rum instantly caught fire, its blue flames licking round the thick velvet curtains. Then everything seemed to happen at once.

'Fight gentlemen, fight!' the Governor was crying, his arms in the air, and in that moment a Maroon stepped forward, aimed his rifle at the Governor's chest, and fired. The Attorney General, who was at the Governor's side, threw himself in the way, but an instant later a second shot rang out and the Governor fell to the ground, clutching his chest.

Bedlam erupted.

'Kill them all!' screamed Alba, his face twisted with rage, and as crashing volleys of rifle fire all but burst my eardrums, men fell all about me. At the Governor's cry I'd jumped up and onto the piano, and as smoke and gunpowder filled the air I felt a sharp sting in the back of my leg as though I'd been bitten, and I fell to the ground on the other side.

Looking back, I can't help thinking that Alba's plan was to ply people with so much drink they would struggle to resist. But if that was his plan, it backfired spectacularly. All around, as the first volleys subsided, men launched themselves at the Maroons. A desperate hand to hand struggle ensued. Rifles twisted in the air, chairs were thrown and everything that came to hand – ornaments, vases, candlesticks and in one case even a clock – found service as a weapon. I jumped onto the back of one Maroon, reigning blows down on his head, while another fellow smashed a chair into his stomach and wrestled away his rifle.

I wish I could say the heroic actions of the men in that room turned the tide, but the truth is that the Governor's gift of fire did more than anything else. By now the curtains were ablaze, the flames flaring out to the pairs on either side and up over the ceiling to the centre of the room. Smoke billowed, clouding the struggle in a pall of confusion.

The situation could not continue long, and even as the Maroons fought strong and hard, panic flickered in their eyes until, with a cry of fear, one of them broke off and launched himself at one of the windows. There was a loud crash as the glass shattered. The wooden frame splintered, and he was through and out onto the lawn. The sudden rush of air roared the flames on and two more Maroons followed; and then, with the room beyond control, I spied Alba slipping through the door at his back.

I blundered across through the sparks and smoke, over broken furniture and bodies and shook that door half off its hinges. But he'd locked it fast. The room was an inferno by now, and dozens lay dead or dying. From the floor beside me I hauled the bewildered Attorney General to his feet and together we dragged Sir Henry through the carnage, then out through a window to the grass below. The Governor's blue sash was singed and thick with blood, and as I lifted his hand from his chest I was met by the sight of a mortal wound clean through his brave heart. For a moment he gazed with a look of serene indifference upon the chaos all around, the bright flames flickering over the surface of his eyes, and then he was gone.

My next thought was for the Attorney General kneeling at the Governor's side. He was pale as a ghost, his eyes wet with tears, his shattered left arm hanging limp.

'How is this happening,' he mumbled.

'You're gravely injured sir,' I shouted, tearing away the Governor's sash for a tourniquet, 'I need to stop your bleeding.'

He recoiled in horror at my act of desecration, but I insisted; and in a heartbeat I had his arm bound, though it would soon have to come off above the elbow. It was only then it occurred to me to look to my own injured leg, but by an almighty piece of luck the bullet had struck a buckle at the top of my boot and deflected. The bleeding from the impact was still bad though, and I bound up the wound as best I could with the sash from my own uniform.

All this time, others were crawling from the windows, coughing and spluttering onto the grass, while out over the grounds

Maroons were shouting to one another and regrouping. Just then, however, the first crack of gunfire echoed down the driveway as the redcoats arrived. The leaderless Maroons hesitated and were melting into the trees when suddenly, with a single bound, Crawford McCunn leapt clean over my head and sprinted into the gloom.

44

Instinctively I raced after McCunn to the edge of a sugar cane field and along to a cluster of buildings. For a moment I lost him, then a door banged shut off to my right. I followed the sound, passing two wide-eyed slaves as I did so, and came to a large barn of a place, its door swinging.

As I slipped inside the heat struck me like a wall. Smoke stung my eyes and there was a stench of treacle. Six vast cauldrons stood in a row over woodchip fires, each filled to the brim with what looked like bubbling tar. Beyond them a towering steam piston rose and fell, the ground trembling as it drove rusted iron rollers. This was the estate's refinery, and the grim reality of sugar making opened before me like a vision of hell.

More slaves, naked to the waist, worked the mixture in the cauldrons with long wooden paddles, while others heaved baskets of chopped sugar cane down onto the rollers. A few turned languid, lifeless eyes in my direction, as if beyond surprise by anything that life could offer: but one fellow flicked a glance to a gantry above, its branches criss-crossing the roof space, and following his gaze I spied a dark figure clambering to the top of a ladder.

'McCunn!' I shouted.

He stopped and turned but pressed on as I clambered after him up the narrow rungs. By the time I stepped onto the rusted gantry he was sprinting away. The whole structure was swaying like a ship at sea and I grasped a flimsy wooden handrail on my left, leaning too heavily as I did so. With a crack it began to give way and I was out, balancing on my toes, with nothing but thin air between me and the ground far below. My arms flailed, I arched my back, and somehow kept myself upright. Even so, the gangway was less than a foot wide and, dropping to my knees, I crawled forward.

I passed two branches left and right and carried on, eventually summoning the courage to get back on my feet. Another branch lay ahead, but as I teetered towards it McCunn stepped from the dark with a look of sheer malice. All traces of Alba's smooth secretary vanished, and I saw him for the murderer he was.

'You just won't take a telling, will you?' he smiled, drawing a knife from his belt and stepping towards me. But I had the pleasure of seeing fear flicker in his eyes as I drew the Major's sword.

'Get back!' I cried, the razor tip glinting a foot from his chest, 'or, so help me God, I'll kill you where you stand.'

He hesitated but stood his ground. 'Careful, Doctor Lyon. One swing and you'll be over.'

He took a step closer and raised his knife, daring me to react, but I inched back, gripping the sword for all I was worth. In that moment I made the mistake of glancing to the cauldrons below. My arms and knees began to tremble.

'You haven't got it in you,' he mocked, and shook the gantry for all he was worth. Arms flailing I lost my footing, and as I fought to stay up I dropped the sword and McCunn kicked it away. Down through the air it fell, disappearing into one of the cauldrons below.

I was on my knees now, clinging on for dear life, and seeing his advantage McCunn made a sudden lunge, blade flashing. I grabbed his wrist and our arms arched in the air. His face was just inches above me now, his breath on my cheek as he struggled to topple me. It was do or die when, roaring like a beast, I punched him in the flank and knocked him first to the edge and then over the gantry.

A look of confusion came over his face, only to be replaced by terror as he realised the only thing holding him up was my left hand.

'No! No!' he cried, his mouth puckered, his eyes bulging from his head; and for all his evil deeds, the murder of Sandy McLeod not least among them, I fought with both hands to keep hold of him while my heart pounded in my chest. But, as his legs flailed, my grip slowly began to slip from his wrist, up over his hand, across his fingers, until finally there was nothing left to hold.

Down to the cauldron he fell and slammed onto its simmering surface, his bloodcurdling screams grating over the pounding of the steam piston. I can't begin to imagine the horror of that death as he twisted and sank, every inch of his body burning, his lungs, nose, eyes and ears filling with molten sugar. But hard as it is, I can't say I pitied him. It was a violent end for a violent man, and he richly deserved his fate.

By the time I'd won my way to the ground and followed the terrified slaves out of the building, an ominous orange glow had lit the sky. Burning cinders drifted like snow in the night air and I didn't have to wait long to discover why because, when I climbed past the fields and reached the lawn, it was a very different Denholm House which met my eyes. The fire had spread up and out from the drawing room until it engulfed the entire building. Flames flared from every window, towering through the roof and reaching to the heavens, making a vast bonfire of Alba's dreams.

Redcoats and civilians milled about the lawn. Terrible cries of anguish rose up from loved ones, however, as they cradled the dead and dying; and pressing forward through the crowd I passed the Attorney General sitting on the ground, clutching his wife and two daughters close to him. He'd regained his composure, however, and looked at me with the light of recognition in his eyes.

'We have a lot to thank you for, Doctor Lyon,' he whispered. 'He looked round. 'But where is Major Crombie?'

I quickly explained, and his mouth fell open as I first described the surgery, then everything that followed.

'But we must return to Port Royal at once, sir,' I said. Alba's allies may yet make their attempt. I glanced at his arm. 'And I think you know what I need to do about that.'

He looked to the Governor's bloodied sash and nodded.

'You saw it, Doctor Lyon,' he replied grimly. 'Sir Henry gave his life for the island. Whatever the cost, we can't fail him.'

As he struggled to his feet I reached to help him, but he waved me away. Then embracing his wife and daughters he motioned them to the remaining carriages which were filling with the wounded and their families.

'Wait,' I called as they drifted away. 'There was a young Scotswoman, Fiona Cameron.' They stopped and turned while I gave a hasty description. 'Have you seen her?'

Their eyes widened then one of the daughters, a girl of about sixteen, slipped her mother's hand and stepped forward.

'You mean you haven't heard?' she cried, pointing to the blazing building.

My heart skipped a beat. 'Heard what?'

'I tried to pull her out, Doctor Lyon,' replied the girl's mother, her lip trembling, 'but she was frantic, screaming that her daughter was locked in an upstairs room.' Tears welled in her eyes. 'She broke away from me and ran.'

Blood drained from my face.

'I tried to go after her,' she sobbed, 'but the heat—'

I didn't hear the rest of her words because I was sprinting toward the house.

With flames roaring all around I shielded my eyes and plunged into the great hall. Thick smoke hung in the air choking my lungs and the chandelier had crashed to the floor. As I pressed toward the staircase, however, a tall figure emerged from the gloom. It was Fiona, her daughter over her shoulder.

Together we hurried out as the ceiling crumbled and fell.

'Katie!' cried Fiona, laying her daughter on the grass and shaking her shoulders. 'Please Katie, stay with me!' And she shot me a look of fear.

The girl's lips were blue and she wasn't breathing. Without a second thought I pressed my mouth to hers. There were gasps from onlookers, and I admit I'd never tried to resuscitate anyone in my life. I'd no idea if it might work but, in that moment, I knew it was the right thing to do. Fiona watched in astonishment as I fought to win her daughter back to life. I breathed again and again and then, just as the first sense of despair began to creep over me, Katie coughed and opened her eyes.

'How in God's name did you do that?' spluttered an astonished soldier close by. 'That lassie was dead!' To him, it must have seemed a conjuror's trick.

I slumped to one side. By now Fiona was clutching the girl to her breast, her eyes closed.

Something seemed to catch in my eye and I blinked hard several times, then cleared my throat.

Fiona opened her eyes and looked at me, as if seeing me for the first time. 'Thank you,' she whispered.

It was the happiest moment of my life.

45

Nothing stirred in the darkness before dawn, neither breath of wind nor creature of the night. The sky turned grey, then coal-flame yellow, then pink, and as the sun's rays lanced over the Caribbean to the accompaniment of the parrots' cries I gazed out from the summit of Port Royal.

A soldier shuffled to my side and pressed a tin cup of coffee into my hand. I gulped it down, its bitter tang sharpening my mind. It had been a frenetic night, during which soldiers and civilians alike had hurried to the fort by every means possible.

To the north, behind Kingston, a plume of smoke marked the ruins of Denholm House. But the idea that the battle for Jamaica was over was dispelled by seven warships lying off the coast, their guns run out on every side, their red pennants snaking in the breeze. Whether those ships owed allegiance to any nation or none remained a mystery to us. While one had the low lines of a French corvette, another the agility of a Spanish frigate and a third the shape and speed of a Portuguese brigantine, no colours flew from any mast. Alba's words were not a bluff, but the question remained whether they would dare an assault once they realised Port Royal remained under British control.

With everyone inside it fell to the Attorney General to take command, but not before I had amputated his left arm, with only a slug of morphine and brandy to dampen his pain, and a strip of leather to bite upon. After the operation I bound the remains of his arm to his chest. With his jacket draped over his shoulders he rose to his feet, fixed his buttons in place and insisted on overseeing the island's defence.

In the hours that followed, preparations were made against any assault by the Maroons over land, and any incursion by sea. The gates of the fort were barred, the cannons loaded and the redcoats summoned to battle stations for the closing act of Alba's insurrection.

The flagpole behind me was bare, but with the dawn light the Attorney General now gave the order to sound the reveille. A dozen redcoats marched to its base. The sergeant major bawled an order, his cry drifting off into the air. In the silence that followed one of the young lads raised a brass bugle to his lips and, closing his eyes, blasted out the short pips of the morning call to arms. With the last note he brought the bugle to his side. Two of his comrades then stepped forward and hitched on the flag. As it slowly ascended, the Attorney General gave a nod. Drums rolled and the flagpole company raised cymbals, trumpets and fifes as the flag unfurled in the light wind. Then the slow Highland march, *The Garb of Auld Gaul*, rang over the ramparts.

As the last echoes of the refrain faded, all eyes turned to see what reaction there might be from the enemy. The ships were no more than a mile distant, their main sails trimmed. They showed no sign of a response.

'Run out the guns,' ordered the Attorney General.

A soldier came running across the ground from the far side of the fort and made a hasty report. The officer listened, then turned and saluted the Attorney General.

'Sentry from the north side sir,' he murmured, 'reports Maroons on the coast road advancing towards the fort. Hundreds of 'em,' he added.

The Attorney General gave a curt nod. 'Very good Captain. Give the command for volley fire at three hundred yards.' He turned to the artillery officer. 'Try a range shot,' he ordered.

I felt the hair prickle on my neck as the order was bawled and an artilleryman raised a torch to the nearest cannon. The slow match was lit, the twine fizzled then disappeared into the vent. There was a terrible moment of anticipation followed by a deafening boom and a streak of flame from the muzzle. My ears rang as the cannon recoiled in a haze of smoke and all eyes searched the sky and the sea. A plume of water rose at the impact point, hundreds of yards beyond the ships.

As the artillerymen got to work adjusting and reloading, the repeated crack of rifle fire echoed from the north side. The situation was now critical. If Alba's ships were to go through with an attack on the harbour then a full-scale battle would follow, with the combined forces on land and sea closing round the fort like pincers.

My heart thudded in my chest. The acrid stench of gunpowder drifted in the breeze. A second cannon exploded into life, this time dropping the ball within a hundred yards of the enemy ships.

Then it happened.

One of the seven, the furthest from the bay, began to unfurl its topsail in a long, languid drop like a Sunday tablecloth; and as the sail tightened into place to reveal a red crusader cross, the ship made a lazy turn toward the open sea. One by one, its sister ships followed suit until they formed a line, retreating from the coast.

All around me men erupted in a riot of cheers and launched their hats into the air. The island still remained in peril, however, and the Attorney General remained steadfast in his determination to regain full control. He quickly quelled the celebrations, barked fresh orders and hastened men to support the landward side.

Events had meanwhile provoked panic in Kingston, and everyone who was able to do so had descended to the harbour and taken to the water. The upshot was the bay teamed with merchant ships of every class, lingering in a state of uncertainty, but looking to the mouth of the channel I saw one brig under full sail, racing for the open sea.

I grabbed a telescope from an officer and peered at its prow as it cut through the water. The spray rose along the planking and up towards the painted letters of its name. The *Méduse*. I called to the Attorney General.

'Doctor Lyon?'

'That brig, sir,' I said, handing him the telescope. 'It seems in rather a hurry.'

The Attorney General raised the telescope to his eye and frowned.

'I know the *Méduse* well,' he said. 'It sails the Caribbean circuit. But I know its owner even better.'

Suddenly they came back to me, the words which the ill-fated nobleman aboard the *Julietta* had recorded in his journal.

Five leagues out of Kingston ... we met the brig Méduse at anchor.

'It's Alba's ship, isn't it?'

He nodded.

I looked from the *Méduse* to the seven ships sailing towards the horizon.

'He's on board!' I cried out. 'I'll stake my life on it. He's turning tail with his allies!'

Moments later I was sprinting along the fort's twisting passages with a team of twelve redcoats. Their captain was the very man who'd arrested me that first night on Jamaica, but now he was ready to follow my every command. Catching up with the *Méduse* would take a herculean effort of rowing, but the team was strong and willing, and if anyone could do it now it was these men.

At the foot of the last staircase an officer of the guard slipped the bolt, and we emerged back into dazzling sunlight just a few feet from the water's edge. Far off to our right the Maroons continued their attempt on the walls of Port Royal, and as we scrambled into the patrol boat, slipped the tender and dipped the oars, a small group of them cried out and ran towards us, their rifles blazing. We were obliged to return fire and dropped half a dozen, but not before one of my men took a shot to the shoulder. It wasn't a fatal wound, but he couldn't row. I switched places with him and hauled away for all I was worth.

Twice I turned my head towards the prow and caught sight of the *Méduse* far ahead, her sails billowing; and as we left the channel and began rolling on the sea, the distance only increased. The oar slipped in my hands, I missed the stroke and my shoulders ached. But just as the task began to seem impossible, a boom resounded from the ramparts. There followed a sound like a rush of steam from a kettle and a cannonball streaked over our heads. An instant later it exploded in the water, fifty yards short of the *Méduse*. Another followed, but again pitched short. Then came a third but this time, to the sickening crack of timbers, the ball struck home.

The *Méduse* listed heavily, somehow managed to stay afloat, but returned to an even keel with a gaping hole in her side and her mainmast broken.

Inspired we pulled harder, putting everything into the strokes until the gap was two hundred yards, then a hundred, then fifty. With lungs bursting we finally reached her side, flotsam from the impact drifting on the waves. The shattered hull loomed above, creaking and turning in the swell. Our redcoat captain looped a grappling hook and launched it over the main deck. Two more followed, and we shinned our way up. A handful of her crew sought to cut our ropes, but the men below fired off a volley and they instantly retreated.

I clambered over the gunwale in time to see her crew gather on the far side of the deck. They were wrestling with a rowing boat in an effort to escape. By the time half a dozen of us had scrambled on deck, however, they turned and raised their hands. They were a mixture of French and Hispanics, and they cried out in broken English.

'Alba!' I shouted, rushing towards them. 'Where is Alba?'

At first they shrugged and shook their heads, but when a redcoat at my back raised his rifle they began to cry out again and pointed to a doorway beneath the bridge. I grabbed a sword and disappeared below.

Stairs led down to an abandoned galley and pushing past benches and tables I pressed on towards the stern. By now torrents of water were flooding the lower decks and the hull groaned as the ship listed ever more to one side. I opened a set of swing doors, staggering against the wall as I did so, and fell forward into the captain's cabin. There was a desk in the middle and behind it, as I entered, stood Alba.

He glanced up from a heap of documents he was tearing to shreds, lifted a pistol and fired. But by a combination of his haste and poor aim, he missed. Seizing my chance I leapt across the room, and before he could make another move the tip of my sword was pressing into his neck.

'It's the gallows for you now, Alba,' I breathed, my chest heaving, 'unless, of course, you'd rather die here.'

He tilted his head and bared his teeth.

'Traitor,' I whispered.

His face twisted scornfully.

'Fool! You're the traitor, Lyon,' he mouthed, spitting emphasis on my name. 'You're the traitor to your own people. And for what? So a foreigner can reign in our land? So British rule can continue a little longer in Jamaica? So slavery can continue?'

He laughed. 'After all, I doubt your redcoat friends will thank you, now you've shown them up for the fools they are.' He shook his head. 'No Lyon. You should have made your cause with me.'

'You have no cause,' I answered. 'Only vanity and greed. And the idea that you're a friend to slaves is an insult. I've seen your plantation first hand, just as you'd promised me. Or had you forgotten? Now get your hands up.'

He slowly raised them, licking his lips as he did so, and for the first time fear flickered in his eyes.

'Look, Lyon,' he whispered, his voice mellow, 'There's gold on this ship. It's yours if you want it.'

I kept my gaze on him, saying nothing.

'What do you say, Lyon, eh? Or is it something else you're after?' His eyes narrowed. 'Ah, I see it now, yes. Fiona Cameron! Take her. She's nothing to me.'

Amidst the turmoil I'd managed only a brief conversation with Fiona. But it had been enough.

'You mean the servant girl you dishonoured?'

His eyes widened but he didn't reply.

'Oh, Fiona told me,' I shouted, the sword trembling in my hand now as my passion rose. 'She told me everything about your violent obsession. Of how your father threw her from the house when she went to him, and how she made a new life for herself and hoped never to see you again. But you hunted them down because you never lost the desire to own them, just like this island and your precious gold.'

By the time I finished a trickle of blood was starting at his neck, but a look of defiance remained in his eyes. Footsteps sounded in the corridor, then two redcoats were at the door, their rifles trained on his chest.

I dropped the sword to my side.

'You'll pay for your crimes, Alba. But not here.'

He rubbed his neck and seeing the blood gave me a venomous look. Then glancing from me to the redcoats he made his way to the door.

'You'll pay for this, you and that cripple of a sister of yours.'

The sword in my hand was an old-fashioned kind. It had a great basket hilt which curved round my fist, and I crashed it into his face with every ounce of strength I had. For all his size, I had the pleasure of watching him collapse like a half empty sack, and he was unconscious before his head hit the ground.

'You really shouldn't have said that,' I told him.

46

A cannon boomed in the distance.

I stopped in the act of adjusting my cuffs and tilted my head. For a moment I was there again, far across the ocean on the ramparts at Port Royal.

This cannon, however, was the gun at Edinburgh Castle, and it was time to give my report. Two days earlier I'd stepped ashore at Leith on the final leg of my return journey. I was home.

I followed the club's old retainer as he led me up the stairs.

'Henderson, you haven't changed a bit,' I smiled.

He stopped and turned toward me. 'No, sir, I don't suppose I have. But if you will forgive me for saying so, sir, you look a little different. Have you been away?'

'Oh, you know, just over in the west,' I grinned. 'Nothing special.'

We crossed the landing to the Day Room where I'd first met the Lord Advocate. There he was again, seated in an armchair, and by the look of things, in the midst of a conversation. Two high backed chairs faced him, and he glanced up as I entered.

'Here he is!' he beamed. 'Good to see you again, Lyon.'

The occupants of the other two chairs turned to face me. One was Sir John but the other came as a surprise.

'Commander Birkmyre has agreed to join us.'

I shook Sir John's hand.

'Well done, Lyon,' he smiled, giving me a wink. 'Capital bit of work.'

I turned to Birkmyre and we exchanged a curt nod. Then the Lord Advocate beckoned us to sit.

'Well well,' he began. He opened a dossier on his lap. 'I suppose I should begin by going through your report, Lyon.'

I sat back and lit my pipe.

'I think we can skip the account of everything up to the capture of Lord Alba,' he murmured. 'I've taken Sir John and Commander Birkmyre through that already.'

'Quite a tale,' said Sir John as he lit a cigar. Birkmyre, without looking at me, gave a tight smile.

Henderson arrived with a decanter of sherry then left, closing the doors behind him.

'Now, let me see,' continued the Lord Advocate. 'Alba's allied ships were repulsed and the Maroon uprising petered out, yes?'

'Correct, my lord,' I replied. 'They retreated to the hills but continue with their guerrilla tactics.'

'Indeed'.

'And as you know,' I added, 'Sir Henry was laid to rest with full military honours.'

'A brave fellow,' murmured Sir John.

'And the Attorney General and Major Crombie? Both made good recoveries?'

'I'm glad to say they did, my lord.'

'And, eh, our other agent, Miss Cameron?' he asked. 'And her child?'

'They returned to London on board the *Valiant*. Once Lord Alba was delivered into the Tower they took ship to Glasgow.'

For a moment I thought of our farewell by the Thames, and my last glimpse of Fiona as her ship faded into the fog.

'What about Hare?' asked Sir John. 'What became of him?'

I smiled. 'I still don't know the answer to that. He picked the lock of our cell door the night of the uprising and hasn't been seen since.'

Sir John smiled but Birkmyre shook his head. 'I still can't say I approve of that villain's involvement,' he muttered.

'Good, good,' said the Lord Advocate, ignoring him. 'Well now. About those papers. The ones you mention recovering from Alba's desk on board the *Méduse*. Talk us through them, Lyon.'

'Papers?' said Birkmyre in surprise. He looked to the Lord Advocate. 'What papers?'

'I interrupted Alba in the act of tearing them up,' I explained, 'and afterwards I pieced them back together. They included his records of the *Julietta's* shipments, some letters from McCunn and a letter from the leader of the Maroons confirming their support of his insurrection. But there was something else.'

I looked to each of them in turn.

'There was a coded letter written in Spanish, which has just been deciphered by an agent in Whitehall. It was written by a nobleman, who signed himself 'Inspector of the Order of the Double Eagle'. The seal at the foot of that letter was a perfect match for the seal from the signet ring of the French nobleman who perished aboard the *Julietta*.'

I took a breath, then continued. 'The letter was to Alba, who is likewise addressed as 'Inspector' by the nobleman. So it appears that both he and Alba held the same rank within their secret society. What the nobleman proposed to Alba, with the aid of their Order, was a joint venture for the recovery of gold from a sunken Spanish galleon.'

'So that's where he sourced it,' murmured Sir John.

'The letter explains that nearly two hundred ago, during a violent tropical storm, the galleon sank on a reef off Jamaica.'

'In its days as a Spanish colony,' added the Lord Advocate.

I nodded. 'Indeed, my lord. This was the venture that drove Alba to develop his technique of underwater exploration. He lied, you see, when he told me he had carried it out for the first time at Dunearn. He'd already perfected it over a year earlier, in the Caribbean.'

'Astonishing,' exclaimed Birkmyre.

'And you say,' said the Lord Advocate, 'that from the outset they plotted to overthrow Jamaica?'

'Yes, my lord. The letter states as much. Alba would provide both the means for recovering the gold and converting it into currency, for the Order's benefit. In return, the Order gave every support possible to Alba's insurrection. That was why Alba needed to develop his underwater apparatus, and also why he needed to melt the gold and convert it into sovereigns. Alba then used the gold to fund arms deals at home and to buy the loyalty of the Maroons on Jamaica.'

The Lord Advocate nodded slowly.

'I think it's time you enlightened us, Lyon. What can you tell us about the Order of the Double Eagle?'

As I gathered my thoughts to answer his question, that powerful symbol formed in my mind once more. It had run like a refrain through everything from the very start. The tattoos on the *Julietta*'s crew, the nobleman's signet ring, the crest in Birkmyre's office and outside Sir Guy's study, the nobleman's journal, the Julietta portrait in Alba's cabin, and even the words of the strange toast he'd made that evening in Denholm House. Just as the text from Glasgow University had warned, its significance hadn't always been clear and I'd certainly made mistakes. But, at long last, my grasp was closing round the truth.

'There were hints, of course, among Alba's papers. But it was only after a visit to London that I was able to confirm my suspicions.'

I leaned forward.

'Gentlemen, the Order of the Double Eagle is the world's oldest secret service. It has an almost mythical status in diplomatic circles. Its origins lie in Roman times, when it was first known to have served the Byzantine Emperors at Constantinople in their dealings with east and west alike. But when that empire fell to the Ottomans in the fifteenth century, the Order's far flung network of spies were rumoured to have transferred their allegiance to King Ferdinand and Queen Isabella of Spain. Another rumour, however, tells of the Order's members journeying to China, and pledging their loyalty to its Emperor a century later, while yet another rumour puts them at the heart of America's revolutionary war. Whatever the truth about the Order may be, this affair demonstrates it remains a powerful force, capable of supporting any cause it wishes.'

The Lord Advocate frowned. 'And you're quite sure that Alba was a member of this, as you say . . . Order?'

'There's no doubt about it, my lord. His family has a long connection with the Order, which allows men and women to serve at every level. His grandmother, Maria Julia Constanza Martinez, was the youngest daughter of the Duke of Aragon. She was known within her family as Julietta. She fell in love with the Earl's grandfather and they settled at Dunearn. They supported the Jacobite cause, but after Culloden and her husband's execution she returned, heartbroken, to Spain.'

Sir John gave a long sigh and sat back. 'Well, it's the silk noose for Alba and no mistake. There's no cheating the hangman.'

The Lord Advocate cleared his throat.

'Not quite.'

'What do you mean, my lord?' asked Birkmyre.

'What I mean is this. The day after Alba was committed to the Tower, the *Times* noted in the Court Circular that his lordship appeared before the King at the Palace.'

He waved his hand. 'That, of course, only happened after I'd spoken with the Prime Minister.'

I smiled. 'So you were in London too.'

'The day after Alba's visit to the Palace,' he continued, 'the *Times* recorded two things. The first was the news of an unfortunate Maroon uprising on Jamaica which had been supressed, but which claimed a number of lives including that of the island's governor, Sir Henry Barrie. In the aftermath of the uprising, a board of inquiry has been established to consider its causes. And I can confirm,' he added, glancing to me, 'that the board will consider carefully the question of the abolition of slavery throughout the Empire.'

'Welcome news, my lord,' I replied. 'And what, may I ask, was the second thing?'

'It was that due to ill health, the Right Honourable Robert Beaufort-Stewart, fifteenth Earl of Alba, had vacated his title in

favour of his cousin the Honourable Sir Guy Stewart with immediate effect, and retreated abroad to an estate on the island of
Sicily.'

'Extraordinary,' murmured Sir John.

The Lord Advocate sat back, puffing on his pipe. 'It's the
British way,' he said.

I couldn't help grinning at the thought of how pleased Lady
Octavia would be, now that she was Countess of Alba.

There was a long silence. Birkmyre finished his sherry.

'Well that's it I suppose,' he said. 'I have to admit, Doctor
Lyon, that we had our differences, but yours has been an extraordinary piece of work. Now, if you'll forgive me, my lord,
gentlemen, there's the canal boat. I'm afraid I have to go.'

I exchanged a look with the Lord Advocate.

'Just a moment please, Commander,' he said, extending his
hand. 'I think there is one final piece of information which
Doctor Lyon has yet to provide.'

'Oh?' he replied, dropping heavily into his chair. He looked
to each of us in turn. 'And what might that be?'

The Lord Advocate sipped his sherry, then looked to me to
continue.

'There was a further letter among Alba's papers. It, too, was
written in code, but a much more challenging one.'

'And did you succeed in deciphering it?'

'We did,' I replied. 'Though I must acknowledge the debt I
owe to my sister, Margaret. You see, gentlemen, the letter was
double coded, an added layer of concealment that neither I nor
our agent in Whitehall could untangle. Only Margaret proved
equal to the task and succeeded in deciphering it late last night.

By that time, I'd already submitted my report to you, my lord, but I sent a further message this morning—'

'Which I received,' he acknowledged. 'I must say, you should've informed me of your decision to involve Miss Lyon. The way you went about that was rather irregular.'

'Yes, my lord. Apologies, my lord.'

'But no matter. Go on, Doctor Lyon.'

I glanced at each of them, took a breath, and continued.

'The first thing to note was the nobleman's journal from the *Julietta* was addressed to someone he referred to as 'Inspector General'. Since he was himself an Inspector, the unnamed recipient was therefore a more senior figure in the Order.

'Now, I'd always assumed that the person to whom the nobleman had written his account was Alba. But my suspicions arose when I discovered, in that separate letter, that the nobleman had addressed Alba merely as Inspector. So who was this higher ranking Inspector General, if not Alba?'

My heart thumped in my chest.

'It was only last night,' I continued, 'when Margaret had deciphered it, that the identity of the Inspector General became clear. In that letter, as the Inspector General personally assured Alba, everything had been arranged. Firstly, the selection of Machrihanish as the *Julietta*'s landing place. Secondly, the recruitment of Crawford McCunn to be Alba's secretary. Thirdly, arranging the secret use of the Campbeltown pottery both for melting the Spanish gold and minting sovereigns. And fourthly, arranging the transfer of Tom Hamilton to the Cumbrae Lighthouse.'

I looked up. The Lord Advocate was staring at me through a haze of smoke. Birkmyre reclined, arms folded, his one good eye trained on the ceiling. Sir John contemplated his sherry on the table in front of him, head bowed.

'This person,' I said, 'who is a double agent in the service of the Order, was the prime mover behind Alba's plan to take Jamaica. A plan which was, in itself, merely the first step in an even more ambitious plan, touching upon the safety of the Crown itself.'

I looked beyond my listeners towards the dark mass of Edinburgh Castle.

'This person,' I added, 'is in fact the real Double Eagle, at the heart of the Establishment.'

I paused for a moment, then turned my gaze to Sir John.

'He even welcomed the idea of a novice agent to conduct the Crown's investigation. An idea which Commander Birkmyre, quite reasonably, considered unwise.'

In the silence that followed neither Birkmyre nor the Lord Advocate spoke.

Sir John raised his head and looked me in the eye. His face was serene.

'You thought I was bound to fail, Sir John. And to make doubly sure, you set your men to hunt me from the very start. Why?'

He lifted his sherry and sipped. Then he carefully laid the glass back down, took a long draw on his cigar, and reclined.

'There were bigger issues at stake,' he replied at last. 'And I'm afraid you were expendable.' He drained the sherry and extinguished his cigar. 'There is nothing left for me to say except well done, Doctor Lyon. I underestimated you.'

There was an awkward silence, eventually interrupted by the Lord Advocate.

'I presume—' he began, but Sir John shook his head.

'I understand of course, my lord,' he replied, 'and I know what you're about to suggest. But really, there's no need. Thank you. I'll see to the matter myself.'

'If you are quite sure?'

'I am, my lord. Thank you.'

He stood and made a stiff bow to Commander Birkmyre and the Lord Advocate. To my surprise, he shook my hand.

'Goodbye, Doctor Lyon.' He turned to leave. As he reached the door, however, he hesitated and looked back over his shoulder.

'Just one thing, Lyon, if I may. Our, ehm, that is to say, your fellow agent, Fiona Cameron. I want you to know I never meant for her to come to any harm. Ever.'

He gave a nod, turned the handle and left.

I never saw Sir John Foster again. A week later, it was announced in the pages of the *Caledonian Mercury* that he'd been swept out to sea during the routine inspection of a tea clipper anchored in the Firth of Forth. I knew the truth, of course, but his good reputation was permitted to follow him to the grave.

Who can read the hearts of men?

But I will say this. Many years later, in the course of a candlelit University dinner, I was seated beside an ancient Highland minister. For some reason which I can no longer recall, the subject of the Customs arose. The good minister spoke warmly of Sir John, but as he raised his wineglass to his lips a distant look came into his eye.

'Aye, Sir John Foster,' he said slowly. 'His grandfather was out in the 'Forty-Five, of course.'

He then related to me the sad tale of an adjutant, who had been aide-de-camp to the Prince.

'Aye, my father always said he was a brave young callant that one,' said my companion, with a shake of his head. 'He hid in our kirkyard when the battle was lost, but the redcoats caught hold of him. Och, but I just cannot recall his name.'

Suddenly the light of memory came over his face. 'Patrick. Aye, that was it. Patrick Foster. He was true to the cause lang after the Prince had fled the field, and he was hanged, drawn and quartered in London within a month of the battle.'

He stared at the food on his plate, then pushed it away. 'Such a terrible waste o so many young lives.' Strange thing was though,' he said, 'Patrick Foster's own brother was one of the redcoats that laid hold of him in the kirkyard.'

The minister closed his eyes and bowed his head, as if offering a silent prayer.

'Aye,' he added at last, pushing back his chair and shuffling to his feet. 'But that was the way of the whole thing.'

POSTSCRIPT

The autumn sun came lancing through the windows on Morningside Place.

'Well,' said Margaret, as I placed the *Caledonian Mercury* to one side and sliced the top off a boiled egg, 'aren't you going to open them?'

I glanced at the silver tray Lizzie had just left. There were two letters.

'You do it,' I said, dipping a soldier into the yolk. 'I'll listen.'

Margaret tutted and smiled. 'Big feartie!'

She reached for the top letter and opened it.

My Dear Doctor Lyon,

Following the conclusion of your investigations into the deep waters of both the River Clyde and the Caribbean, I am pleased to inform you that His Majesty has personally taken note of your service.

Your interest in marine inquiry, so essential to the interests of Empire, is one that His Majesty considers will require a number of studies in locations across the globe. Naturally, when you travel, it will be convenient that you hold a suitable appointment. His Majesty has accordingly instructed me to offer you His newly created Chair of Marine Science at Edinburgh University, with all the usual emoluments which such a position will bring.

His Majesty does so, of course, on the understanding that your inquiries, wherever they may be, will coincide with significant national interests which His Majesty anticipates you will support.

No doubt you will wish to take time to consider this most generous offer Doctor Lyon, but in the meantime I await your reply and beg to remain sir,

Your obedient servant,

The Right Honourable Sir William Rae PC MP, His Majesty's Advocate

Another note was scrawled beneath the signature:

. . . I should add, Doctor Lyon, that, in addition to the assistance of your highly experienced and equal ranking colleagues Miss Fiona Cameron and Miss Margaret Lyon, both of whom hold positions in His Majesty's faithful service of many years' standing, as you are now aware, His Majesty has also agreed to place at your personal disposal the services of Mister Jack Dervil. I'm given to understand he has been of considerable assistance to you in your prior endeavours, both here and elsewhere. Those services will continue, at His Majesty's pleasure.

'Marine science?' said Margaret incredulously, rising more confidently now from her chair and gently placing the letter on the fire, in accordance with her training long ago. 'Really, Mungo, what on earth do you know about that? In fact, I'm starting to wonder why I ever recommended you to the Lord Advocate in the first place.'

I poured her tea from the pot with a knowing smile, but my attention was already on the second letter.

The handwriting was delicate but firm. And was that a hint of perfume I detected, as I turned it in my fingers?

My heart raced.

AFTERWORD

Following a Maroon uprising on Jamaica, a government inquiry contributed to Parliament passing the Abolition of Slavery Act 1833, thanks in large part to the enormous efforts of William Wilberforce MP and the earlier Slave Trade Act of 1807. However, the rejection of slavery in Great Britain had begun many years earlier with, in Scotland, the 1687 case of *Reid v Scot of Harden & His Lady* (known as 'the Tumbling Lassie') and *Knight v Wedderburn* in 1778 which declared, in the celebrated case of the Jamaican slave Joseph Knight, that Scots Law did not recognise the institution of slavery. *Knight* followed the 1772 ruling of Scottish judge Lord Mansfield in the case of *Somerset v Stewart*, to the effect that the status of slave was also not recognised at Common Law in England.

ACKNOWLEDGEMENTS

There are many, many people to whom I am greatly indebted for their help and encouragement in writing this book, including my sister Janet Russell for her historical knowledge and insights into all things related to Scotland's west coast, and my brother Dr Brian O'Rourke for his medical and surgical insights. I'd especially like to thank Robert Davidson, Moira Forsyth and everyone at Sandstone Press for their faith in publishing this book, Camilla Seddon for her superbly illustrated maps, Hugh Andrew, Alan McLean QC and his colleagues at *The Tumbling Lassie* (the charity to which one third of any royalties paid to me from the sale of this book in the UK will be donated), Willie McColl, Ronnie Renton, Sandy McCall Smith, Professor John Cairns, Maureen Bell, Ruth Baird, Charles Drummond, Ginny and Alex Scott, Robert and Sara Scott, Alan and Deborah Davidson, Frank and Emma Fowlie, Scott and Susan Bennett, the Rev. Steven Manders, John Scullion QC, Iain McSporran QC, Alex Prentice QC, Jane-Frances Kelly, Stuart Kelly, Michael Fry, David McManus, John Nimmo, James Fraser, all the O'Rourkes, Barnetts, Hunters, Russells, Crabbs, Flanagans, Morrises and Bairds, and, of course, the Crown Agent David Harvie for borrowing his title.

I'm especially grateful to Joanna and Martha for putting up with me writing in my study all this time and spending so long in the nineteenth century. Martha also created the initial drawing for the book's cover. Most of all, credit is due to my father James because without his encouragement, enthusiasm, ideas and imagination this book would not have happened. The last words, however, belong to my mother, Patricia, 1946–2016. They are *amor vincit omnia*.

www.sandstonepress.com

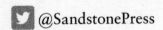 facebook.com/SandstonePress/

@SandstonePress

Mosquito Point

Hunt's Bay

Port Royal Harbour

Salt Pond Hill

Salt Pond

Port Royal

1829

Central Scotland

Munro Men's Journey

of Miles

10   15